THE
GOOD LIFE

THE
GOOD LIFE

STORIES

Erin McGraw

A MARINER ORIGINAL

HOUGHTON MIFFLIN COMPANY

BOSTON · NEW YORK

2004

For information about permission to reproduce
selections from this book, write to Permissions,
Houghton Mifflin Company, 215 Park Avenue South,
New York, New York 10003.

Visit our Web site: www.houghtonmifflinbooks.com.

ISBN-13: 978-0-618-38627-7
ISBN-10: 0-618-38627-0

Library of Congress Cataloging-in-Publication Data
McGraw, Erin, date.
The good life : stories / Erin McGraw.
p.   cm.
"A Mariner Original."
Contents: The beautiful Tennessee waltz — A whole
new man — Ax of the Apostles — Appearance of
scandal — Aruba — Lucky devil — Daily affirmations —
Citizen of Vienna — The best friend — The penance
practicum — One for my baby.
ISBN 0-618-38627-0
I. Title.
PS3563.C3674G66   2004
813'.54 — dc22   2003056892

Book design by Melissa Lotfy

Printed in the United States of America

MP 10 9 8 7 6 5 4 3 2 1

Lyrics from "Tennessee Waltz" copyright 1948 Sony/ATV Songs LLC.
All rights administered by Sony/ATV Music Publishing, 8 Music Square West,
Nashville, TN 37203. All rights reserved. Used by permission.

FOR ANDREW

It ever was, and is, and shall be,
ever-living fire, in measures being
kindled and in measures going out.

— HERACLITUS

ACKNOWLEDGMENTS

"Ax of the Apostles" originally appeared in *STORY*, "Appearance of Scandal" in *Daedalus*, "The Beautiful Tennessee Waltz" in *Boulevard*, "Aruba" in *Shenandoah*, "Daily Affirmations" in the *Georgia Review*, "The Best Friend" in *Image*, "Lucky Devil" in *Witness*, "The Penance Practicum" in the *Kenyon Review*, and "Citizen of Vienna" in the *Southern Review*.

Thanks are due to several friends who offered help and wisdom with these stories, especially Murray Bodo, Michelle Herman, Tim Parrish, and Lois Rosenthal. My gratitude to all of you.

My agent, Gail Hochman, and my editor, Heidi Pitlor, extended kindness, good sense, and enormous good taste, and I am happily in their debt.

To my husband, Andrew, I owe more thanks than I can ever give. Though I can try.

CONTENTS

THE
GOOD LIFE

THE BEAUTIFUL
TENNESSEE WALTZ

THE DAY AFTER Alice and Dik's second wedding anniversary, Alice called to tell me how they had celebrated: cross-legged at sunset, hand in hand, chanting melodies that Dik had composed. I loved Alice, but this was rich, and I called my friend Martin as soon as she hung up. "Hoo-*ooh*. Hoo-*ooh*," I chanted for him. "It's the cosmic wind that holds us all together."

"Don't winds blow people apart?"

"Alice and Dik? Not far enough."

He fell silent, and I understood that I had violated one of Martin's unstated rules, a code of acceptable discourse that changed with his moods. I spent half of our conversations scrambling to figure out what was currently permissible. "*Hoo*-ooh," he finally intoned.

"You're not doing it right," I said, relieved. "Pay attention. This is Dik's gift to the universe."

"Dik has a wide heart," Martin said, quoting Alice.

"He brings joy. He restores balance," I said, riffing.

Neither of us could stand Dik, and we worried about his sway over Alice, but he provided first-rate conversational fodder. With savage mimicry, Martin was now recalling Dik's discussion of the crucial, too-often-neglected role of ritual in daily life. Dik lit candles every night to usher in the darkness and chanted every morning to usher it back out again. In a moment I would bring up how he had gone from "Richard" to "Dick" to "Dik" as a way of honoring his desire for simplicity. Martin would remind me of the tray heaped with mulch that Dik had placed before a pine tree in his front yard to apologize for the travesty of Christmas. "You don't need to be so ugly about it," Alice had told Martin helplessly when he and I came over with holiday brandy. Martin was elaborately bowing to the tree.

"Did Dik give you a present?" Martin said, straightening up.

"He doesn't believe in presents." Catching Martin's look, she said with exquisite wryness, "Being together is a gift."

"Martin's a traditionalist," I'd murmured to her after he charged off the patio. "He believes in presents that come in boxes you can unwrap."

"The kind you can return and exchange. Just ask his ex-wife," Alice said, in a flash of her old, sharp self, which heartened me, though I wouldn't share the moment with Martin.

He was combustible on almost any topic, but he was incendiary about marriage. His ex, Charlotte, had left him four years before, and though we all thought he should be getting over her, he still brooded and drank, revisiting every humiliation. Sometimes he broke plates. She had left him not just for another man, but for a man and his horse, her riding teacher across the bay, in Oakland. "Stallions, probably. Certain jokes present themselves," Martin said when he broke the news. "Please don't tell them."

"I don't see any jokes," I said.

"Does he wear spurs, do you think? Can you hear those little metal teeth jingling when he walks from room to room?"

"You're only hurting yourself."

"I hope he wears them to bed," he said.

Martin's wife had insisted on a court hearing, where she testified in a whisper about manipulativeness and mental cruelty, but in the end the fair-minded judge weighed her boisterously successful catering company against Martin's several unacquired screenplays and awarded Martin alimony. "At least there's that," I said when we left the courthouse, Martin's jaw still locked. Since then, if I happened to be around when the check arrived, he would hold the envelope in front of me. "At least there's this," he'd say.

My husband, Jeff, said that Martin was feeling sorry for himself, as of course he was. But Jeff didn't understand how thoroughly Martin had been blind-sided. He had loved his marriage vows. A cynical man, he nevertheless had faith in marriage — for its difficulty, he said. For the pure challenge. For the action of getting up every morning and recommitting to a promise made one or twenty or fifty years before. He made marriage sound like a prison sentence, but I knew what he was driving at and admired his standards. He and I believed in marriage. We just didn't believe in Alice and Dik's marriage.

"It's not up to you to believe in it," Jeff said the night I demonstrated the anniversary chant, throwing in some arm motions to amuse him. "She's your friend. Be happy for her."

"Secretly she's miserable. She only thinks she's happy."

"I'm sure she's delighted to have you around to point out her errors in perception." Jeff had put on a clipped accent, cribbed from 1960s movie thrillers. In college he had majored in film studies, although he worked as a loan officer now, "supporting my dainty wife." He used to use the phrase all the time. He said, "Tell me again why Alice puts up with you."

"We're her best friends. Worrying about her is our job. Do you remember that she used to eat hamburgers? I've never seen Dik give up anything for her."

"Maybe she likes having somebody tell her how to live. A lot of people do."

"One of these days she's going to wake up and grope around, wondering where her personality went," I said, quoting Martin.

"She won't need to grope long. You'll be right there to tell her," Jeff said.

I picked up sleek gray Toulouse, our cat, who was slithering figure eights around my ankles. "I'm not bent on her and Dik's destruction, okay? In case you're interested, Martin and I talked today about giving them an anniversary party."

Jeff had been shredding carrots for a salad. He stopped mid-grate. "Okay, I'm nervous."

"She likes parties. At least she used to. And Martin can stand around and talk, which he'd be doing anyway."

"Does he talk about us?" His voice sounded comfortable. On the other hand, he was mangling the carrot against the grater.

"Not to me."

"Why not?"

I pulled down Toulouse, who was trying to sit on my head. "You and I are like one of those ice-skating couples. When he jumps, she jumps. When she spins, he spins. There's nothing to talk about with us. We don't even have to look at each other to know when to start skating backwards."

He shook his head, a smile crimping his lips. "You're good, Lisha."

"We're good together." Some thick emotion swelled between us, and I talked into it. "Martin thinks the second anniversary is a watershed. People can get to the first one on the wave of sheer newness — new relatives, new tax forms, all those new appliances. By the second year, though, you start watching yourself change. You see the new grooves and calluses in your brain from rubbing every day against this other person. You realize you've signed on for the duration. Martin calls it the Panic Anniversary."

"I don't remember panicking," Jeff said.

"You, my darling, are blessed with a lack of imagination."

He tried to scowl, an expression his even, pale features could never pull off. "So what are you going to do for this party? Provide topographical maps of Alice's and Dik's brains?"

"Champagne. Cake."

"I'll toast the happy couple. Am I invited?"

"It's at our house," I said, kissed him on the ear, and took off to call Martin.

I had told Jeff the truth. The party Martin and I had in mind was old-fashioned and generous, with mixed drinks and music and dancing. Back when I first met Alice, she went square dancing on Tuesday nights, ballroom dancing Wednesdays. All that had stopped since Dik, and I wanted to give her the chance to strap on her dancing shoes again. Of course, I also looked forward to watching Dik, who moved as if he were assembled out of Tinkertoys, box-step around the room.

Already Dik had told Martin that he couldn't wait. "Dik likes to glide," Martin reported over breakfast. Martin had a new temp job, taking inventory at a consignment store in San Rafael, so we met at a nearby diner, where we shared the long counter with pensioners and truants. "I thought Dik would want to do interpretive dance to the music of the spheres, but it turns out he loves to waltz. He's at home right now, polishing his Earth shoes."

"So who are you going to waltz with?" I asked.

"My partner's off dancing with somebody else."

"It's high time for you to find yourself another partner. Try reading the personals. The Bay Area is loaded with gals ready to take a chance on love."

"Bully for them."

"Why do I bother? You're in love already. You're in love with your own misery." I saw no reason to add that this was Jeff's speech; we'd been talking about Martin the night before. "You're like a dog that's found something disgusting to roll in. You're ecstatic about how awful you can make yourself feel."

He set his cup down. When he looked at me, his square face was rigid. "You didn't talk this over with Alice, did you?"

"Settle down, Martin."

"You didn't invent little schemes, audition a lineup of women ready to take a chance on love?" His rough features roughened even more. His eyes went flat and his mouth twisted. Even after years of practice, I flinched from talking to that face and so looked at my plate, its old ceramic worn to gray at the center.

"Think about who you're talking to here, would you? I sat in your living room every night for six months after Charlotte left. I made rice pudding for you. I cleaned your toilet. I *know* you." I held off the urge to tell him I loved him. Though it was true — no other friend built up in me such shimmering excitement — the last time I had told him this he overturned an ashtray in my lap. I said, "These days Alice and I don't see each other all that often. When we get together, we don't talk about you."

"I don't believe you. I don't know a single topic as riveting as me."

"Alice has so much to tell me about Dik, and I have so much to tell her about Jeff."

"Tell me. You never talk to me about him."

His voice sounded nonchalant, but he was never nonchalant. I took care with my response. "We eat take-out and watch TV. We have extended conversations with Toulouse. Jeff does a terrific imitation of Cary Grant. It's a good life."

He let that comment hang for a moment before telling me, "You were born to be married."

"Here's a news flash: so were you."

"And that's just my bad luck." He gestured at my half-finished omelet and cold toast. "Are we finished here?"

"Nearly. But you should know that I'm not letting you into the party if you don't come with a date. And this is not a party you're going to want to miss."

"You'll let me in, all right. Otherwise I'll howl outside and embarrass Jeff."

"You sulk. You don't howl."

"You think you know so much." Tilting his head back, he opened his mouth and let out a yodel that was long, intricate, and chilling. He rode the notes until they quivered, then shattered, and then he started again. Every conversation in the restaurant stopped, and waitresses started toward us from three different directions. He grinned at me, and I grinned shakily back.

"You know what you are?" I said.

"The man of your dreams," he said.

"Bad dreams," I said. We said it all the time.

To my surprise, Alice agreed to go shopping for a party dress. We spent two hours before she found what she was looking for, a pink confection of a frock with a skirt that would twirl. To celebrate, she suggested a mineral water at High Five, a sports bar across from the mall. I looked at her clear glass with its bobbing lime slice, called back the waitress, and ordered a Singapore sling.

"When I told Dik we were going shopping, he told me to get something pretty," Alice said. "He told me that celebrations are external as well as internal. He thinks it will open the door to new energies. That's as good a way as any to get him to a party."

"I was trying to decide on music," I said. "Do you still have your square-dancing tapes? The only country music I have is Patsy Cline."

"I learned the two-step to Patsy Cline. I never hear her without wanting to tap my feet."

"You hear 'I Fall to Pieces' and want to dance?"

Alice ate her lime rind. Back when she was a secretary for a temp agency, she was plumply pretty, her dimpled face set in a corona of springy yellow curls. She went to singles bars and never left alone. Now her face was thin and brown as bark from the hours she and Dik spent in their immense garden. Her hair looked like straw, but her smile could still make heads swivel. "I haven't turned into a total flake, you know," she said.

"I wouldn't have a party for a flake."

"I'm trying out some new ways of living, and Dik helps me with that."

"I've got eyes, Alice."

"Well, some eyes need glasses. He isn't — the easiest person to live with." She swirled her water, and I counted to five to keep from saying anything stupid.

"Who is?" I said. "Apart from us."

"He's this terrific optimist. The universe makes him an optimist. If he wants rain, we get rain. If he wants asparagus tips, they're pointing through the dirt the next day."

"Does he want Alice to get what she wants?" I murmured.

"Shoot. I want Dik, and there he is, every morning, out on the deck." She gave her water glass another swirl. "Don't leave me out here all alone. What do you want, you and Martin?"

I clutched my throat. "*Jeff.* You're supposed to be my friend. Don't marry me off to Martin."

"Freudian slip. You and Jeff," she said. I didn't know another soul who blushed.

I said, "Can you even imagine living with Martin? One minute everything's fine, the next minute you're in the volcano. I love the guy like I love my right arm, but I wouldn't want to live with him."

"I meant to say Jeff."

"You want to know a secret? I sided with Martin's wife in the divorce. Who couldn't look at Martin and tell he'd be hell to live with?"

"You don't want to talk about Jeff, do you?"

Plucking the thin red straw from my cloying drink, I flattened the plastic into a stick. "The only problem with Jeff and me is that we don't have any problems." I looked up in time to catch Alice's extremely expressionless face. "If this is denial, tell me what I'm denying. Jeff and I tell each other jokes. We divide up the chores. We see the same world."

"I'll bet this party wasn't his idea," Alice said.

"It wasn't. But he can't wait to see you."

"Tell him I can't wait to see him, either." She nibbled at her fingertip and glanced up at me through demure eyelashes.

"Why, Alice. I didn't think you remembered how to flirt."

"I'm married, not dead. You told me at my wedding shower not to forget the difference."

"Tell Martin," I said.

"You first," she said.

I drove home feeling a little sick from the liquor pooled balefully in my stomach. Jeff was stretched across the couch, watching *All About Eve*, Toulouse slung over his shoulder like a stole. "Your night to cook," Jeff said.

"Yeesh. Forgot. I've been off getting half plotzed with Alice. You should see the dress she got. It'll send the whole party into insulin shock." I watched him watch the TV, Toulouse snoring beside his ear. "How long have you been zoned here?"

"Since the last half-hour of *Whatever Happened to Baby Jane?* It's a Bette Davis festival. That was one terrible movie."

"You want me to call for a pizza? You don't have to get up — I'll feed it to you a bite at a time." Even I couldn't decipher my tone.

"Up to you. *The Little Foxes* is on next." He waited until I was settled on the couch next to him before asking, eyes still on Bette Davis's bow-tie mouth, how Alice was.

"You'll like this. She thinks that you and I are secretly miserable."

"There's a lot of that going around."

His eyes didn't waver from the TV screen, and I reached over to scratch Toulouse under the chin, a caress that always made him extend his claws. "Martin would say we need misery. He'd say it's how we know we're alive."

Jeff extracted the cat's claws from his neck and sat up. "I wonder what it would be like to go through a day without hearing Martin's name."

"He thinks you're a lucky man. He says I should tell you so. If I don't, he says, he will." I meant to sound saucy, but I could feel the words slipping as they left my mouth. Jeff's face was stiff and peculiar, and my stomach felt as if cold air were pouring into it.

"Lucky. What a word." His voice clotted, and the cold feeling spread across my lungs. "Here's a Martin story for you. Back when things were getting so rocky between him and Charlotte, she called me about getting a personal loan. Her name only. Martin had broken all of her antique serving dishes — not in one big rage, but across months. She would come home and find another tureen in pieces. He used to scream at her until he wasn't even saying words anymore, just howling. She was terrified. Your friend Martin." He blinked at me, then looked away. "You and I had been married two years. Charlotte and I didn't last long. Six months."

"What." My voice was dry as wind. "What are you doing?"

"I'm telling you my secret despair. An homage to Martin."

"Stop talking about Martin."

"I can't stop talking about Martin. He's over every inch of our life."

The image of a slow, creeping stain in the air between us came immediately, as if I'd been holding it ready. "Does he know?" I said.

"Why else would I tell you?"

"So you're acting out of kindness."

Jeff closed his eyes. "I haven't seen her since then. Not a phone call or an email. Zip."

"Congratulations."

"Aren't you itching to get on the horn and tell Martin, 'Guess what I just found out?'"

Jeff's face, even his eyes, were pale as dust. He might blow away any second. I said, "What do you think I am? I don't want him to know this. I don't want to know this."

"But now you do. You know everything Martin knows. And I think it will be very hard for you not to tell him that." He sat Toulouse up on his lap and addressed him as if he were conducting an interview. "Felicia has a secret. What do you think Felicia will do?"

"I didn't ask for this," I said.

"Think of it as a gift," he said.

Dik had given mulch to a pine tree. I had given Alice brandy. Jeff had given me wretchedness, mortification, five straight nights without sleep.

I pondered his gift instead of thinking about divorce lawyers or separation, ideas that I could not give weight, though I tried. Perhaps if I had caught Jeff and Charlotte together, lunching in Sausalito with their ankles entwined, I might have stormed to an attorney's office and dictated page after legal page of demands. But Charlotte had galloped away, leaving only memory, which had no smell or substance. Memory was nothing at all.

In the thin dark of the study where I lay on the fold-out bed, I stared toward the nubbled ceiling and remembered, of all things, phrases of Dik's. "Every moment is movement toward wholeness." "Rejoice in discord, for it leads to harmony." What kind of person could look at his wife's friends' marriages — one already vanished, the other blistering — and rejoice?

If I could become that kind of person, I might stop imagining how Jeff must have kissed Charlotte, his fingers caught in her long black curls. I might stop replaying the hundred conversations that he had strewn with plump hints. Already I was taking the outrage and turning it into something else — wisdom or defeat, if there was a difference. The emotion that wedged unabsorbably, like a muscle in my chest, was embarrassment. Once I had bragged to Martin about how Jeff came home from work smelling like strange spices. "Those downtown restaurants!" Now, in the dark, I felt my face turn the pillow hot.

I didn't tell Martin what I knew. Even in simple times, letting on that Jeff and I had been fighting, or had come close to fighting, or might soon be fighting, would be like giving him a gift-wrapped hand grenade. But at the restaurant where we met for breakfast, Martin caught my wavery gaze and nervous fingers.

"Come on. You can tell Uncle Mart. Jeff lost his job? Toulouse got beriberi? You're pregnant?"

"Interesting parallels." I stared unhappily at my syrup-bloated waffle. As the party grew nearer, Martin and I were meeting daily.

"Well, I hope you'll name the baby after me."

"Are you kidding? My child will be named after someone with a pleasant nature and a helpful manner." I couldn't banish all of the quiver from my voice. "Now tell me that you've found a date for the party."

"I told you, the only date I want is already taken. Have you and Jeff been brushing up that waltz?"

"Not exactly. Look, Martin, this is an anniversary party. It's all about couples. You can't just moon around the punch bowl."

"It beats dragging some poor gal to a wingding where she doesn't know anybody and gets to watch me drink myself cross-eyed."

"The whole *point*—" I took a breath and started again, more softly. "The whole point of having a date is to have fun with her. So you don't need to get cross-eyed."

"You really don't know," he said, shaking his head. "You really don't know what you're asking me to do."

Too easily I imagined Jeff mimicking Martin's words, his slump, his voice creamy with self-importance. I'd been hearing that imitation a lot in the past few days, as every object of Jeff's anger tumbled loose like items from an overstuffed closet. Eventually, I assumed, anger of my own would tumble out. I said to Martin, "I'm asking you to try to be happy, all right? I'm asking you to reach out your little hand in the direction of pleasure. Just this once."

"What do you think I'm doing here? This morning? With you? Do you think it's normal for a man and a woman to meet every single day and just *talk?*" His chin was thrust out, his lips curled back from his teeth. I looked away first.

"Martin, you know I love you."

"Stop right there," he said.

"You are my best friend."

"So, Best Friend, you've been helping poor Martin through a rough patch? Been kind of a long patch, wouldn't you say?"

"Yes, as a matter of fact."

"Maybe that should have told you something. Jesus." He shook his head. "You don't pay attention."

"You're not the first one to tell me that."

"But you keep drifting along, expecting all of us to look out for you. Why are you crying?"

"Headache," I said.

"I'm only telling you the truth."

"Thank you."

"I pay attention to the world that's in front of me, not the one I want to see." He waited for me to respond, then said, "Give it a try sometime. No telling what you'll find out." He left the diner without yelling. Even so, a waitress came over and rested her hand on my shoulder.

"You need me to call anybody?"

I wiped my eyes. "We're friends," I said. "We do this all the time."

Once the party got started, the guests laughing and the music not yet too loud, my spirits surprised me by lifting. Dik and Alice danced like gangly angels, and I was glad I'd resisted the frightened, last-minute impulse to call things off.

Across the room, beside the drinks table, Martin banged his hands together to laud the happy couple. At his side, peering at the crowd with interest, stood Lora, his date.

"How nice that you're here," I'd said at the door. "Where did you and Martin meet?"

She smiled crookedly. Her hair, almost white, stuck out in feathery tufts. "The Hot Spot. I don't usually go there. Marty says he usually doesn't either."

"That's right," I said, stopping myself from telling her that Martin invariably called the place The Wet Spot. He went there more often than he told her. "Marty," I said.

He kissed me on the cheek. "The place looks nice. I like the balloons. Where's Jeff?"

"Pouring a drink."

Martin took off across the room, and I grabbed Lora's hand before she could follow him. "I'm very, very glad you're here."

Perhaps she was tipsy enough not to hear the pressure in my voice. She said, "I like parties. I go to every party I can find."

"We don't have them very often," I said. "You tell us if we're doing something wrong." I was tipsy myself, high enough on gin to be unsure whether I was feeling delight or dread. "Promise me you'll tell."

"You've been drinking," she said. "That's a good start. Make sure everybody's drinking."

As if surveillance were required. Guests hardly paused at the door before they steamed over to our little bar. I smelled scotch, bourbon, lots and lots of gin. Martin stood with a glass in each hand. Even Dik popped open a beer, which might have accounted for his toreador spin at the end of "Walkin' After Midnight." Once he started dancing, the man was as light on his feet as a sunbeam. When he and Alice whirled by, he said, "Dancing puts us in harmony with all creation."

"Preach on," I said, and he winked.

Jeff was circulating, telling jokes, freshening drinks. From across the room I noticed for the first time that his yellow shirt, which I had never liked, lent his skin a summery glow. I caught up with him on the way to the kitchen for more ice.

"Did you see Martin?"

"And Lora," he said. "Lora Ruth, first of four daughters. Never divorced, grows tomatoes on her patio, rides a Kawasaki."

"Blood type?"

"I'd say she's a universal donor."

"I hope so," Martin said, leaning around the other side of the kitchen door. "Felicia thinks I need some new blood."

"Your old sources have dried up?" Jeff said.

Martin smirked amiably, and even through my ginned-up haze, I was alarmed. Martin was rarely amiable. "Show some respect. Felicia is wise. She knows many things."

"Sharpen up, buster," I mumbled. "I know everything."

"For instance, she knows how to give a party for her best friend," Martin said. "A dancing party. Why aren't you two dancing?"

"All we can do is the waltz." I motioned toward the living room. Someone had put on Herb Alpert. "This is a cha-cha. I guess."

"No one will be giving a grade. Get out there."

"What about you?" Jeff said to him. Absurdly, I felt comforted, as if Jeff were trying to protect me by throwing the spotlight on Martin. "Where's your date?"

"Easy come," Martin said, and shrugged. "Guess she found more congenial company. My fate to be alone."

"Don't be a jerk. Felicia will dance with you." He didn't look at me, which was prudent: no auctioneer should look at the flesh on the block. Confused by my train of thought, I stopped it. Jeff wasn't selling anything. He was giving me to Martin, who was giving me back. My face buzzed with blood and liquor.

I said carefully, "Felicia is sitting this one out."

"You're a good dancer, babe. You should get out there." Jeff sounded almost sober, but he never called me babe.

"Both of you. Show us how it's done," Martin said.

"Up to you, man. You're supposed to dance with your hostess," Jeff said.

"Is that how Cary Grant does it?"

"Shut up, Martin," I said.

"You love his Cary Grant."

Jeff said, "Martin, this is not the time to remind us of everything we ever loved. You're like hell's matchmaker."

Martin's smile was a cherub's. "It's a good time to remember what you've loved. What else is a party for?"

I said, "Celebrations are external as well as internal. We are opening the doors to new energy."

Martin and Jeff stared at me. "When did you learn to channel Dik?" Martin said.

"I told you: I know *everything*." My voice rang across two rooms — somebody had taken off Herb Alpert in mid–"Tijuana

14 · THE GOOD LIFE

Taxi." After a moment came dreamy strings and Patti Page, her voice warm as breath. "I was waltzin' with my darlin' —"

Not lightly, Martin pushed me toward Jeff. "There's your waltz."

"Ease up, Glad Hand. We'll dance when we feel like it," I said.

"Do it for me," Martin said. "As a favor."

"I don't recall owing you a favor."

"Then I guess I'll just be in your debt," he said. I flinched, but his voice remained small. His hands and lips were shaking.

Jeff gazed into the living room. He said, "Alice looks like a princess."

In front of the picture window, Alice and Dik and Lora were swaying, arms linked, singing along with the old lyrics — "Yes, I lost my little darlin' the night they were playing the beautiful Tennessee Waltz." Alice's pink skirt billowed, enough fabric there to wrap up the three of them.

"Jesus, this is a sweet song," Jeff said. I was prepared to go refresh my drink, but before I could move, Martin had his arms around us both, shoving my shoulder into Jeff's armpit.

"Come on, now. It's your song." Martin's breath across my shoulder was rough as a file. I twisted my head to look at Jeff, whose eyes were full of tears. He always cried when he drank too much, although I didn't know how much he'd drunk tonight. The three of us swayed, a dangerous activity for people so drunk. We tottered across the room, stumbling into a lamp and a chair until we came to rest against the bookcase. When I closed my eyes, my head swam, and when I opened them I was dizzied by Jeff's yellow shirt.

The song seemed to last for hours, as songs in drunk time do, and until the last note we kept swaying. Then we slowly came unstuck, Jeff's hands sliding down my back, Martin still unsteadily singing that he'd lost his little darlin'.

"Nobody is lost here," I snarled. "Nobody is going anywhere. Do you hear me?"

From across the living room, Dik's high voice: "This is the center. Get used to it," he said. "This is joy, whether you like it or not."

A WHOLE NEW MAN

O N A DIFFERENT DAY, Frederick Weiler might not have been bothered by the puffs of chintz his daughters had recently installed above the kitchen windows. The puffs replaced the quilted, energy-efficient shades he had put up when his oldest daughter, Laura, was still a baby. On another day, his feet might not have longed for the friendly prickle from the sisal floor mats that his daughters had covered with throw rugs. But today his column about sustainable energy had been rejected by the editor of the *West Haven Hills Advocate,* who pointed out that he had just taken a whole series of articles by Frederick. Maybe he should try again in a year.

The editor couldn't see that the column was meant to go *with* the articles, a series on Xeriscaping — energy-conscious, water-saving gardening. Already Frederick knew that the articles would be cut and botched and jammed into back corners of an inside page, edited beyond recognition. Next to them, the newspaper would probably feature an article like the one in today's paper, on hybrid tea roses — simpering, frail, fertilizer-dependent plants that some hybridizer should have been fined for developing. The headline read "Your Garden's Glory!"

"I'm a dinosaur," he told his wife, Pat, over the dinner table.

"You're not extinct, just unfashionable," she said. "Like beneficial bacteria. People would miss you if you weren't there."

"I was hoping for something of greater stature than a microorganism."

"Microorganisms don't have ponytails," said Laura.

"I like my ponytail," Frederick said mildly.

"So that's one vote," she said. "You know, Dad, we have to look at you. If you're not part of the solution, you're part of the problem."

Bett, the next oldest, got up for more spaghetti and flipped Frederick's ponytail as she passed. "Problem. Definite problem."

He counted to five, then said, "Who would like to tell me one interesting thing that you learned in school today?"

The girls sighed chestily around the table. "Like talking to a brick wall," the oldest said, and Pat lowered her eyes and smiled.

Frederick gazed at her: long, wavy hair and pretty eyes, a pert nose unlike his own long one, which all the girls had inherited and fussed about. Every time they complained, he gravely apologized, though Pat said he shouldn't. Frederick felt that an apology was in order — if not to his daughters, then to the universe. He hadn't intended to have so many offspring. Who could have known that Pat, who rarely raised her voice and whose opinions were mild and generous, would be a creature of such rampaging fecundity? After Laura, their planned child, seventeen years ago, Pat had managed to conceive through a condom, an IUD, and the pill — the last only 94 percent effective, as her gynecologist defensively reminded them.

Now, at the dinner table, he said to ten-year-old Tina, the youngest, "Pay attention to what people do, not how they look," and to Laura, "We've been over this."

"And you haven't given me one reason for you to keep going out in public looking like a used-up hippie," she said.

"I haven't had to pay for a haircut in years."

"That's not really something to brag about," said Bett.

Laura set her elbows on the table and assumed her concerned expression. "You know, Dad, we'd like to be proud of you, but it's hard when you have stringy hair and go out wearing corduroys that you bought when Nixon was president. You do own a tie, right? One? I don't know it personally."

"I think I do plenty for you to be proud of," he said softly, thinking of the committees, the letter and petition drives that Pat helped him with, the volunteer hours every week that far exceeded his time in the classroom. In the statement of support his department head had written for Frederick's tenure years before, it was noted that "Professor Weiler's best teaching is embodied in his community service." Frederick heard the barb but cherished the comment anyway.

Laura let the silence between them grow boggy before she said, "My friend Marcia saw you handing out dry milk at the food bank. She went there for Social Awareness Day and couldn't wait to call me when she got home. She said some of the clients were better dressed than you, and she wanted to know if you were making some kind of statement."

"Your friend Marcia should concentrate on her homework."

"I told her yes."

He shouldn't have asked further, but when the question occurred to him, it seemed to be produced by intellectual curiosity. "What kind of statement?"

She shrugged. "Same as always. There's a fun way to do everything and then there's your way, and everybody is supposed to do it your way. It's really irritating, if you want to know." She shook her wavy hair back from her face. "Go on, now. Tell me that I'm wrong."

"Not me," he said. He glanced at Pat and wished she would stop smirking at her plate. This was the kind of thing that always amused her, even when it undercut the lessons they had agreed they should teach the girls. "You got it about right."

After a long walk, Frederick came to think of the conversation as a watershed. He would tell Pat so. Now he and his daughters might have a real talk about values and priorities, about the outward symbols that defined a full interior life. But the next night, dinner conversation rippled at its usual breathless level, the girls chattering about a television show that all of them had watched that afternoon.

"I wish you'd do something a little more constructive with your time," he said reflexively.

"One hour a day," said Laura. "My friend Marcia says I live in a prison."

"Pretty low security. You get TV and fruit juice," Frederick said.

"*The Jack Carey Show* rules," said Bett. "Couples get makeovers. After haircuts and new makeup and clothes, their own families don't recognize them. They're crying, they're so happy."

"You're just trying to get me to react, aren't you?" Frederick said.

"People's families send their names in. The ones who get on the show are mostly shy at first, but once they come on stage with the new clothes and all, you should see them."

"They give the phone number all the way through the show. Toll free," said Laura. "If you ask me, it's a public service."

"These people — you'd never believe where they started," said quiet Trish, the third youngest. "Before the makeover, they look like you, Dad. After the makeover, they're movie stars."

"You're going to have to work harder than that to insult me," Frederick said.

"I think they know that, dear," Pat said.

"Everybody supposedly knows they have options," Laura said. "But this show lets people see them. If you don't like what you are, then change. It's very empowering."

"'Empowering.' Sweet Jesus," said Frederick. Catching Pat's look, he added, "Remember when that meant something more important than hairdos?"

Pat smiled. He smiled back at her. She had spent the afternoon, he knew, stuffing and Zip-Code-sorting envelopes with flyers he had made about an antidevelopment proposal that would be on the next ballot. He hoped that the girls were watching and learning about real relationship — about respect, reciprocity, a love too deep for words. He said to his daughter, "Don't even think about it."

"You can't keep them from thinking," Pat said.

Over dinner three weeks later, Pat told them about the phone call from the show's producer. The girls were cheering as if they'd just discovered a new life form. Frederick said to Pat, "You could have hung up."

"This is the answer to my prayers," Tina kept saying, although she did not, as far as Frederick knew, pray.

Bett's chatter rattled on like a telegraph machine. "They have designer clothes, or close, anyway, and real hair professionals, not just the Supercuts morons. I'd die for this."

"So we're on the same page," said Frederick.

"Don't be a party pooper, Dad."

"I'm not going on TV. Your mother and I aren't. Isn't that what you told the producer, Pat?"

"I indicated some problems would have to be addressed," she said. Dinner was tabouli, and she was working a shred of parsley from between her teeth. While he waited, she presented him with a smile that told him nothing.

"Look, Dad." Laura was using her clear, logical voice, which he knew was an imitation of his. "You say you don't think that appearance is important. Well, there you go. This isn't important, so you can just do it. For fun."

"A person who goes on the show says that these things *do* matter. I'm not going to make that statement." He imagined his Citizen Action Committee colleagues watching the show — not that they would — and felt the quick sheen of heat.

"But Mom wants it! And she promised the producer!" wailed Tina, whose tears were always nearby.

"This isn't the kind of thing Mom wants," Frederick said lightly, still trying to catch a glance from his wife. "I'll bet she didn't make any promises."

"Naturally not," she said. Her smile was beginning to frighten him. "They are nice people and didn't ask me to make any commitments. I just answered their nice questionnaire over the phone. Nothing was invasive or personal. Things like *Do the people have duplicates of the same items in their wardrobe?* and *Has either person changed hairstyle in the past year?*"

"Invasive *and* personal," Frederick said.

"Nothing that anybody with eyes couldn't tell her," said Bett.

"She said we'd make fine candidates," Pat said.

"You cannot want this," Frederick said. He didn't say the word *betrayal*, but he would later, in the bedroom.

"She got me thinking about change. I've made this tabouli exactly the same way for twenty years." As usual, her voice was mild. Thick and soft as a snowbank, it barely revealed the shape of what might be beneath it, whether a fallow garden or a scythe. "Dinner when you want it. The sideboard covered with your pamphlets. The newspapers you want, the radio shows you like."

"You make me sound like a dictator."

"Well, no. Not that." Pat finally let go of her smile. "Don't you ever get tired of casting exactly the same shadow?"

"Do you think it's easy for me to keep our standards high?" Too late he heard the self-approval in his voice, and he wasn't surprised when Pat said yes. He would have done the same.

"So you want me to go on TV and get dolled up with new clothes and haircut and eyebrows plucked just to prove that I'm not stuck in the past. To show you that I'm worth keeping up with," he said. The girls, now that he would have appreciated the protective cover of their clamor, had shut up.

"You can be a whole new man," she said.

"I don't need to be new."

"And I'll get a new dress, a manicure. Sometimes a girl likes to look pretty."

In twenty-two years he had never heard her call herself a girl. He said, a shade desperately, "I think you're beautiful."

"Well," she said, standing to clear the plates. "That's one."

The show was taped in Chicago, fifty miles away. At first Frederick expected he and Pat would return home that night, but then he heard about the dinner and hotel, the night on the town. Pat's eyes sparkled when she told him, and all he had to do was remain silent.

When they got to the studio, they met the two other couples who would share the stage with them — a welder and his wife, each of them easily fifty pounds overweight, and two dog groomers who kept making jokes about coming in for the puppy clip.

Frederick let himself make one crack to Pat about bread and circuses, then he closed his mouth.

The studio was not as glossy as he had expected. In fact, it was shabby, with paper coffee cups heaped in the trash cans and snakes of cable held in place on the floor with duct tape. In the harshly lit mirrors of the white-painted "green room" (he hadn't expected it actually to be green; he wasn't a complete rube) his face looked truly dreadful, every wrinkle like a crevice. The other two couples pretended to be scared of their reflections, the welder solemnly saying, "Sow's ear." On Frederick's other side Pat was silent. She leaned toward the mirror and touched the skin around her eyes — dry, the color of weak tea. He watched his wife finger her skin until one of the show's subproducers came in and arranged the couples in the order they would go on stage.

The show would be made up of two parts — the morning taping, designed to show off the guests' lackluster attempts to claim a personal style, and then the live broadcast in the afternoon, when six Cinderellas would float across the stage. During the morning segment the host — lustrous shirt and tie, huge hair — asked, "Aren't you excited?" The dog groomers squealed, the welder and his wife spread their hands and laughed, and Frederick looked at Pat, who was looking at the light blue carpet. The heavy moment pooled around them. Then the cameras stopped, the handlers stepped forward, and Frederick was separated from his wife. He felt slightly panicky, as if he were bidding her farewell from a dock, a feeling not helped by her flirtatious wave as a man with a tight goatee led her away.

But no one was going far. Backstage, cubicles were set up, each with a barber chair. The guests were escorted to their chairs, the curtains then discreetly drawn. "I'm Faïence," said the black-haired woman who slipped into Frederick's cubicle. She was wearing a sleeveless dress, so he could see how her shoulders, under the skin's dewy sheen, were sculpted like fists.

"Isn't that a kind of china?"

"Not many people know that. We'll get you on *Jeopardy!* after you're finished here." She stood with her head cocked, and Frederick could guess at her checklist: hair, beard, T-shirt. He'd heard the litany from his girls often enough. Only when he imagined similar narrow, assessing eyes trained on Pat did his chest grow hollow.

"Women tend to do this kind of thing better than the men, right?" he said.

"Sometimes yes, sometimes no. People will surprise you. Now come with me and we'll work on losing ten pounds of hair."

Frederick was only mildly nervous, which pleased him. The worst he felt was a ripple across his stomach, some small trouble breathing. Faïence chattered about how much simpler he would find life with his new hair, the short length such a breeze to wash and dry. "What do you like to do with your time?"

"I'm an activist," he said.

"Should have guessed. Well, you'll have more time to be active. You'll wonder why you waited so long. You're going to meet a whole new you."

"It's just a haircut," he said. He probably should have said more, but his lungs felt squeezed.

He had read about prisoners of war who survived their ordeal by focusing on whatever was directly in front of them. One man had counted the bricks on the wall he faced. After he counted them, he named them — U.S. presidents, British monarchy, state capitals. Frederick would have liked a task so specific. For three hours, he concentrated on the slap of heavy creams across his face, the cold blade of the scissors snicking against his neck, the lapful of coarse wool as his beard was cut. "This isn't even trimming," Faïence said. "This is shearing. When was the last time you shaved?"

"1841."

"You could have an AK-47 hidden in here."

"I don't believe in guns."

"Right. You could have a MAKE LOVE NOT WAR sign hidden in here."

"My daughters would like you," he said. Faïence was rubbing a silky lotion into his stinging cheeks and jaw. The lotion was green and smelled like honey. "They're the reason I'm here, in case you wondered. I wouldn't have come on my own."

"I don't want to shock you, but every guy who comes on the

show has a wife or daughters or girlfriend behind him, shoving. We had a guy in his sixties come in — beard like yours, bald at the top and then a yard of fuzzy hair. The whole hippie toot. His mother sat out there in the audience, eighty-four years old. When he came on stage with a haircut and a sports coat she yelled, 'Thank you, Jesus.' They tried to dub her out, but you could still hear her."

"So I'm a type?"

Faïence shrugged. "There are a lot of guys making your fashion statement."

Frederick nearly started to explain the difference between statement and fashion statement, but Faïence said, "Hold still. I'm layering."

Frederick fixed his eyes on the green cape draped over his knees. Perhaps Pat would appear with her hair arranged in the curly bubble that suburban housewives had worn when he was a boy. He had never touched hair like that and couldn't even guess how it might feel. Most nights he fell asleep with his hands wrapped in sections of Pat's hair, which had certainly been cut off by now. Trembling briefly overtook him. "Sorry," he said, before Faïence could chide him.

"We're done," she said, whipping the chair around so that he could see the mirror. He had to watch himself raising his hand to his cheek to recognize the reflection as his own. Without its brushy beard, the face looked squared off and purposeful: "Colonel," he first thought with disdain, and then, despairingly, "President." The hair rose in a crest from his straight forehead, and he needed a moment to take in the streaks of deep auburn Faïence had applied, and the etched layers that made his formerly no-color hair look as abundant and rich as loam.

"This is the part where you compliment the stylist," Faïence said.

"You're good at your job."

"You haven't sold your soul here."

"I know. I left my soul at home." He gazed at the square face before him, which would look comfortable with the suit and tie that were waiting in the dressing room. He had seen this man all his life, on the opposite side of podiums and picket lines. The trembling became a shudder, which Faïence either didn't see or ignored.

"You've gone for too long without a change. A person can lose track of all that he's capable of."

"I haven't done *anything*," he said too fiercely. He kept his eyes on the mirror, looking first at her attractive face, then at his own unrecognizable one. Nearly unrecognizable. In their new context, his familiar wrinkles looked full of character. "Have you ever changed yourself this much?"

"Honey, last week I was a blonde. Now, quit ogling yourself or you'll be late for your own show. You don't want to disappoint your wife."

He also didn't want to be disappointed by her, a thought that shamed him as soon as it appeared. It was a thought that belonged to this man in the mirror — this corporate superstar, this mover and shaker, who found in his dressing room a suit in three parts, with pinstripes. The shirt had French cuffs, and on the little dressing table sat gold cuff links the size of dimes. "You can't be serious," Frederick said.

"It's Corbin," said the woman assigned to his clothes. She wore black glasses, black skirt, black stockings. He worked on a joke about mourning, although a woman with a face like this wouldn't laugh.

"It looks like you're making me the president of Chase Manhattan."

"Bank presidents dress a lot better than this."

"I teach college. The most formal event I go to is dinner when my daughters talk me into Long John Silver's. Where in the world would I wear a suit?"

"On television." She pushed her heavy black glasses up her nose. He waited for her to step back before he took off Faïence's smock and put on the shirt, whose crispness felt foreign but not unpleasant. He would remember to tell Pat that.

He had supposed himself finished after he put on the shoes — formal and shining, "cap toed," according to the handler, in for a dollar — but then she made him stand on a small dais and rotate before her. Pulling straight pins from a cushion on her wrist, she tightened the seat of his pants and the shoulders of the suit coat, and Frederick felt his tiny store of patience give out. When she fussily tugged on his cuff, he actually slapped at her, though he missed. "Jesus *Christ*, that's enough."

From the other side of the green curtain a woman said, "Oh!" His handler pulled down his cuff again, and then again. Again.

At the cued music, action swooped down in a rush. The audience applauded and the trumpets repeated their flourish and the host said that no one would ever believe the changes. He'd said so three times already. Then Frederick was on the stage, feeling an embarrassed smile strain at his mouth while the women in the audience — there seemed to be only women — cheered. The host drew him to the edge of the stage and made him turn around, showing off the suit. Audience members stamped the floor. Somebody catcalled, and to Frederick's horror his eyes dampened. Where was Pat?

The host wanted to chat. How did Frederick like his new hair? Wasn't that a fine suit? Did he feel like a whole new man?

"Yes," Frederick said, and hoped that the host could overlook the acid that filled his tone. "I'm eager to see my wife."

"Pat," said the host, sliding his eyes to the TelePrompTer. "She's had quite a day."

"Is she all right?"

"Pat Weiler," the host mused. "Wife, mother, activist." On the screen at the side of the stage, a video clip showed Pat standing with an unhappy smile in a dressing room, her long hair straggling over her shoulders and her hands hidden in her jumper pockets. She kept them there as she turned around, and Frederick noted for the first time how the soft fabric bagged across the seat and how her flat sandals made her ankles look stumpy. She had worn that jumper, or one just like it, for years.

"Meet the new Pat Weiler: Style Queen!" cried the host. Music surged, and from the far side of the stage Pat burst out, nearly running. Later people would ask Frederick whether he had recognized her, and he would be insulted. A haircut and a new dress couldn't conceal the woman with whom he had built his life. Still, she tore at his heart. Her hair trailed in feathers over her ears and down her neck, and her face's sweet softness was lost. She was wearing a sea-green evening gown whose sequins caught the light, and beneath it he glimpsed green sandals with heels so high that her ankles wobbled while the audience wolf-whistled. Frederick's eyes flooded again and he stared at the floor to compose himself. When he looked up, he was the only person in the room still seated.

"What do you think?" the host cried over the commotion. "Are these our biggest makeovers ever?"

Pat had almost made her way to Frederick, her step light. As members of the audience shouted their approval, she twirled. The skirt flared up her calves, and he was jolted by her legs' unnatural color — shaved, he realized. When she reached him, he finally stood and took her hand. Her smile was more than a smile; for the first time he understood what it meant for a person to look radiant. He could hardly keep his eyes on her. "You look like a princess," he said. His voice was high and strained.

"Style Queen," she said. "But you!"

Before he could ask her what about him, the host was at their elbows, making both of them turn around again for the cacophonous audience. "Who knew?" he said. "Who could have foreseen these beautiful people?"

He turned to Pat. "What are you going to do with that jumper when you get home?"

"Burn it," she said.

"And your new hair and face? Do you think you can keep this up on your own?"

"Or die trying." She gestured at the huge "before" picture on the screen. "I think it's time to retire her."

"You're talking about the woman I love," Frederick said, and the host cuffed him on the shoulder. "What about this guy?" the host said to Pat. "Did you ever think you'd see him looking so fine?"

"Never," she said, setting off another roar from the audience. Frederick tried to exchange a glance with her — a promise, an affirmation — but her bright eyes slid away, she twirled again, and he was left trying to straighten his idiotic French cuffs.

"We have a present for you," the host was saying to Pat, who said that she needed nothing more. "You already know that we're sending you and Frederick out on the town tonight, to show off your new looks. But we want to send you home with a memento." Frederick's black-clad handler strode from the wings with a plastic bag for Pat, who pulled out something lank and grayish that looked like a dead cat.

The audience howled, and the host cried, "We were going to give you his beard, too, but we didn't think it would fit in your suitcase," setting off another roar from the crowd. Pat, too, was shaking with laughter, dabbing at her green-lidded eyes and wagging the ponytail in the air. "Look," she said to Frederick. "There's twenty years."

Twenty-two. With a little cry, he bent over against his constricting vest, pressed his manicured hands to his smooth face, and burst into tears.

That night at the restaurant, where the network limousine had taken them from their hotel, Frederick's emotions had dried up. Bathed in creamy light, he listened to the muted string quartet and the murmur of the French sommelier moving from table to table — wealthy sounds, paid for by the show. He hoped that the show would also pick up the tab for Pat's long phone call from the hotel to the girls, in which she had detailed every stroke of the cosmetician's brush. He had lain on the bed, cold along the chin, and listened for some reference to his tears, but Pat spent most of the time telling them about her hair stylist, a navy man.

"They're very excited," Pat told Frederick now. She sucked at a white Russian. Laura and Bett had told her to order it. "They wanted to make sure that we'd gotten directions for all of the makeup and hair drying. They're afraid that we're going to come home tomorrow just the same, as if none of this ever happened."

"It'll take a while to grow that hair back."

"They love that I got to keep your ponytail. They all want some of it to braid and wear as bracelets."

"I was thinking about giving it a proper burial."

"We could burn it, along with my jumper. A purification ritual."

"Not bad," he said. "We could smear the ashes on our faces."

"And ruin my makeup? No way." Her laugh was a trill, and she ducked her head girlishly as she sipped her sweet drink. He had made her happy, as he had meant to do. Surely couples owed each other happiness. He looked at his own drink, a double scotch, more liquor than he usually drank at a sitting. So now did their lives stop, resting on the platform of her happiness?

He said, "If we're going to hold a ritual, we'll have to check the calendar for an opening. It's already time to start thinking about the recycling initiative. The new waste-removal contract is coming up before city council." He saw her drop her eyes, and he softened his voice. "In Rock Hill they missed the deadline, remember? They went three months without curbside pickup. I hate to think of the waste."

"I don't think that will happen to us," she said.

"Constant vigilance," he said, their old battle cry.

"The girls are keeping up the fight in our absence. I have reason to believe that they are spending tonight putting a faux finish on our recycling bins."

"You want me to be charmed by that, don't you?"

"That would be nice."

The sight of his own groomed hand and buffed nails unnerved him, although at least he'd changed into a shirt with button cuffs. Pat had insisted on visiting the hotel's boutique, and he had taken the opportunity to buy another shirt. "I don't want to fight," he said.

"Remember what Jack Carey said? We're supposed to have fun."

"Who's Jack Carey?"

The smile died on Pat's mouth. "He's the host of *The Jack Carey Show*, Frederick. It's a television program. You were on it."

"I'm sorry. I never caught his name."

"It was all over the set. And people said it about a hundred times."

"You know I'm not good at names." He nudged his glass, noting the damp impression it left on the thick tablecloth.

"And I shouldn't ask you to change, should I? I shouldn't ask you to be what you're not," she said. He knew this voice. She had used it when Laura, age eight, came home in tears after throwing a rock at her best friend.

He said, "What do you plan to do now? If we have to picket about waste removal, are you going to walk in high heels?"

"I think so, yes. I like them. If I make the 6:00 news, we can keep the videotape with the one of you talking to city council."

No, they couldn't. One of the girls had taped a cartoon show over the old tape of Frederick's speech, a fact he had uncovered one afternoon when he was alone in the house. Still, he remembered how he had looked on TV, as if a prophet had come before the clean-shaven council members in their dark suits. He closed his eyes against the sharp tears.

"What do you want me to say?" Pat said.

"'Honey, are you all right?' 'Frederick, is there anything I can do?'"

"I'm sorry," she said. He lifted his stinging eyes to see her, blurry and green. "I truly am."

"If I knew you were crying, I would have done something." He absolutely should not have gone on to the next sentence. "I wouldn't have let you cry on TV."

"What are you talking about?"

In his shock, Frederick had plenty of time to watch the young waiter hastening to their table. His broad, welcoming smile had been installed all the way across the dining room.

"You know that your charges here have all been taken care of by the network," the waiter said as soon as he was tableside. "If I were you, I'd keep the champagne coming. You look like movie stars. I'll bet you spent the last two hours in front of a mirror."

Maybe he misinterpreted their silence. He lowered his voice to the level of a confidence. "The show sends most of its makeovers here. Sometimes the people look like they're wearing costumes. You can tell that they just let the crew on the show do things to them. The important thing is to let people's true selves shine out."

His smile blazed. Pat looked stunned. To Frederick he said, "You were the most honest thing I've ever seen on television."

Frederick said, "There was a close-up, wasn't there?"

"You looked good."

"That wasn't exactly what I was asking."

"I said, 'There is a man who knows his truest self.' No one who saw that show will ever forget you."

"Thank you," Frederick said unsteadily.

Pat's voice, speaking to the waiter, was suddenly tart; her white Russian must have already dived into her bloodstream. "Haven't you ever seen this show? Tomorrow somebody will get his hair dyed red and his wife will get a miniskirt, and everybody will clap again, and nobody will remember that Frederick's beard took up most of a trash bag once it was off his face."

"They'll remember the ponytail," said the waiter.

Pat shook her head. "Did you see the show when Jack Carey gave a guy's overalls a funeral? Another time he weighed all the makeup a woman wore every day to work."

"Three ounces, with the eyelashes," the waiter said.

"A ponytail is nothing," she said.

"Hang on," Frederick said, and cleared his throat. The tremble was back. "Everybody's been telling me all day that I was being made into a new man. I thought that was the point. The gal who cut my hair kept saying that you'd never know me."

"Frederick, no one would ever be able to miss you." She nodded at the waiter. "Just ask him. You're the most unchanging thing he's ever seen on television."

"That's not what I said," the waiter protested.

Frederick said, "Are you saying that I can't be different? No matter what?"

Perhaps because of the lipstick, Pat's smile looked strange — saucy, appraising. "Prove it," she said.

"I know how to make a good thing last a long time," he said.

"Same guy."

"I appreciate what I've got."

"Same, same, same."

What was going on today with his shirt cuffs? Now they were

twisted around his wrists like shackles. "I'm trying to give you what you want. You're not making it easy."

"Good."

The waiter brushed his fingers over the tablecloth and made a sizzling noise. "If you two had talked like this on the show, they would have had to bleep you out."

Pat raised her slim new eyebrows suggestively. "This is the part of the show that doesn't get advertised, where the couple starts fresh. They decide whether they want to get started with each other."

"And?" said the waiter.

"Negotiations are under way," said Pat.

"The worst is over," said Frederick. He waited, but neither Pat nor the waiter agreed.

On the ride back to the hotel Frederick and Pat's silence was rich. The limousine driver turned off his radio, and the doorman at the curb stepped back, swallowing his "Good evening" before it left his mouth. The Weilers ascended the elevator in silence and entered their room in silence. Perhaps Pat was happy. Perhaps even Frederick was. It seemed unlikely, but he was a little drunk and wasn't going to exclude any possibilities.

Though the night was sweltering — pure Chicago August, with the smell and feel of rubber — Frederick sat out on the balcony while Pat took off her evening gown. He liked the cling of the humid night air, which erased the lingering aroma of emollients and hair spray. From nearby a car alarm started up, and somewhere behind it the El clanked past. Frederick hadn't sat outside in a city for years, and the mechanical shrieking and sighing were oddly satisfying. He had an urge to get even closer to it — to go back down to the streets, into a bar. Into a bar fight. He wanted to rub his smooth new face against gritty surfaces.

Three feet in front of him, the edge of the balcony was faced with cheap, rough stone. Frederick had read once that jumpers in cities often suffered massive abrasions on their way down. If the impact didn't kill them, the loss of skin would. No one knew whether they simply hit the building or were trying to reach out and cling. Frederick stood up and ran his hand along the outside of the balcony, brushing the rough surface until his palm stung. Then he slung his jacket over his shoulder and slipped back into the cool room.

Sitting on the bed like a dollop of froth, Pat watched television. She had bought a filmy green peignoir at the boutique, and her pale shoulders bloomed from the green flounces. She still wore her makeup.

Frederick whistled, then made his voice soft. "Come here often?"

"Maybe. Looking for a sharp-dressed man."

"Be smart. Clothes are just the start." He opened the honor bar and pulled out a finger-size bottle of VSOP. She made room for him on the bed, but not much. He had to sit close.

Either the show had included perfume in her makeover, or one of the lotions smelled like pine and honeysuckle, traced in a line behind her ear. The smell deepened as he moved his mouth down her throat and licked the tiny cup at its base. He opened the cognac, dabbed it across her breastbone, and started to lick it off.

"Is this smart?" she said.

"Highly." Wetting his finger again, he wiped the cognac across her cheek, taking a stripe of the makeup with it. She closed her eyes, but he was afraid to go after the mascara, which might sting if he wet it.

"I have to leave tomorrow," she said.

"Me too." He slipped his fingers through her hair, now so smooth and short it had almost no weight.

"I'm married," she said, pressing her head against his hand.

"Me too. But we'll always have tonight."

"Who would ever think we could be lucky enough to find each other?" she said. Then he put his mouth over hers, so she couldn't ask any more.

AX OF THE APOSTLES

AFTER FOUR HOURS spent locked in his office, gorging on cookies and grading sophomore philosophy papers, Father Thomas Murray seethed. His students, future priests who would lead the Church into the next century, were morons.

"Kant's idea of the Universal Law might have made sense back in his time, but today we live in a complex, multicultural world where one man's universal law is another man's poison, if you know what I mean." *So there are no absolutes?* Father Murray wrote in the margin, pressing so hard that he carved the letters into the paper. *Peculiar notion, for a man who wants to be a priest.*

They didn't know how to *think*. Presented with the inexhaustibly rich world, all its glory, pity, and terror, they managed to perceive only the most insipid pieties. If he asked them to discuss the meaning of the crucifixion, they would come back with *Suffering is a mystery, and murder is bad*. Father Murray looked at the paper before him and with difficulty kept from picking up his pen and adding *Idiot*.

He had planned on spending no more than two hours grading and then going over to the track to put in a couple of overdue miles. But flat-footed student prose and inept, flabby, half-baked student logic had worked him into a silent fury, and the fury itself became a kind of joy, each bad paper stoking higher the flames of his outrage. He reached compulsively for the next paper in the stack, and then the next, his left hand snagging another of the cookies he'd taken last night from the kitchen. They were not good — lackluster oatmeal, made with shortening instead of butter — but enough to keep him going. *What makes you think,* he wrote, *that Kant's age was any less complex than yours?*

Still reading, he stretched his back against the hard office chair, which shrieked every time he moved, and started to count off the traits lacked by the current generation of seminarians: Historical understanding. Study skills. Vocabulary. Spelling. From down the hall he heard a crash and then yelps of laughter. "Oh, Alice!" someone cried. Father Murray closed his eyes.

A month ago one of the students had sneaked into the seminary a mannequin with eyelashes like fork tines and a brown wig that clung to its head like a bathing cap. Since then the mannequin had been popping up every day, in the showers, the library, at meals. Students mounted it on a ladder so that its bland face, a cigarette taped to its mouth, could peer in classroom windows. Now a campaign to turn the mannequin into the seminary's mascot was afoot. Savagely, Father Murray bit into another bad cookie, then stood, inhaled, and left his office.

At the bend in the hallway, where faculty offices gave way to dormitory rooms, five students clustered beside an open door. The mannequin, dressed in towels, half reclined in the doorway to Quinn's room. Blond, morose Quinn, a better student than most, tugged the towels higher up the mannequin's bosom. The customary cigarette had fallen from the doll's pink plastic mouth and now dangled by a long piece of tape. "You should have seen your *face,*" Adreson was saying to Quinn. Father Murray knew and loathed the sort of priest Adreson would become: peppy, brain dead, and loved by the old ladies. "I thought you were going to faint. I thought we were going to lose you."

"Jumped a foot," added Michaels. "At least a foot."

"Went up like a firecracker," Father Murray suggested, and the seminarians turned, apparently delighted he had joined them.

"A Roman candle," Adreson said.

"Like a shooting star," Father Murray said. "Like a rocket. Like the *Challenger.* Boom."

The laughter slammed to a halt; Adreson stepped back, and Father Murray said, "You men sound, in case you're interested, like a fraternity out here. I would not like to be the one explaining to the bishop what tomorrow's priests are doing with a big plastic doll. Although I could always tell him that you were letting off some steam after your titanic academic struggles. Then the bishop and I could laugh."

"She fell right onto Brian," Adreson murmured. "Into his arms. It was funny."

Father Murray remembered a paper Adreson had written for him the year before, in which Adreson had called Aquinas "The Stephen Hawking of the 1300s," not even getting the century right. In that same paper Adreson had made grave reference to "the Ax of the Apostles." From any of the other men Father Murray would have allowed the possibility that the citation was a joke. Now he looked at his student, twenty years old and still trying to subdue a saddle of pimples across his cheeks. "You have developed a genius for triviality."

"Sorry, Father."

"I'm giving you a piece of information. Think about it."

"Thank you, Father."

"Don't bother thanking me until you mean it."

"Oh, I mean it, Father." Adreson pursed his mouth — an odd, old-maidish expression. "Sorry we disturbed you. Guess we're too full of beans tonight. Hey — you want to go over to the track?"

Father Murray felt a plateful of oatmeal cookies churn in his stomach. "Another time. I've still got work to do."

"*Corpore sano,* Father."

Father Murray snorted and turned back toward his office. He cherished a measure of low satisfaction that the one Latin phrase Adreson seemed to know came from the YMCA slogan.

He should, of course, have taken up Adreson's offer. By ten o'clock his stomach was violent with oatmeal cookies; his error had been in eating even one. As soon as he'd tasted that first sweet bite, he was done for. He could eat two dozen as easily as a single cookie. Tomorrow he would have to be especially strict with himself.

Strictness, as everyone at St. Boniface knew, was Father Murray's particular stock-in-trade. Fourteen months before, his doctor had called him in to discuss blood sugar and glucose intolerance. "You have a family history, is that right?"

Father Murray nodded. His mother — bloated, froglike, blind — had had diabetes. By the end, she had groped with her spongy hand to touch his face. He had held still, even when she pressed her thumb against his eye. "Doesn't everybody have a family history?" he said now.

"This is no joke. You are at risk," the doctor said. "You could start needing insulin injections. Your legs are already compromised. You could die. Do you understand that?"

Father Murray considered reminding the doctor that a priest's job entailed daily and exquisite awareness of his mortality. Nevertheless, he took the doctor's point: Father Murray's forty-five-inch waist, the chin that underlaid his chin, his fingers too pudgy for the ring his father had left him. If he let the disease take hold, he would deteriorate in humiliating degrees, relying on others to walk for him when his feet failed, to read to him when the retinopathy set in. A life based wholly on charity — not just the charity of God, which Father Murray could stomach, but the charity of the men around him. The next day he began to walk, and a month later, to run.

For a solid year he held himself to 1,100 exacting calories a day, eating two bananas for breakfast and a salad with vinegar for lunch. His weight plummeted; his profile shrank from that of Friar Tuck to St. Francis, and the waist of his trousers bunched like a paper bag. The night Father Murray hit 150, ten pounds below his target weight, Father Radziewicz told him, "You're a walking wonder." They were standing, plates in hand, in line for iced tea. Father Radziewicz's eye rested on Father Murray's piece of pork loin, slightly smaller than the recommended three ounces, stranded on the white plate. "How much have you lost now?"

"One hundred twenty-four pounds."

"Enough to make a whole other priest. Think of it."

"I'm condensed," Father Murray said. "Same great product, but half the packaging."

"Think of it," Father Radziewicz said. His plate held three

pieces of pork, plus gravy, potatoes, two rolls. "I couldn't do it," he added.

"It's just a matter of willpower," Father Murray said. "To the greater glory of God."

"Still, isn't it time to stop? Or at least slow down. Maybe you've glorified God enough."

"I've never felt better in my life."

The statement was largely true. He had never in his life been quite so satisfied with himself, although his knees sometimes hurt so much after a twelve-mile run that he could hardly walk. He bought ibuprofen in 500-count bottles and at night, in bed, rested his hand on the bones of his hips, the corded muscles in his thighs. Out of pure discipline he had created a whole new body, and he rejoiced in his creation.

So he was unprepared for the muscular cravings that beset him shortly after his conversation with Father Radziewicz. They came without warning, raging through the airy space below his rib cage. The glasses of water, the repetitions of the daily office, all the tricks Father Murray had taught himself now served only to delay the hunger — five minutes, fifteen, never enough.

One night he awoke from a dream of boats and anchors to find himself pushing both fists against his twisting stomach. Brilliantly awake, heart hammering, he padded around the seminary, glancing into the chapel, the storage room that held raincoats and wheelchairs for needy visitors, the pathetically underused weight room. Finally, giving in, he let his hunger propel him to the kitchen, hoping that food would help him get back to sleep.

Holding open the refrigerator door, he gazed at cheesecake left over from dinner. He was ten pounds underweight. He had left himself a margin; probably he was getting these cravings because he actually needed some trace of fat and sugar in his system. And the next day he could go to the track early and run off whatever he took in tonight. He ate two and a half pieces of cheesecake, went back to bed, and slept as if poleaxed.

Since then Father Murray had hardly gone a night without stealing downstairs for some snack — cookies, cake, whatever the seminarians and other priests, those locusts, had left. He stored his cache in a plastic bag and kept the bag in his desk drawer, allowing himself to nibble between classes, in the long afternoon lull before dinner, whenever hunger roared up in him. Twice he broke the hour-long fast required before taking communion. Each time he sat, stony faced, in his pew, while the other priests filed forward to take the host.

At meals he continued to take skimpy portions of lean foods, so stuffed with cookies that even the plate of bitter salad seemed too much to get through. Father Bip, a Vietnamese priest he had often run with, told him that he was eating like a medieval monk. Father Murray slapped himself hard on the rump. "Brother Ass," he said. That rump was noticeably fleshier than it had been two months before, and he vowed again that he would recommence his diet the next day. That night, anticipating the stark hunger, he quietly walked the half-mile to a drugstore and bought a bag of peanut butter cups, several of which he ate on the walk back home.

As he lay in bed, his teeth gummy with chocolate and peanut butter paste, his days of crystalline discipline seemed close enough to touch. The choice was simple, and simply made; he remembered the pleasure of a body lean as a knife, a life praiseworthy and coherent. Yet the next night found him creeping back to the kitchen, plastic bag in hand, not exactly hungry anymore but still craving. Already his new black pants nipped him at the waist.

After his one o'clock Old Testament class the next afternoon, Father Murray returned to his office to find Adreson waiting for him. The young man, who had been absently fingering a flaming blemish beside his nose, held out his hand toward Father Murray, who shook it gingerly and ushered Adreson into his office.

"How was your class, Father?"

"We entertained the usual riotous dispute over Jerome's interpretation of 2 Kings." Then, looking at Adreson, he added, "It was fine."

"Your O.T. class has a real reputation. Men come out of there knowing their stuff."

"That's the basic idea."

"Sorry. I'm nervous, I guess. I want to apologize for making all that racket in the hallway last night."

"Thank you."

"I knew we were being —"

"— childish," Father Murray offered.

"— immature. I just thought you should know that there was a reason. Brian's mother has multiple sclerosis. Advanced, but he just found out last week. She's at home by herself with four kids, and she keeps falling down. I know it's killing Brian, but he won't talk about it. He just keeps going to class and services. It isn't healthy. That's why we put Alice in his room."

"He may find it comforting to keep up his usual schedule. This may be his way of coping," Father Murray said, autopilot words. Genuine surprise kept him from asking Adreson how a towel-wrapped mannequin was supposed to help Quinn manage his sorrow.

"He needs to talk, Father. If he talks to people, we can help him."

"You have a lot of faith in yourself."

"We're here to help each other." His hand fluttered up toward his face, then dropped again. "If it were me, I'd want to know I could count on the guys around me. I'd want to know I wasn't alone."

"He prays, doesn't he? He may be getting all the support he needs. Not everything has to be talked out."

"We're not hermits, Father."

"A little more solitude wouldn't hurt anybody around here."

A burst of anger flashed across Adreson's face, and Father Murray leaned forward in the chair, which let out a squeal. He was more than ready to take the boy on. But after a complicated moment Adreson's mouth and eyes relaxed. "Of course you're right. I thought I should apologize for disturbing you." He stood up straight, clearly relieved to have put the moment behind him. "I'm going for a run this afternoon. Want to join me?"

"You're doing a lot of running lately. I'd suggest you take a few laps around the library."

"You're great, Father. You don't ever miss a lick." He produced another grin. He seemed to have a ready-made, toothy stockpile. "Track meet's coming up. I'm running the relay and the 440. The 440's your event, isn't it?"

"Distance," Father Murray said.

"I'm a little obsessed about that 440. Sometimes in practice I can get close to the conference record, so now it's my goal: I want to put St. Boniface in the record books."

Father Murray held his peace, but Adreson must have read his expression.

"I'll have plenty of time to be pastoral later. Right now, running's the best talent I've got." He winked. "I know what you're going to say: not a very priestly talent, is it?"

"I wasn't going to say anything like that. You are the model of today's seminarian."

Father Murray waited for Adreson to leave the office before he swiveled to gaze at the maple outside his window. Hundreds of tender spring leaves unfurled like moist hands, a wealth of pointless beauty. Where, he wondered, was Quinn's father? Had he run off after the fifth child, or had he died, snatched away in midbreath or left to dwindle before the eyes of his many children? Cancer, heart attack, mugging. So many paths to tragedy. Now Quinn's mother was trapped inside a body that buckled and stumbled. Before long she would rely on others to cook for her, drive for her, hold a glass of water at her mouth.

"Too much," he muttered, his jaw so tight it trembled. He didn't blame Quinn for not wanting to talk to Adreson, who knew nothing about pain. He didn't have a clue of sorrow's true nature or purpose: to grind people down to faceless surfaces, unencrusted with desire or intent. Only upon a smooth surface could the hand of God write. Every priest used to know that. Father Murray knew it. Quinn was learning it.

Turning to the desk, Father Murray began to reach for the stale cookies in his drawer, then pushed back his chair. If an overdue visit to the track would make his legs hurt, so much the better. He couldn't take on any of Quinn's suffering, but at least he could join him in it.

Weeks had passed since Father Murray had last gone for a run.

His legs were wooden stumps, his breath a string of gasps. He flailed as if for a life preserver when he rounded the track the fourth time. Adreson, out practicing his 440, yelled, "Come on — pick 'em up, pick 'em up!" and Father Murray felt his dislike for the boy swell. After six laps he stopped and bent over. Adreson sailed around twice more. Father Murray waited for his lungs to stop feeling as if they were turning themselves inside out. Then he straightened up and began again.

At dinner he stood in line for a slice of pineapple cake. "Oho," said Father Bip. "You are coming down to earth to join us?"

"I should be earthbound after this, all right."

"Should you be eating cake?" Father Radziewicz asked. "Wouldn't a piece of fruit be better?"

"Of course it would be better, Patrick," Father Murray snapped. "Look, one piece of cake isn't going to make my feet fall off."

Father Radziewicz shrugged, and Father Murray stomped across the dining room to a table where Father Tinsdell, a sharp young number imported this year from Milwaukee to teach canon law, was holding forth. "You're all thinking too small. We can sell this as an apparition. Trot Alice out after mass and get the weeping women claiming that their migraines have gone away and their rosaries have turned to gold. We'll have the true believers streaming in. Pass the collection basket twice a day; next thing you know, we're all driving new cars. We'll buy one for the bishop, too."

Father Antonin leaned toward Father Murray. "He found the mannequin in his office. Hasn't shut up since."

"The women are always grousing about how there isn't enough of a feminine presence in the church," Father Tinsdell said. "Well, here they go. Five feet, six inches of miracle-working doll. We can put her in the fountain outside. Stack some rocks around her feet: Voilà! Lourdes West. Bring us your lame, your halt. If enough people come, somebody's bound to get cured. That should keep us rolling for the next century."

"You know," Father Murray said, setting his fork beside his clean plate, "Rome does recognize the existence of miracles."

"Somebody always stiffens up when you start talking marketing." The man's face was a series of points: the point of his needley nose, the point of his chin, the point of his frown set neatly above the point of his cool smile, directed at Father Murray. "Don't get in a twist. I'm up to date on church doctrine."

"People have been cured at Lourdes."

"I know it." Father Tinsdell leaned forward. "Have you ever seen a miracle?"

"No," said Father Murray.

"There are all kinds of miracles," Father Antonin broke in.

Without even glancing at the man, Father Murray knew what was coming: the miracle of birth, the miracle of sunrise, those reliable dodges. He looked at Father Tinsdell. Father Point. "Never. Not once. You?"

"Yup. Saw a fifteen-year-old girl pull out of renal failure. She was gone, kidneys totally shot. Her eyeballs were yellow. Even dialysis couldn't do much. For days her grandmother was in the hospital room, saying rosaries till her fingers bled. She got the whole family in on it. And then the girl turned around. Her eyes cleared. Her kidneys started to work again."

Father Murray stared at the other man. "That can't happen."

"I know. But I was there. I saw it."

Father Murray pondered Tinsdell's mocking gaze. How could a man see a miracle, a girl pulled from the lip of the grave, and still remain such a horse's ass? "I envy you," Father Murray said.

"Keep your eyes open. No telling what you might see." Father Tinsdell stood. He was thin as a ruler. "I'm getting coffee. Do you want more cake?"

"Yes," said Father Murray, though he did not, and would ignore the piece when it appeared.

Several times in the next week Father Murray paused outside Quinn's door, his mouth already filled with words of compassion. But Quinn's door remained closed, separate from the easy coming and going between the other men's rooms. Father Murray respected a desire for solitude, the need for some kind of barrier from the relentless high jinks of the Adresons. He pressed his hand against the door frame, made ardent prayers for Quinn's mother, and left without knocking.

He should, he knew, have saved at least one of those heartfelt prayers for himself. His hunger was becoming a kind of insanity. Food never left his mind; when he taught, he fingered the soft chocolates in his pocket, and at meals he planned his next meal. Nightly he ate directly from the refrigerator, shoveling fingerfuls of leftover casserole into his mouth, wolfing slice after slice of white bread. He dunked cold potatoes through the gravy's mantle of congealed fat, scooped up leathery cheese sauce. He ate as if he meant to disgust himself, but his disgust wasn't enough to stop him. Instead, he awakened deep in the night, his stomach blazing with indigestion, and padded back to the kitchen for more food.

With the other priests in the dining room he carried on the pretense of lettuce and lean meat; his plate held mingy portions of baked fish and chopped spinach unlightened by even a sliver of butter. He ate as if the act were a grim penance. For a week now he hadn't been able to button the waist of his trousers.

One night after dry chicken and half of a dry potato he made his ritual pause outside Quinn's door, then continued down the hall to his own room. Fourteen papers on the autonomy of will promised to provide ugly entertainment. But when he opened his door, he jumped back: propped against the frame stood the mannequin, wearing his running shoes, his singlet and jacket, and his shorts, stuffed with towels to hold them up. From down the hall came a spurt of nervous laughter, like a cough.

Father Murray waited for the laughter to die down, which didn't take long. Adreson and three other men edged out of the room where they'd positioned themselves. They looked as if they expected to be thrashed.

"My turn, I see," Father Murray said.

"We didn't want you to feel left out," said Adreson.

"Well, heavens to Betsy. *Thank* you."

"We thought you'd like the athletic motif. It was a natural."

"An inspiration, you might say."

"I was the one who posed Alice running," Adreson said. "Some of the other men suggested your clothes. Hope you don't mind." He leaned against the wall, hands plunged into the pockets of his jeans. Relaxed now, the others ringed loosely around him.

"Did Quinn have suggestions for this installation?" Father

Murray looked at the mannequin's narrow plastic heels rising from his dirty running shoes, the wig caught back in his dark blue sweatband, the face, of course, unperturbed.

"Didn't you know? He's gone home to help out." His voice shifted, taking on a confiding, talk-show-host smoothness. "I don't think it was a good idea. His mom may be getting around now, but over the long run, he needs to make arrangements. Immersing himself in the situation will give him the sense that he's doing something, but he isn't addressing the real problems."

"Maybe he wants to be there."

"Not exactly a healthy desire, Father. Multiple sclerosis, for Pete's sake. I don't want to be brutal, but she isn't going to get better."

"No," Father Murray said.

"But you know Brian. He said he had to go where he's needed. I told him that he has to weigh needs. He needs to ask, 'Where can I do the most good?' He can't fix everything in the world."

"You weren't listening to him. Every need is a need," Father Murray said, chipping the words free from his mouth. "If you're hungry and you remember that children in Colombia are starving, do you feel any less hungry?"

"Sure. When I'm on vacation, I always skip lunch and put that money in the box. And you know, I never feel hungry. Never."

"One of these days," Father Murray began, then paused. The tremble in his voice surprised him. He felt quite calm. "One of these days you'll find that your path isn't clear. Choices won't be obvious. Sacrifices won't be ranked. Needs will be like beads on a necklace, each one the same size and weight. It won't matter what you do in the world — there will still be more undone."

"My dark night of the soul." Adreson nodded.

"Your first experience of holiness," Father Murray corrected him.

Adreson flattened his lips, and his friends looked at their shoes. "Zing," Adreson said.

"Pay attention. I'm trying to get you to see. If you could take on Quinn's mother's disease tomorrow, if you could take it for her, would you do that?"

"We each have our own role to play, Father. That's not mine."

"I know that. Would you reach for this other role?"

Angry, mute, Adreson stared at the carpet. Father Murray understood that the young man was exercising a good deal of willpower to keep from asking, "Would you? Would you?" and he meant to ensure that Adreson remained silent. If the young man asked, Father Murray would be forced to confess, "Yes, yes, I would," his desire to save just one human life caustic and bottomless.

"I'll go ahead and get Alice out of your room, Father," Adreson was saying.

"Leave her for now," he said wearily.

"I'm sorry. It was just supposed to be a joke."

"I know that. I'm not trying to punish you." Father Murray watched the ring of young men shrink back. He was sorry they were afraid of him, but it couldn't be helped. "She's something new in my life. I'll bring her down to your room tomorrow. Besides, I need to get my clothes back."

The men retreated toward the student lounge, where they would drink Cokes and discuss Father Murray's bitterness, such a sad thing to see in a priest. None of them, Adreson least of all, would imagine himself capable of becoming like Father Murray, and in fact, none of them would become like Father Murray. Only Quinn, and he was gone.

Father Murray turned and studied the mannequin, which looked awkward, its angles all wrong. When he adjusted one of the arms, the mannequin started to tip; its center of balance was specific and meant for high-heeled shoes. Quickly he tried to straighten it, but it inclined to the right. In the end, the best he could do was prop the plastic doll against the bureau and berate his painfully literal imagination, which had flown to Quinn. He wondered how often the young man had already steadied his mother on her way to the bathroom or the kitchen. Father Murray's singlet had slipped over the mannequin's shoulder. He pulled the garment up again.

Adreson and the others must have gotten a passkey and skipped dinner so they could sneak in and rifle his bureau drawers. Father Murray didn't care about that — he kept no secret magazines that could be discovered, no letters or photographs.

Then he remembered the nest of candy wrappers, the thick dust of cake crumbs. And he himself, talking to Adreson about hunger.

"Mother of God." He paced the room in three familiar steps, turned, paced back. The mannequin's head was tilted so that the face gazed toward the flat ceiling light, its expressionlessness not unlike serenity. A bit of paper lingered where a cigarette was usually taped, and Father Murray leaned forward to scrape it off. But the paper didn't come from a cigarette. Carefully folded and tucked above the mannequin's mouth, as precise as a beauty mark, was placed a streamer from a chocolate kiss. When Father Murray touched it, the paper unfurled and dangled over the corner of the mannequin's mouth like a strand of drool, and the doll pitched forward into his arms.

He thrust it back, resisting the impulse to curse. The mannequin's balance, he finally saw, was thrown off by extra weight in the pockets of the jacket. They were distended, stuffed like chipmunk cheeks. How had he not noticed this? Father Murray stabilized the mannequin with one hand and rifled the pockets with the other, his heart thundering.

He knew upon the first touch. Handfuls of dainty chocolate kisses, fresh-smelling, the silver wrappers still crisp. He dropped them on the bureau and let them shower, glittering, around his feet. The air in the room thickened with the smell of chocolate; he imagined it sealing his lungs. A full minute might have passed before he fished out the last piece and sank to the floor beside the pool of candy.

He thought of Adreson: grinning, amiable, dumb. Seminary record-holder in the 440, possessor of a young, strong body. He didn't look capable of true malice. He didn't look capable of spelling it. But above Adreson's constant, supplicating smile sat tiny eyes that never showed pleasure. They were busy eyes, the eyes of a bully or a thug. Eyes like Adreson's missed nothing, and Father Murray had been a fool to think otherwise. He had attributed the nervous gaze to self-consciousness, even to a boyish desire to make good, a miscalculation that might have been Christlike if it weren't so idiotic. Like mistaking acid for milk, a snake for a puppy.

Pressing his fist against his forehead, he saw himself illuminated in the silent midnight kitchen, the overhead light blazing as he shoveled food into his mouth: a fat man making believe he had dignity, and the community of men around him charitably indulging his fantasy. Only Adreson withheld charity.

He fingered the candies on the floor. Unwrapping one, he placed it on his tongue, the taste waxy. He unwrapped a second and held it in his hand until it softened.

The next day, Father Murray waited in Adreson's room, hunger making his mood savage. Before him on the desk sat two textbooks and a dictionary that Father Murray found in the furthest corner of Adreson's single bookshelf. Father Murray's legs, clad only in running shorts, spread pallidly on the hard wooden chair. He had propped the mannequin against Adreson's closet, draped in a sheet for modesty's sake.

"Whoa! Father, you don't get it. The whole point is not to be caught in somebody else's room." Adreson's smile lacked anything like mirth, as Father Murray supposed his own did.

"I read your paper," he said. "I'm here to save you."

"I'm doing fine in all my other classes," Adreson said.

"That's hard to imagine," Father Murray said. He gestured toward the desk chair, but Adreson did not sit down.

"You're not dressed for teaching, Father."

"I thought we might have an exchange. I'll help you, then you can coach me at the track. I need some coaching."

Adreson needed a moment to process this. Once he did, the expression that crossed his face made Father Murray shiver.

"Don't look to me to cut you any slack," Adreson said. "I take running seriously."

"It's your great gift," Father Murray said.

"I just want to make sure you know what you're getting into."

"I know," Father Murray said. He hoped that Adreson could not hear the light edge of fear in his voice, but even if he could, it would change nothing. Father Murray was committed. "But I'm going to help you first."

Appearance of Scandal

After the screaming and the poisonous accusations, after the broken vase and rib, after the gonorrhea, waking up to find Anthony gone was not the hardest thing. It was not the hardest thing to sleep on the fluffy clown rug between the girls' beds or to come to school to pick up Stephanie the day a rash bloomed across her chest. It was not even so hard to forward Anthony's mail and to review the bar association's list of divorce lawyers, so many of whom Anthony had gone to law school with, and mocked.

The hardest thing was sitting in church, where the scalding sense of failure shot from Beth's hairline to the soles of her feet. Surrounded by intact families with husbands who looked proud of their wives — Anthony had not looked proud, ever — Beth read the ads on the back of the bulletin for funeral homes and CPAs, leafed through the hymnal, distracted herself in every way she could think of until the hour was over and she could race to the parking lot, always one of the first to gun it out.

"You don't know how hard it is," she said to Father Marino. "If it weren't for the kids, I wouldn't come back here."

"Then thank goodness for the kids," he said.

The easiest thing after Anthony left was Beth's talks with Father Marino. Every week he made room for her in a schedule filled with Social Justice Committee meetings and intramural soccer and daily hospital visits — needs more legitimate than her small loneliness and sorrow. Every week he opened his office door and produced his cracked-tooth grin, and she saw the sort of boy he must have been, round-headed and cocky, sure of the world's affection.

He had long ago captured the affections of everybody at Holy Name. After cranky Father Mestin had retired and nervous Father Torbeiner had been whisked away with so little explanation — people still murmured about him — parishioners recognized their good fortune in Father Marino. He had a friendly habit of snapping off his Roman collar in midconversation. "Enough of this. Let's *talk*." People confided in him — guilty teenagers and angry mothers and the whole Men's Club, which took Father Marino on a trout-fishing trip every June, returning sunburned, hung over, and sheepishly low on trout. Beth wondered whom Father Marino confided in, but she recognized her curiosity as the question of a freshly divorced woman half in love with her priest and kept it to herself.

Instead, she told him about her job at the Women's Services office on the weedy outskirts of town. Now she was working as a receptionist and sometime counselor, but she was planning to become a paralegal and, after that, an attorney. "That would kill Anthony," Father Marino said.

She said, "My point, exactly."

Anthony had already asked her how she, a Catholic, could work in such a place, a question she thought rich, considering that he had been the one with the girlfriend. "The women who go there need help," she said shortly. She wasn't about to give him details on the sullen, exhausted mothers who edged through the office door, needing health care, legal advice, babysitters. Sometimes they needed abortions, and Beth counseled them about facilities, a fact she'd confessed to Father Marino and that he told her didn't need to be confessed. More than anything, these women worried about their children, and Beth told them with real compassion, "Children are the fear that steals your heart. I know just what you mean."

When she said this, her eyes slid to the desk photo of her two daughters, laughing and proud on their new Rollerblades. They were older now and laughed less. The divorce had hurt them. Ten-year-old Alison threw tantrums like a first-grader, and seven-year-old Stephanie refused to read her colorful schoolbooks. Beth told Father Marino about this, too. "Ali screams until she's blue. Anthony would never have stood for it."

"No kidding. He left." He leaned forward, resting his bony elbows on his thighs. Despite his apple-round face, he had a lean frame, freckled skin stretched over long bones. "Don't you feel like screaming?"

"No more than ten times a day. But for the last six months Anthony was home, I wanted to scream all day long, so I should be grateful."

Father Marino shook his head. "You don't ask for enough."

"I ask for plenty," she said. "I just don't get."

"We'll have to see about that," he said.

Beth understood that she should not take Father Marino's vague promises too seriously. Everybody knew that he liked to make promises. He especially liked to make them on the telephone, at night, when people heard the sound of ice cubes rattling in a glass not far from the phone.

There weren't rumors, exactly, and no incidents — unlike the case of Father Toole at St. Agnes, who had been pulled over for DUI and was abusive to the officer: the whole parish council had had to swing its weight to keep the story out of the paper. Still, so many people had run into Father Marino at the Liquor Barn. At so many parties he had gotten tipsy. Holy Name parishioners were accustomed to a priest who took a drink — if anything, they liked the little touch of worldliness — but sometimes when they called the rectory late, they heard a wildness in Father Marino's voice — too much laughter, too-quick sympathy. He spoke very knowledgeably about wine.

Beth's own mother had drunk too much and had died of it. Beth knew the signs. Still, she didn't blame Father Marino. Lately, when the girls were at Anthony's condo, Beth had been learning about the stillness of an empty house, how a person could wade through loneliness as if through mud. One night she'd sat in front of the blank TV until one in the morning, unwilling to turn it on because eventually she'd have to turn it off again and hear the silence sweep back down. Who could be surprised if Father Marino took a snort too much now and then?

Nevertheless, when the Parish Life Committee started planning Father's birthday party, Beth voted with those who said the only liquor should be jug wine, and not too much of that. Already teens from the youth group were writing a skit, and the Men's Club had planned a roast. It would be the sort of evening that a pastor should enjoy, and Beth meant to make sure Father Marino enjoyed it. "Sorry," she said to Frank Burding, who wanted to bring his special punch. "This is family entertainment."

"What are you, the den mother?"

"That would make you a Boy Scout?" She meant it as a joke. Father Marino would have laughed.

Maybe Frank had a party for Father before the party, or maybe Father had a little party for himself — as soon as he entered the parish hall, to applause, Beth could see how his eyes wandered and slid. "Happy birthday to me," he said at the door.

"How old are you, Father?" said Amy Burding.

"A gentleman never tells."

"You're not a gentleman. You're a priest."

"And that is where my troubles began."

Amy didn't so much laugh as cough, and Father Marino, companionable, did too. Beth strolled over to the refreshments table. It pained her to watch her pastor pretend to be sober.

The party was moving now. All over the hall people were laughing, and a pile of gifts sat near the door. Beth knew what some of them were — two pounds of smoked trout from the Men's Club, a soft wool cardigan from the Altar Society. From Beth, a card that said only *Happy birthday*. She was confident that he would be able to read into it her larger feelings — if not tonight, then tomorrow. For now, she busied herself with refreshments, cutting cake and making sure everyone had a napkin. She spotted Father approaching her but didn't meet his gleaming eyes until he said, "Can a fella get a Sprite around here?"

"I think we can manage that."

He hoisted the can she handed him. "Alcohol zero percent. Do you approve of me?"

Beth glanced up, but no one was standing quite close enough to hear. "For now."

"What a whip cracker you are."

"My ex-husband said the same thing."

"He was a jerk. Forgive me, but I always thought so."

"I forgive you." She ambled toward the end of the table, away from the knot of people beside the wine. If she had been more concerned for his reputation, or her own, she would have led him into the group. Already she could see the flickering glances, parishioners noting how Father Marino spoke so closely to the divorcée.

"You forgive. That's a great virtue."

"I forgive *you*. Anybody else is on a wait-and-see basis."

"I'll bet it's a long line. The only thing people should want is to be forgiven by you. Well, not the only thing." His face was blazing, light pouring out of the skin, and Beth knew exactly how she and the priest looked at that moment.

"Your appearance of scandal is going off the chart," she said.

"'Appearance.' I get the name without the game." In answer to her look, he added, "From *Clever Phrases for All Occasions*. It's a cheat book for priests, to make us look like we've got the common touch."

"As if you needed it. Everybody loves you."

"Beth doesn't love me."

She felt the blush spreading across her face and throat, ignited by dismay and drumming, triumphant joy. "Of course I love you," she murmured. "You know that."

"And what does your love lead you to do? Pour me a Sprite?"

"Hush."

He lowered his voice, which was almost worse; Beth had to lean close to hear him. "I wasn't going to come tonight. I could have called somebody and said that I had the flu or there was a crisis at the hospital. My feet fell off. But I knew you would be here. Knowing I would see you here, I got up and put on my clothes. Do you understand what I'm saying?"

"Would you shut *up?*"

"People have to make choices in their lives. Anthony made one when he left you. He found a door in his life and opened it."

"Thanks for the reminder."

"But he opened a door in my life, too. All I have to do is walk through. Should I do that, Beth?"

"You should open your presents, go home, and sleep." She was proud of the evenness of her voice over a heart that was clanging like a fire alarm. "You need to get a grip."

"I'm trying." He brushed his hand across his glistening eyes. "I'm trying to hold on. But it's up to you now, not me. Will you hold on to me, too?"

At least those were the words Beth thought she heard. Noise banged through the high-ceilinged, uncarpeted room, matching the din inside her skull. She wanted to ask Father Marino to repeat himself, but it seemed crass to ask a man to declare himself twice. Anthony had hardly done it once.

"Yes," she said.

"Excuse me, you two," said Amy Burding, materializing beside Beth. "Can I steal Father away? The kids are ready to start their skit."

"Of course," he said. "I've been looking forward to it. I've been looking forward to everything tonight."

"We hope so, Father," Amy said, steering him away. "We wanted to give you exactly what you wanted." Not a glance back at Beth. Not one.

Following that night, when she did not sleep, she woke the girls with the promise of chocolate French toast, usually only a special-event breakfast. She saw them onto the bus from the front porch, then called the Women's Services office and told them she had the flu. Waiting for the phone to ring, she took apart and scrubbed the stove hood. She removed the china from the hutch and washed it, piece by piece.

By noon she was polishing the chandelier. The house's silence turned her joyful anticipation into unease and then, as the afternoon lengthened, into panic. Beth could well imagine the guilt Father Marino might be experiencing, the jolting fear — or, worse, the uneasy memory. He mustn't shut her away from him. Not now of all times. At two-ten, before the girls came home, she reached for the phone.

She was prepared for a diminished voice, but he was full of sass. "Thanks for the card. I put it on the mantel, to remind me that I'm getting decrepit."

"Did you enjoy your party?"

"I love parties. But I don't think the kids showed me enough respect. At the next Youth Fellowship we're going to have a sensitivity session on the word *geezer.*"

"That wasn't the part of the evening I paid most attention to."

"Did I miss something?"

"You. Asked me to go away with you."

Though he laughed, the stiffness in his voice was instant. "Every single guy in this parish should want to go away with you."

"You said opportunities make new doors in our lives. All we have to do is walk through."

"Maybe Frank Burding? He was feeling his oats."

"You said you were trying to hold on." She couldn't get her mouth to stop. "You asked me to hold on to you."

"Listen, Beth. Everyone understands how difficult things have been for you."

The hand holding the telephone against Beth's ear began to shake, and her brain was flooded with bright heat. "Do you have any idea what you have done?" she said.

"I haven't done anything," he said. "You're not listening to me."

After she hung up, Beth sat at the kitchen table for a very long time. She smiled when Ali and Stephanie clattered in. Sensing an advantage, they asked if they could play now and do homework later, and she nodded.

Every inch of her — skin, organs — ached, and her lungs seemed to have narrowed to the circumference of a thread. What she could hardly tolerate was the unfairness.

As a boy, Father Marino — Joseph, the man's name was Joseph — had once won a competition for flying a toy airplane farther than any of the other boys. His prize was a movie pass, which he used to see *Carnal Knowledge*. The movie was forbidden to every child he knew, but the theater, when he entered, was filled with furtive ten-year-olds. As a teenager, he had driven a violent green Buick and wore his hair down to his shoulders. He liked peanut butter and honey sandwiches and linguini *con vongole*. All this Father Marino had told her, and every detail she had cherished.

In the end, he had given Beth nothing. She'd been an imbecile to believe otherwise.

For the next two weeks she answered the telephone at Women's Services with tight courtesy, hearing but not able to amend the sharpness in her manner. The clients who came in asked to talk to other counselors.

Her daughters shied away from her, though she spent extra time with them, listening to Stephanie's endless stories and sitting up with Alison to watch the girl's favorite TV show. The handsome doctor saved one life after another, in the operating room and beside a hospital bed and at the scene of a car wreck, where thrilling, photogenic mouth-to-mouth resuscitation was called for. When Alison asked if Beth would volunteer for resuscitation from the doctor, the first question the girl had volunteered in weeks, Beth nodded curtly, and the girl didn't ask anymore.

Had she been able to talk to Father Marino as she used to, Beth could have told him that she was trying to listen to her daughters, to walk a narrow bridge of love and communication through this dark time. She and her priest could have talked about darkness, which always implied, somewhere, the presence of light.

When the girls got home from school, they slung their backpacks into the living room and raced back outside to join other children, sometimes not bothering to call out a greeting to her. Standing in the doorway, Beth grew angry, then felt her heart soften painfully at the sound of their squealing laughter, blocks away. Soon, she thought, picking up Alison's backpack, she would have to remind them to take sweaters, as the October afternoons faded. Soon. Not yet.

She shivered. From a distance, she heard a high, long shriek — a child, screaming to be screaming, making noise because she could. Beth listened to the keening for a few moments in furious sympathy. Then she was through the living room, out of her house, running as fast as she could, but not fast enough.

On a neighbor's lawn Alison sprawled under a drooping fir, her neck propped painfully on a root. There was no blood. Her knees jerked, out of rhythm with her screams, and above her the tree stretched like a column, thirty feet at least. No telling how far she had fallen.

"Hush, sweetheart. Hush, baby girl. I'm right here. You're all right." Beth touched her daughter's shoulder while her brain, frosty with terror, ran down the table of contents from the first-aid manual she'd memorized for work: shock, head trauma, neck injury. She looked around for Stephanie, but the littler girl was not in sight — either hiding from her mother or lying at the bottom of her own tree.

"Listen, Ali. Stop crying, baby. I'm going back to the house. I'm going to make a phone call. I'll be right back. Don't cry, angel. You'll see."

A brave girl, Anthony's favorite, Alison tried to stop screaming, though her body shuddered with every racking breath. Smudged across the back of one dirty hand were the remains of a face she had drawn at school, its smile showing a single tooth. Beth bent to kiss that hand. Then she stumbled to the neighbor's house and planned the next hours: first the ambulance, then the emergency room. Then Anthony. Already, underneath her fear, she felt the stirring of guilt. She understood that it would only grow, a fact that in her terrified eyes seemed natural and right.

Alison had fallen head first, her arms outstretched before her. Both her wrists were snapped, but her back was untouched; she was able to walk out of the emergency room, tapping her casts together. Later, when she could, Beth planned to make jokes about Superman. First she had to stop shaking.

In the emergency room and in x-ray, doctors and technicians and three nurses told Beth how lucky Alison had been. "You should have a party," said the radiology attendant, her Hispanic accent softening her vowels. "You should celebrate." Beth thanked her and turned away. The woman meant well.

Only Anthony understood. "I keep imagining her dropping

out of that tree. When I think of what could have happened —"
he said.

"Stop," she said. "Save yourself the anguish."

In the pause she could imagine his crooked smile. "I thought
you wanted me to have anguish."

"I do. But not about this." She made her own flickering, rue-
ful smile. She had read the articles by women who claimed their
ex-husbands had become their best friends. Beth believed those
women were deluded, but nevertheless, she saw how intimacy between two people was never quite erased.

"I miss," he said, and cleared his throat. "I miss the girls. I think
it's time for us to talk about custody."

"We did that already."

"Circumstances have changed."

"Don't be a jackass, Anthony. It was an accident."

"That's not what I'm talking about."

Through the sudden roaring in her ears, Beth tried to scruti-
nize Anthony's voice, but, lawyer trained, it revealed nothing. He
routinely worked fourteen hours a day. He couldn't think of
changing the girls' custody unless he was getting married again.

He said, "It's time to move on."

"I'm not going anywhere." The words were out before she
could reel them back, and his laugh was honestly mirthful. "It's a
great big world, Beth," he said. "Get out a little."

Predictably, Alison was a handful that night. Holding up her casts,
she refused to attempt even the tasks she could manage, bullying
Beth into feeding her and brushing her teeth. Stephanie took her
sister's cue and tugged at her mother, whining about television
and school and a diorama for her reading class until Beth's remaining speck of patience exploded. By nine o'clock both of the
girls were in bed, tucked in so hard they couldn't move. The house
was filled with their raging resentment, the emotion that would
make their lives easier when their father announced his news.
What was the name of the girls' stepmother-to-be? Beth had read
that men were drawn to sibilant names — Susan, Cheryl. She fixed
herself a glass of water with a splash of Dewar's from a bottle Anthony had left. When the doorbell rang at nine-thirty, she was re-

membering with irritation that two of Anthony's secretaries had been named Sandra.

Father Marino said, "I came as soon as I heard. You should have called me when you got to the hospital."

"She was in good hands," Beth said, barely able to hear herself over the slamming of her heart. "Come in." She went to the kitchen and brought him a Sprite, which he smiled at and set aside. Almost certainly he had been drinking. He wouldn't be here otherwise.

"People are saying it was a miracle that she fell just right," he said.

"She was lucky," Beth said.

"Same thing." Father Marino leaned toward her. "How are *you?*"

To her horror, she felt her face crumple and tears race to her eyes. "Terrible," she whispered.

"It's too hard," he said. "No one should have to go through what you've been through. You of all people."

"Please stop."

"I should, I know," Father Marino said. "I just want to talk to you. Every day I want to pick up the phone. 'Did you see that sunset? Did you see that double play? Did you see that God-awful hat Louise Skipper wore to Mass?' The second I saw it, I thought about how you would laugh. Everything I look at brings me back to you."

"And here I am," Beth said. "The priest's friend. Poor thing, she doesn't get out much."

"What can we do?" he said. "We have no choices left."

His voice lapped happily at its self-pity, like a pet cat given its cup of cream. Angrily, she got up and poured him a scotch. He looked at her hand, not her face, when she gave it to him. "I need you," he said.

"This is hardly the time."

"I need you to talk to someone. A woman I know," he said, and for a moment she was convinced that her heart stopped beating. She had not realized that another disappointment could be so stunning.

He said, "You're the only person I trust. I told her to talk to you at Women's Services, but you won't be there now that Alison's home."

"Is this woman you know pregnant?"

"Yes." The hand that raised his glass to his mouth was unsteady, and scotch sloshed onto his chin.

"Oh, Joseph," she said, and watched him flinch. "What have you done?" Something, maybe the half-finger of Dewar's, was affecting her ability to focus. Father Marino's face was a watery blur, but the room around him — the green chair, the knife-pleat curtains, the Sunday newspaper that Stephanie had cut into pieces the size of fingernail clippings — was sharp and hard as glass.

"The thing that always drew me to you was your kindness," he was saying. "Even when things were at their worst, you had the impulse for giving and helping. I could turn to you."

She cleared her rippling voice. "Anthony had two names for me: Cupcake and Frau Gestapo. You'd be surprised how early he moved from one to the other."

He looked around at the mostly tidy room. "You've turned my life inside out. You never meant to, I know."

"For Pete's sake, Joseph," she said. "What do you think I am?"

Because he was looking at the photos of the girls on the wall, she couldn't see his face. "People call me Father."

When he turned back nothing had changed — not his watery eyes or his trembling, swollen mouth. She could see that he was filled with regret and she wished, as she had wished so many times, that she could keep her heart from opening like a mollusk to him. She said, "Your friend might have been pregnant before. I know you don't want to think about it, but that's the pattern with certain women." Seeing Father Marino's wrecked expression, Beth couldn't keep her voice from softening. She hoped he did not take encouragement from that. "What's her name?"

"Cecily. Cessy." He smiled. "I liked playing with her name. Cessation. C-Span."

Cesspool, Beth thought, but said instead, "Adoption services need babies."

"Not this one," he whispered, and then, "Do you want me to pay you for counseling her?"

In the moment before the insult took hold, her uncooperative brain pondered all she was owed. Father Marino could not pay those debts. "Anthony's got a girlfriend," she said. "Talk to him. Tell him that she's endangering his position in the church. Tell him she's got the clap. Tell him you'll withhold communion."

"I don't think anybody's been able to do that since the 1500s."

"It's less than you're asking of me."

The speech hung formally in the air between them. Beth slipped from the fire of her anger into woolly embarrassment, which would probably mean that she would talk to Cessy and draw her a map to the nearest clinic, fifty miles away. Father Marino said slowly, "When did this happen to you? Was it me?" His face looked strangely excited, which Beth thought was the wrong reaction. She was about to tell him so, but Alison cried out, the hoarse squawk that signaled a nightmare. "Please go home now," she said.

"I can go in and talk to her."

Too easily, Beth could imagine her daughter's terror if she woke to the sight of her priest bending over the bed. "It's time to go home."

"You'll help me?"

"I have to talk about adoption. It's the law."

"That's not what she needs to know."

"I'm sure you're right. I'm sorry, Father. My daughter needs me." She steered him toward the door, then hurried to her child, who was crying but not feverish. Beth smoothed back Alison's clumped hair and said, "Father Marino was here. He wants you to get better right away."

"Is he still here?" Alison said.

"I told him to go home."

"I guess I should feel special that Father came to see me. Even if I didn't see him."

"You don't need to see him," Beth said. "I can tell you everything you missed."

After twelve years, Father Marino mostly remembered Beth in nights of brilliant, corrosive dreams, from which he woke up sizzling. On those nights he rolled out of bed and counted off push-ups until his arms gave out, then drank glass after glass of water. He'd been taught the techniques in rehab, and they helped.

Beth had left the parish not long after Alison's wrists healed, and the bishop had offered Father Marino a sort of vacation — six months at a facility in Mexico, drinking iced tea under swags of purple bougainvillea where green hummingbirds darted as if stitching the air. The other priests talked ceaselessly about margaritas and piña coladas. "Even a beer," muttered Father Spurling, Thad. "Wouldn't you sell your own mother?"

"Don't think about it," said Father Marino.

"If you start talking to me about detachment, I'll take that slice of lemon and shove it up your nose."

Father Marino felt sorry for the other man, who one night at dinner had clenched his water glass so hard he snapped its stem. "I'm lucky, that's all. You wouldn't believe the things I cannot think about."

During the sharing sessions, he acknowledged his misdeeds: Cessy; the blurry nights; the inappropriate jokes; and Beth, a misdeed he didn't know how to name. He wished he had more. Other priests described their police records and suspended driver's licenses. Thad Spurling had walked out of a department store carrying three silk shirts still on their hangers — one, he recalled wistfully, had been yellow. Of all the men there, only Father Marino had never been transferred to another parish.

He had broken no marriage, created no crisis, not even dented a fender. During his whole life nothing had happened, just as nothing was happening now. Like a boy having a tantrum in an empty room, he had struck furiously at the air around him and hadn't been able to scrape a knuckle. He should have been grateful, but a peevish sense of loss spread through him. At the end of a sharing session, the priests were encouraged to shake hands or embrace, but Father Marino walked stiffly out, stiffening further when he saw Father Spurling's approving face.

He came home after his six months, and a noisy crowd waited for him at the rectory with balloons and cake and sweet punch. Frank Burding offered him a soft drink. This was how it would be from now on, Father Marino realized with a spark of fury, but then the spark winked out, and that was all.

Gradually he understood that Anthony had bankrolled the holiday. Anthony never stopped attending mass at Holy Name, and he donated handsomely to the Bishop's Annual Appeal. His law firm bought advertising space on the church's weekly bulletin. He passed two years in admirable parish service before making a private appointment with Father Marino, and then he started talking as soon as he sat down. He was ready to marry again. He was ready to make a lifetime commitment, in his own eyes and the eyes of the Church. But first he needed to have his marriage to Beth — never a real marriage, Anthony said — annulled. "I can't do anything about that," Father Marino said. "Do you think I have pull? I don't."

"I know," Anthony said. "I went to the chancery office and read up on procedure. But you can speak for me."

"They want statements from people who knew both parties. Who knew the marriage well."

"Beth talked to you enough," Anthony said. He did not bother to smile, so Father Marino didn't either.

After the other man left, Father Marino read through the questionnaire Anthony had left — six pages — with mounting dismay. Why had Anthony and Beth decided to marry? it asked. What occurred on their wedding night? Did Father Marino have reason to believe that the marriage had been entered into without proper understanding? He couldn't begin to answer the questions, although he would answer them anyway. To the paragraph asking about his qualification to make such judgments, he wrote, *I was their priest.*

The annulment was granted fourteen months later, and Anthony leased Father Marino a new car. "This will help you get around, Father. It's for the good of the parish."

"Like everything you do," Father Marino said. Anthony looked surprised, but he didn't fire back. Nobody ever did. Sometimes Father Marino lay in bed, appalled at himself for having told Marnie Francis that her son wasn't smart enough to go to medical school, Elaine Williamson that she was drinking too much. But

Marnie's son did go to medical school — in the Dominican Republic, yes, but he still came back and passed his boards — and Elaine kept right on drinking. Was there a word for a man whose acts were uniquely useless?

Catching himself, Father Marino poured a glass of water, downed it, and poured another. The parish relied on him to baptize infants and bury the dead. Who could mark life's way stations, if not Father Marino? Now, for instance, this steamy morning in July, he was needed to officiate at the wedding of Anthony's oldest daughter.

Alison, Father Marino reminded himself, taking deep breaths of the sacristy's waxy air. He slipped the heavy green vestment over his head and waited for the storm of memories. But he had to strain to recall the girl, her scowl and dual wrist casts, and her mother. Then he remembered Cecily, who had gone away after her abortion — her second, as Beth had guessed. Father Marino had been relieved to learn that, and then ashamed, and then relief had turned to forgetfulness. In the end, nothing had changed.

The rented organist started the familiar measures of "Jesu, Joy of Man's Desiring," and Father Marino strode to the altar. Anthony's new wife billowed out of the pew beside her three teenage sons. Behind her sat Beth, a slim blur dressed in blue. The night before, at the rehearsal dinner, she had shaken Father Marino's hand. Then she and her new husband had joined her daughter's table, while Father Marino spent the evening in conversation with the groom's great-aunt.

Impatient now, he watched Beth read every word of the wedding program. Nothing would have changed if, the night before, he had pulled up a chair beside her, fingered her bright hair, and whispered to her through the meal. Nothing if he had sipped from her glass of champagne — his first drink in eleven years. Nothing if he had followed her home. Still he would be standing in these hot robes, and still she would plan to drive away with her dull husband after the reception. They were all trapped, every one of them, but he, the priest, was trapped in the smallest room of all.

"Hi," he said, when the couple stood before him. "Here's the big day. Did you get any sleep last night?"

"No," said the groom ruefully, getting a chuckle from the congregation.

"That's all right. You'll sleep from here on in. You might sleep more than you ever meant to."

Hearing his words slip into dangerous waters, Father Marino hurried into the wedding liturgy. He generally riffed a lot at weddings, making warm jokes about pets or the new wedding china. It was one of the reasons couples wanted him. But now he stuck to the succession of formal blessings and invocations. To do so was steadying, and he felt his heart settle down. Before him stood Alison and her groom, their shining eyes impatient. From the pews the congregation looked on with mild affection, perhaps half-hearing the weighty words about trust and steadfastness. Beth sat beside her husband and looked at Father Marino, her face like stone. Anthony had been the one to insist that the wedding be held here. Father Marino would not, he knew, have been Beth's choice.

Holding Alison's and the groom's hands, Father Marino looked up from his prayer book. "People think weddings are about permanence, but that's not right. Vows change us. In five years you won't be who you are now, or even who you'd meant to be. In twenty years you won't recognize yourselves. Here you are, looking beautiful, standing at the altar. Can you know what comes next?"

"The blessing of the rings," Alison said, her clear voice so like her mother's that Father Marino closed his eyes for a moment. The memories that had eluded him earlier were now showering down. He had loved his office because Beth came there. He had loved his office telephone because he talked to Beth on it.

"You're in a hurry," he said, and the congregation laughed. "That's good. You should be holding your arms wide open. Today is the day to embrace your future." The groom, who had a roguish side, pulled Alison into a showy clasp, and Father Marino stepped back and led the quick applause for the couple, forestalling the biddies who would later complain that the ceremony had lacked dignity.

"They're examples to us all, these two," he said. "Why don't we follow their lead? There's no better day than a wedding for a hug." In the pews, people relaxed and smiled at one another. This was not so different from the weekly exchange of peace at mass, so no one was surprised to see Father Marino fondly embrace first bride, then groom, then move down from the altar to the first few pews. Working the crowd. He was famous for it.

Even Beth must have softened. When he rustled to her, she raised her smiling face to his, and he had the sudden, hectic thought that he could kiss her mouth. What could possibly happen? Father Marino hesitated, then lunged, but at the last second Beth turned, and his lips dragged merely across her cheek. Even then he clung to her for a moment past propriety, until he heard Anthony stand. Only then did Father Marino, his heart plunging, let Beth go.

Anthony's big arms were already open. He clasped the priest in a real *abbraccio* that was as much a blow as an embrace and whacked the air from Father Marino's lungs. Then Anthony turned to kiss his wife, Beth to her husband, and other members of the congregation murmured and touched cheeks. At the altar, Alison and her groom kissed again, as prettily as dolls. Shaken, Father Marino watched what he had set in motion. All around him people embraced. Happiness sang through the hot church air. He felt it himself. Meanwhile, the feel of Beth's lips dissolved from his face.

ARUBA

NOT A QUARREL, exactly. Lili and Ron had exchanged words, that was all, about tonight's guests at their western Maryland B & B: a couple en route to Florida and another couple coming in from Baltimore with their son. Taking the reservations, Ron had forgotten to ask about allergies or food requirements, any medical conditions, even coffee or tea preferences for the morning. "What in the world did you talk about?" Lili said. "You were on the phone long enough."

"I told them this is the best time of year to come."

"Liar. It's fifteen degrees."

Ron gestured toward the window. "Tell me that doesn't beat Baltimore."

Lili laughed. Outside, softened by a foot of blazing, billowy snow, the valley wall reared up as if to crack the sapphire sky, and the sky itself stretched sheer and tight as a window. A thin file of green-black firs sentried the ridge; otherwise the view was all white, all blue, hues so hard they hurt. Guests often told Lili and Ron that they were living in paradise, and Ron always said, "It's more than we deserve," a bit of humility that Lili found both corny and touching.

"We're going to have to take our chances with dinner," she said. "I hope I don't wind up at the last minute trying to whip up something with no wheat, eggs, or sugar."

"The guy I talked to didn't sound demanding. He sounded nice."

"They always sound nice to you," she muttered, but patted his arm as he slipped past her.

Now she swatted back a rebellious strand of hair and tapped her pencil. The notepad was printed with the Heaven's Pride logo Ron had designed — wings cupped around a tree-lined valley. Lili scrounged half-used pads from the guest rooms for grocery lists.

Pork medallions. Even picky eaters picked at pork. To go with fried apples, cornbread, some of the beans she'd put up. She wasn't convinced that her home-canned beans tasted one jot better than the Del Montes at the store, but during their first summer here she'd done everything she could by hand, imagining she was creating a pure life. She hadn't learned to pace herself.

Along with shopping stood the rest of the chores to be knocked down one by one: vacuuming, laying fires, fresh linens. Setting out flowers she had to remember to buy. And there was still dessert to be thought about, and marinade for the pork.

She slipped a Tums from her apron pocket. She did not, of course, resent the guests, although she was already certain they would place unforeseeable demands on her. She did not even resent the demands. But she didn't think she was breaking any hotelier's code of conduct by wishing that she and Ron could have one night off to eat frozen pizza, drink a couple beers, and watch the nickel-colored moon rise over their beautiful valley.

They had discovered the property after their second boy, Kit, had called them — they still lived in Pittsburgh then — to announce he was changing his name to Rain. As an afterthought, he mentioned he had decided to follow in his older brother's footsteps and drop out of school. Showing a little more imagination than his brother, Rain asked Ron for the money that would have covered his remaining two years of tuition. "Life is my college now," he actually said.

"What is he majoring in, melodrama?" Lili snapped after they hung up.

"Fantasy. Let's get out of here."

The first hour south of Pittsburgh they hardly said a word, aside from Ron mimicking Rain: "Life is my college now." But once they'd dropped into the far western finger of Maryland, an area they'd never explored, the clouds broke apart and the air around them grew moist. The wooded hills held them like a sweet hand. Even the occasional dogs trotting beside the highway wagged and woofed instead of skulking back like Pittsburgh dogs. When Ron saw the sign advertising acreage for sale, he said, "Should we take a look?"

"Next right," Lili said.

The land was not well marked; Ron drove past the half-obscured thread of a gravel road twice before he saw the realtor's sign in the bushes. Sumac dragged at the windshield as he nosed in, and thornbushes snagged on the tires. But then the path swerved and broke free of shrubbery, and Ron and Lili gazed into a plush valley thick with grass and tumbling drifts of purple coneflowers. A deer strolled from the single line of trees into the sunlight.

Ron started to laugh. "When does the harp music start?"

Coming back weekend after weekend, they learned the masses of summer wildflowers, the deer and fox and single, noisy bear. In the evenings they sat in their Pittsburgh kitchen, re-adding numbers. He could cash in his 401K, she could draw her minuscule pension. Rain's college fund gave them an extra $5,100. The numbers had no elastic, but she and Ron kept stretching them anyway, recalculating mortgage and building estimates, projecting their cost/earnings ratio with more and more optimism until paradise edged almost within reach.

Six months after Rain's call they lunged, buying fifty acres with every dime they could borrow or put a hand to. That night Ron dreamed he was fishing with his bare hands — grabbing hold of their dream, he explained to Lili, before it darted away. But lately she had begun to suspect that they hadn't been quick enough. Every month she worried about the heating bill, the phone. She rarely had time anymore to hike around the property. She rarely had time to look at it. Instead, she looked at Ron's face growing daily more gaunt; when a flyer from the American Heart Association came in the mail, she quietly memorized the warning signs for heart attack and stroke.

Lemons, she wrote. Sometimes, while she arranged flowers or kneaded bread, she entertained herself with a fairy tale about an enchanted valley that wooed mortals with its beauty and then condemned them to endless labor. *Oatmeal.*

Behind her Ron eased in the back door with an armload of firewood. "Better get cracking," he said. "Storm headed our way. Snow and freezing rain. Pennsylvania's closing roads."

"Are our guests going to be able to get here?" If not, she'd skip the hour-long roundtrip to the Fresh Foods. She and Ron could let in the dog, toast s'mores, and drink the champagne one of their New Year's guests had left, whether as a thank-you or by accident Lili had never decided.

"The first ones will; they just called me from the road, in case I was worried about them." He paused, leaving Lili a comment-sized space in the conversation, which she ignored. He said, "You go on to the store while it's safe — I'll keep an ear on the phone."

She stood up, pulled her coat from the hook near the door, and tucked the shopping list into her pocket. "We live to serve."

"Cheer up. If the roads get as bad as people are predicting, our guests will find themselves spending the next three nights here. Which will take care of this month's cash flow."

"I could stand a night off."

"No rest for the wicked," he said, giving her a squeeze at the waist.

She watched him watching her from the kitchen window as she drove away, a moment he wouldn't normally let her catch. He must never have glanced behind him when he was the one driving away — never have seen how perfectly the glass could hold and frame a face, intensifying the weariness it held.

Unaccountably, Lili's spirits improved during the long drive back from the store. Ahead of her the advancing storm opened like a dark door, but the road was still dry, the air still brilliant, and when she inched down her window, the raw air made her face tingle. She yipped like a cowboy.

Half-frozen rain began to patter on the truck's windshield when she started down the long valley road, and by the time she angled toward the house she was down to ten miles an hour, feeling the back tires skitter. A somber blue BMW — she hadn't known they came so big — sat parked at the porch steps, and Lili fixed a smile in place.

Still smiling, she hauled the grocery bags into the kitchen, where she heard a voice laugh from the living room. "Get down, now. Down. Don't you know 'down'?" Then the scrabble of toenails on the pine floor. She swore and dumped the groceries into the sink.

"I'm *sorry*," she said, hurrying through the swinging door and snapping her fingers at Sailor, their brown and white mutt, named for his swagger. "He knows he's not supposed to be inside."

"My bad. I let him in." The young man rubbing Sailor's ecstatic belly looked up and grinned guiltily. "Whoops."

"You —" Lili said to Sailor, "— just got your bacon saved. Lucky dog." As if she needed to tell him. The animal was a cartoon of pleasure, his tongue and paws dangling and his tail sweeping like a windshield wiper while his belly was scratched by a man Rain's age, so handsome Lili lost, for a moment, her breath. His hair thick and dark as sable, his eyes like blue enamel — Ron should put him on their brochure. "You must be Dr. Connor."

"I'm Brian. Mom and Dad are upstairs, resting. I snuck down to break the rules."

"You're not really breaking anything. We let him in when we're by ourselves, but not all guests like dogs." As Brian worked his long fingers up and down Sailor's belly, the dog wiggled, pawed the air, and loosed a long, sighing fart. "He's not exactly an amenity," she said.

"I love dogs. I don't have one." Brian straightened up. Broad and supple shoulders, a waist considerably tighter than hers. "Think you can show me around, before it gets too icy?"

"I've got a dinner that needs making. But Ron can point out a trail." She looked at Sailor, who wagged his jug-handle tail. "You can take your new friend if you want."

"Tell you what. You come out and show me the sights, and then I'll come back and help you with dinner."

"Sorry. I'd get drummed out of my B & B association if they found out I had a guest in the kitchen."

"I like to cook."

"There are rules. The kitchen's for me, not you."

He smiled, an expression so luminous that Lili's legs swayed a little. "Cinderella," he said.

"Happy ever after."

"I knew this place was happy as we drove up. I could tell just by looking at it."

"I hope we don't disappoint you."

"I'm happy already." He reached down to scratch behind ecstatic Sailor's ears. "I want to stay for a long time."

She glanced out the window at the dogwoods, already slick with ice and starting to bend. "I think we can take care of you there."

Back in the kitchen, she forced her eyes onto the potatoes that needed peeling. After that there was the lemon sauce, and then the pie filling. An hour passed before she looked up to see that every window had become black and still; only the steady *tick tick tick*, like a boy tapping the glass with a stick, reminded Lili that an ice storm was in progress. "Any word from the other couple?" she asked Ron when he came in with more wood. Then, looking at his gray face: "Are you all right?"

"Just cold. I haven't heard anything. We may have to call highway patrol."

"Can't you sit down for ten minutes? You look like you're about to keel over."

He frowned at her, an expression that at least brought some shape to his colorless features. "Stop fluttering at me. I'm cold, that's all." He pinched his own cheek, which remained gray. "It smells good in here, babe."

"Thanks. These things took an hour." Reaching into the oven, she pulled out a tray of ginger-lace cookies, her most delicate and difficult. She worked one free with a spatula and held it out to Ron, although it was still too hot. "You can have one if you'll sit down."

He sank into a chair and held the cookie up, admiring its light shape. "Putting on the dog."

"Might as well. The dog's already in the house, in case you hadn't noticed."

"I meant to ask you about that. It can get us a letter from the association."

"Young Mr. Connor let him in. Have you met him yet?"

"Quite a set of wheels."

"You noticed the *car*? Open your eyes. The guy looks like Prince Charming."

"Hope he's not looking for a princess to take to the ball. Guess we could give him Sailor."

"Nobody takes my dog. Besides, Sailor can't dance for crap." Back at the pie board where she'd been working, Lili edged a knife under a sticky patch of dough.

"Well, I'm not going, so that leaves you. Don't stay out too late. If I remember the fairy tale right, something bad happens."

"The princess burns the morning pancakes." Lili refloured the board and started over. "I haven't seen Dr. and Mrs. Connor yet. I wonder if they want any tea."

"I'll go ask. Anything else?"

"Get some rest. You scare me."

"Rest is for old guys."

She knew without looking that he was smiling, inviting her to smile, too. Instead, until he left the kitchen she paid special attention to the fluting on the pie crust, pushing, not squeezing the dough, as recommended by Julia Child in the cookbook Ron and Lili had bought to celebrate moving into their new house.

Six o'clock was cocktail hour at Heaven's Pride; Ron liked to roll into the living room the little trolley he had found at a kitchen supply house, and Lili popped out of the kitchen long enough to join in whatever toasts were proposed. Tonight's ought to be interesting. Collapsed in the huge wing chairs before the fireplace sat Brian's parents, looking 150 years old apiece. Their hands were veiny and trembling, their skin was the color of dust, and every breath they took seemed a tribulation. Ron gestured at the trolley and asked their pleasure, and they requested cups of hot water with a squeeze of lemon. Small cups.

He was slicing the lemons when Sailor barked twice, and Lili heard a slither, as if of tires. Impossible — the road down the valley must be slick as grease by now. But after a moment, headlights still high on the valley wall wavered into view. She stood at the window for five minutes, watching the lights veer and skid and finally slide straight into the lilacs, not usually a parking spot. The couple whooped across the flagstones.

"George and Jenny Pitts!" called Ron from the door.

"Guilty," said the heavily cheerful man. He and his wife, dressed in brilliant, rustling nylon, burst into the room like a squall. "*Whoo.* That was *driving.* I'm not a religious man, but you should have heard me saying 'Thank God for four-wheel drive.' Is that scotch?"

"Looks like you could use a double," Ron said. Lili watched him hug both Pittses and lead them upstairs. He barked with laughter while George leaned from side to side, showing Ron how the car had skidded down the road. "Those slalom skiers don't have anything on me," he said.

Ron said, "We'll give you a 10 just for making it." He would, too — he'd make up a sign with a 10 and bring it to dinner. He loved the laughers, the hearty ones, the great big bluff guests who told bawdy jokes and got up early to watch the sun rise.

The Connors remained silent through all the *har-har-har*-ing. Watching their mouths, thin lines, Lili went to the trolley and finished pouring their hot water. "Thank you," Dr. Connor said. His voice was not quite as dry as she had expected. "What with Roald Amundsen's arrival, I thought we might get overlooked."

"No one gets overlooked here, Dr. Connor."

"So says our son."

"Where is Brian?" Just as she asked, Brian emerged onto the landing with the Pittses. Another burst of laughter obscured whatever his father might have said and made his tiny mouth tighten even further.

"Let the good times roll!" Brian said.

His father said, "Straight downhill," and Lili held up the teapot.

"More water?"

By dinnertime the battle lines were hard. George and Jenn told jokes and asked questions and praised every new dish that Lili brought out. They heaped bonhomie on the table, all of which slid into the black hole of disapproval where Dr. and Mrs. Connor sat, next to Lili, picking at their food and occasionally shivering.

Lili and Ron didn't generally eat with the guests, but Brian, on his third gin, had leaned on Ron to join them, and the Pittses had added their voices to the companionable persuasion. Now Lili felt part chef, part referee. "Who wants more pork?" She smiled coaxingly at Mrs. Connor. "I made plenty."

"Too rich," Mrs. Connor said, pushing back her plate with a papery hand. She had eaten a few beans.

"I'll take some," Brian said.

George leaned across the table toward Mrs. Connor. "So what brought you here?"

"Our son. He found a brochure."

"A gift! How nice," said Jenn.

"Actually, we don't travel very much."

"It's good to get out, Mom. It's one way to make sure you're alive," Brian said. Ron and the Pittses laughed. Mrs. Connor's face shut. Lili closed her eyes.

"Actually, we choose not to travel very much, and we generally prefer hotels. So you might say we're here under protest."

"Well, I still say it's a generous gift," George said.

"You don't have children, do you?" Dr. Connor asked.

Lili slipped into the kitchen for more gravy before she could hear the response, but she could see what was coming. Brushing his hand across his wife's wrist, George would talk about the two of them being a couple of kids themselves, and the Connors would close their lashless eyes, assenting.

The kitchen door swung open, and Brian wedged his shoulders, draped in a soft green sweater, inside. "If I beg, will you let me help?"

"If I beg, will you let me stay in here?"

"We can hide under the kitchen table together." He shook his head. "I'm sorry. Usually I know better than to inflict my parents on people."

"It's just a bad combination of personalities. They're not monsters." Lili wiped the lip of the gravy boat and held it toward Brian, but he was gazing at the obsidian window, leaving her to study his hair, as thick as a pelt, his ears as neat as seashells.

"Nope. They're monsters."

"Haven't you heard? Parents and kids are doomed not to agree. It's a rule."

"Then parents and kids shouldn't live together. That should be the rule."

"Oh," Lili said carefully.

He turned from the window and shrugged. "They made me an offer if I would come back home. They're loaded; Dad was first to market with three different stroke medications. They didn't want to leave their house, and they didn't want strangers coming in. He told me that if I moved back, they would leave the estate to me instead of the American Heart Association. The first thing I bought was a car. The second thing I bought was a car. I didn't even know I was trapped for the first six months."

"What happened then?"

He shrugged again. "The floor plan of their house allows 5,114 square feet. Before long I'll be able to tell you the wall space, which I'll know from crawling it." He offered her a crooked smile, no less handsome than any other expression available to him. "I thought I'd found the ticket to the good life. Should have known better."

"There aren't many of those," Lili said.

"I saw a brochure for this place and forced them to come so I could see some new walls. Now they're paying me back. You get some of the payback too. I'm sorry about that."

"They're guests. We've had worse." From the dining room boomed George Pitts's laugh, and then Ron's voice: "Lil? You need help in there?"

Brian reached for the gravy boat. "I'll take it. Let me pretend I live here for a little while. It would be a kindness."

"In that case, you can bring out more applesauce, too." She lingered in the kitchen after Brian went out, listening for Dr. Connor's bone-hard voice: "My son has learned that work looks like fun when it belongs to someone else."

"Hi, I'm Brian, and I'll be your server tonight." She cracked the door just in time to see him pour wine into her empty glass while

Ron watched with a face that ceded nothing and Jenn lifted her glass to other people's work.

Lili had counted on the Connors making their silent, stiff way upstairs after dinner, so she winced when they made their silent, stiff way back to the fireplace with the others, ignoring George's long joke about the man who walked into a bar with an ostrich. Mrs. Connor stumbled and Lili reached, too late, to help her. The other woman shook off her hand, settled into her chair, then looked at the ceiling and asked if anyone could manage to bring her some hot, really hot water.

"Where are you going?" George called as Lili moved back to the kitchen. "The party's in here."

"The party's everywhere," she said, and let the door swing shut behind her.

Outside the ticking had stopped. Waiting for the water to heat, Lili stepped onto the back porch, then grabbed for the railing as her feet slipped under her. At least a half-inch of ice covered the porch boards, the light fixture, the planter boxes. Clicks and groans scratched at the hard air, and Lili knew that every branch and blade of grass wore a sleeve of clean ice. In the morning there would be branches down, but the trees and grass would look as if they'd been dipped in light. "So beautiful," Ron would say, and he would be right.

Hearing the door, Sailor trotted out of the barn, scrabbled for traction on the glassy driveway, then skidded sideways and slammed into a tree. After a shocked moment, he whined, then went silent, then whined again, a sharper sound. Grabbing for branches, Lili picked her way from the porch. She only fell once, but she came down with her whole weight, jarring her left arm from wrist to shoulder. She was still dizzy when she minced the rest of the way to Sailor, who licked her hand.

"*Come* on, boy. Can you move? How many fingers am I holding up?" She fell twice more urging him to the kitchen door, unable to tell in the slick dark whether he was limping. Her arm pulsed; she could kick herself for not being more careful. "Shh, now. Don't let anyone know you're in here." She tapped his hind end, and he scooted across the kitchen and under the table. No limp. Dog could play her like a violin.

After pouring Mrs. Connor's water and glancing once more at Sailor, now a tight doughnut of fur jammed against the baseboard heater, she joined Ron and their guests, cradling her tingling arm. The living room glowed, its golden air hot against Lili's stinging cheeks and hands. George was talking about Bangkok, which was also hot, where he and Jenn had seen an elephant with a headband walking down a side street. The elephant had looked hot too.

"Bangkok," Brian said thickly.

"Our issue hears the siren song of foreign lands," said Dr. Connor.

"It's a good song," George said. "You travel, you get new ideas. Some people just travel around and around, seeing whatever they can."

"And you admire that," said Dr. Connor.

George leaned back heavily. "Why don't you tell us what you admire?" He kept his tone almost cordial, an effort that Lili appreciated. Ugly as things were getting, though, he might as well go ahead and slam the old fossil.

Dr. Connor smiled, displaying a ghastly spread of browned teeth. "Philosophers say that, in order to know a tree, you have to watch it for ten years."

"And then you know a tree," George said.

"At least you know something."

Mrs. Connor's hand fluttered toward her teacup, a gesture Lili ignored.

"Another time," George said, "another time I saw an old man, white hair, white stubble, in a wheelchair outside a café. He was all by himself and crying. Nobody went near him. He sat there, tears pouring down his face."

"I don't remember this," Jenn said.

"You weren't there," George said.

"So much sadness," Brian said, his voice slurring. "Such unhappy stories."

"I've got the other kind too," George said. "I can tell you about cancan dancers."

"Now that sounds like a fun life," Lili half yelled, trying to overtalk George. "Just think of the ruffles."

"I knew a dancer once," Jenn said. "She had it tough. Wrecked knees and no savings."

"Every choice has a down side," Lili said.

Dr. Connor murmured, "Syphilis."

"So if you had to choose between cancan and this place, would you still come here?" Brian said to Lili, propping himself on one elbow.

People always asked something like this, and she had a burnished answer about their first trip to Heaven's Pride and seeing dreams come true. She watched Mrs. Connor's hand wavering above her teacup like a dull moth and felt her arm throb. Her whole side felt strange. "Sure. Choices aren't hard — what's hard comes after. You can make the biggest choice of your life, but you still need to get up and make breakfast the next morning. Things don't change as much as you think."

"Ask any parent," said Dr. Connor, his voice so foul that not even the Pittses could laugh.

"Dad, is it actually necessary? Is it written in a book somewhere that you have to be such a dick?" In the room's abrupt silence Brian flopped onto his back again. "Lili says it is. She says it's the rule between parents and kids."

"I'm being quoted out of context," she said. "I was telling Brian about our two sons."

"They're not part of your Happy Valley enterprise," said Dr. Connor.

"We don't pay our children to live with us," she said.

Ron said quietly, "Lili."

"You wouldn't have to pay me. I would stay here," Brian said, still flat on his back, staring at the beamed ceiling. "I would stay and stay and stay."

"You're welcome," Lili said. "Stay as long as you like."

"I would stay and stay and stay and stay," Brian said.

Like punctuation, something crashed outside the window — a tree limb. Or a tree. Then from the kitchen the racing of toenails on linoleum, and terrified Sailor came banging through the door, churning, dog as locomotive. "Jesus Christ, Lili," Ron yelled, and she grabbed at the dog, missing his back end by inches as he shot for Brian, slamming into his chest with a thud Lili could hear across the room.

"Bad dog!" Ron and Lili cried, but Brian sat up, hugging and crooning at the trembling animal. "Poor dog. Poor old Sailor-boy. I'll save you from the bad noises." Looking up, he added, "See? He came to me."

"Don't take it personally. That dog loves everybody," Lili said, although Sailor was cowering against Brian, plastering himself against the grass-green sweater, rooting his snout under Brian's arm as if he could crawl inside the man.

"This is what I want," Brian said. "This, right here."

"Listen to yourself, son," Dr. Connor said. "Pay attention."

"I've been *paying* attention. All *night*," Brian said. Lili needed a moment to place her sudden memory: Rain, age thirteen, still called Kit then, wanting new shoes. She felt an unwelcome pang of sympathy for Dr. Connor. Brian flipped his hair back from his forehead. "I'm trying to get *you* to pay attention."

"You've got us riveted."

"This is everything I want," Brian said, squeezing the dog, his cobalt eyes filling with quick, boozy tears.

"Everything?" his father said. "I doubt that. Hush, now."

"It's so hard to find what I really want. And the second you know, you won't let me have it."

"Son, you're being unfair," Dr. Connor said quietly. Lili had used to say much the same thing to Rain in response to his wanting, wanting, wanting. So she shouldn't have been surprised when Dr. Connor lifted his gaze from his son and said to her, "If you sold this land, you would never have to look back."

"What on earth are you talking about?" The pain in her arm made Lili's voice sharper than it should have been.

"You're tired, and our son is happy here. As a parent, you understand what your child's happiness means."

"You could go live under a palm tree," Brian said to Lili. "Eat coconuts."

"If you all don't mind, this is our life you're talking about," Lili said. She glanced at Ron, who was snapping his fingers at the oblivious Sailor. "Why, we wouldn't know what to do with ourselves anywhere but here."

"In Aruba you can hire people to carry you across the street if you don't want to get your shoes dirty," George said.

"I crossed the street all afternoon. It was fun," Jenn said.

Ron said, "Lil?" She wondered whether the Pittses and the Connors heard the ripple in his voice, and whether they thought they were hearing delight. Brian's smooth hand stroked Sailor's ear.

She stood and picked up Mrs. Connor's cup with her good arm. "Too much wine with dinner. Let's all go to bed."

"I'm ready," George said.

"You've earned a rest," Dr. Connor said. "Look at you."

"I'm staying up," Brian said to the ceiling. "Nobody can make me move."

At seven o'clock the next morning, her arm quivering, Lili limped out of bed and padded downstairs. Brian was no longer sprawled in the living room, she saw with relief, and she wondered when Dr. Connor had silently helped his big, handsome son upstairs.

She poured herself a glass of water and swallowed four aspirin, let Sailor out, and stood at the doorway, listening to the clicking of icy twigs. The dim moon hung late in the west, throwing watery gray light across the two shaggy firs, the lace of dogwood branches, and the hedge of lilacs, now a leafless stand of drooping canes scratching at the top of the Pittses' huge SUV. Air scraped across her face. Down her left side, her fingers began to tremble.

"I can't sleep either," Ron said quietly. When she turned, he gestured at the sweater he'd pulled on over his robe. "Too hot in bed. Too cold out."

"It's warm in Aruba. We could be carried across the street every day. Where is Aruba?"

"Search me." He pulled his hands from his pockets and started to massage Lili's shoulders. His first touch shot down her spine as if she'd been speared. "Hey, gal. Breathe."

She tilted her head so that he could get better purchase, even though the pressure made her gasp. In a minute, if she could just stay with it, she'd relax.

"I've never loved a place so much," he said. "I used to stand up on the hillside and almost cry. It was so beautiful, my eyes hurt."

"Easy, Ron."

"It was more than we'd ever asked for."

"Don't press so hard. Nobody's going anywhere."

"I just got to thinking. What do you suppose it would mean? To leave paradise. When people leave heaven, they don't go someplace better."

Lili snorted despite the pain radiating from Ron's thumbs on either side of her spine. "What are you imagining — Dr. Connor casting us out with the fiery sword? You heard George. There's more than one beautiful place in the world."

"But this is the one we love."

"I can imagine loving other places." Lili's voice was unsteady. Outside, pearly predawn light seemed to arise from the ice-coated bushes and snowbanks, a landscape made out of crystal. "People do it all the time. When you wake up from one dream, you go back to sleep and have another one."

"I don't," Ron said. "I get more and more awake, trying to make the first dream come back."

"You know it doesn't work that way."

"Lousy system," he said softly. His thumbs dug into her, and the tears that had been gathering at the bottom of her eyes spilled over. He said, "I want to see the copper beeches we planted get to be twenty feet tall. I want to see if the geese come back. I want to carry firewood without feeling my arms shake."

"They're not going to start shaking less," she said.

"You think I don't know that?" Using his knuckles, he kneaded the back of her neck. "But I can't stand it."

"No," she murmured. She couldn't stop the excited rhythm of her heart, the relief that ran like new water. She supposed they would have to get to Aruba before he felt the relief, or would admit it. Then they could quarrel about something else. "Ron, honey, stop — I've got to sit down."

Her feet were cold from the open doorway, and her swollen

arm hung at her side like a club. Perhaps from the fall, her entire side felt swollen now, strange and slow. She'd been foolish to ignore it last night; Brian's father might have been able to make a bandage, tie a makeshift sling, dispense one of his pills. Now she shuffled to a chair, hearing the sudden alarm in Ron's voice.

"Lili, what's going on?"

When she looked out the window, the valley walls shone like beaten silver, almost too brilliant to look at. More than they'd asked for. More than they deserved. "Can you go wake up Dr. Connor?" she said. "I think he should see this."

LUCKY DEVIL

OFFICIALLY, the grocery store was called Weber's Shop All Rite, but everybody called it the Talk All Nite. Set at the dead center of the Long Acre subdivision, the store was poorly stocked but convenient, and most locals wound up passing through two or three times a week. Around the urn of complimentary coffee, news was exchanged — more interesting news than ever wound up in the upbeat columns of Long Acre's newspaper. It was at the Talk All Nite that Janice first heard about Ben Lund's affair with his office manager, and ever since, when she saw Ben, she remembered the coppery taste of sour coffee.

Now Ben was about to turn fifty, sixteen years younger than Janice, which seemed impossible. She was shopping for his party, a potluck supper thrown by his wife, long-suffering Lou. The event had been much discussed at the Talk All Nite, with Janice joining those wives who would rather give a government audit than a party to a husband who had bought a palomino for his equestrian girlfriend.

As soon as she rattled her cart into produce, Janice spotted Alicia Kelso with Saralynn and Chloe Becker. Standing beside the oranges, their carts pushed aside and their faces nosed together, the women whispered and shushed and nodded, touching one another's wrists, their faces gleaming. Later Janice could tell Jack that they looked like an old woodcut illustrating Gossip. For now, she hurried over. "Let me guess: Ben told Lou that he's having another midlife crisis. He's out of money, though, so this girl gets a mule."

Saralynn, eighty years old, actually jerked back. A blush patched across her pleated cheeks and throat. Chloe steadied her sister, then said to Janice, "You shouldn't sneak up like that. At our age we can't take the shock."

"Since when? Usually you can take a thousand volts," Janice said. Chloe usually scorned the ditzy-old-gal routine. Now she was avoiding Janice's gaze, rearranging the lettuce and grapes in her cart.

"So I was just saying — I'm bringing my same chicken salad tomorrow night," Alicia said. "By now you'd think the ingredients could jump into the mixing bowls by themselves." Pushing the shiny dark wing of hair back from her face, she chattered as if she were picking up the dropped skein of conversation, but the words the women had snatched back were practically visible in the air, even if Janice was too hurt now to try to read them.

"Well," she said. "Looks like you're busy."

"Just talking," Saralynn murmured.

"We'll see you tomorrow, right?" Alicia said. "You and Jack?"

"Naturally. We're the life of the party." Janice made sure her words sounded light.

"We were just saying so," Chloe said.

At the checkout counter with her five-pound can of Folgers, Janice stared at the armload of parsley belonging to the woman ahead of her. Maybe this would be a good party to sit out. She and Jack rarely missed one. Maybe they had become a neighborhood joke, the nice old couple whose only social life came from block parties. Maybe they were the reason *for* the parties.

Catching herself, she shook her head. She really was losing perspective if she thought the Talk All Nite was keeping track of her and Jack's social life. Still, when she got home and Jack didn't bestir himself, she slammed cupboard doors and dropped the coffee. After ten minutes he finally roamed out of the den, his slippers making a *shff, shff* sound on the linoleum. His eyes wore the slightly unfocused look they took on after a session with the computer. "His highness emerges," she said.

"Jay-nice," he said. "Be nice."

"Didn't you hear me come home?"

"I was in the middle of something," he said. "You usually yell if you need me. Was there a lot to bring in?"

"No. I just wanted to be grouchy."

"Finished now?"

"Maybe."

He sat down on a kitchen chair and drew Janice onto his lap, where she squirmed for a minute, then sat still. He tended to let her go quicker when she didn't move. "Jay-nice. Nice girl. But when you're not nice" — he touched his finger to the end of her nose — "you're naughty. Aren't you?"

"Jack."

"Aren't you naughty? Let's play pretend. Then you can be as naughty as you want."

She glanced at the windows and the back door, even though no one could possibly hear them. Then she stood up and pulled him, hard, into the bedroom, where nothing would happen.

"Brace yourself," her sister had warned. She'd been through it with her own husband's retirement: no work to do, no projects or promotions on his mind. He would be after her constantly.

Constant pursuit sounded pretty good to Janice. Over the years, her intimate time with Jack had dwindled to parched, efficient encounters — fifteen minutes, twice a month. Two weeks before Jack's retirement dinner from the office-supply company where he was vice president, Janice lightened her hair.

But her sister was wrong. Janice kept the same habits she always had, cooking, cleaning, washing clothes, present in every room in the house. She was all set to meet Jack in any of them. But once he faced long days with his wife, Jack's appetites shrank, and his eyes grew shy. He skirted her in the hall, and before they went to sleep he gave her fond, grandfatherly pats. Twice a month stretched into once a month, then less.

Instead of reaching out to touch her, he seemed to want to *glimpse* her. He dawdled in the bedroom while she was getting dressed, and she sometimes looked up from her pantyhose just in time to see him glancing away. She stepped out of the shower and saw his eyes fixed on her heavy breasts before he slipped out the door. Janice shivered. His behavior didn't make her feel desired so much as scrutinized — selected, at age sixty-six, to act out Jack's personal peepshow. Lately she'd been forcing him to the bedroom when the glassy look came over his eyes and he started in on the naughty talk. She would tug his shirt up while he tugged it back down again. "I'm not a youngster anymore. But thanks for your faith in me."

"You looked young a minute ago."

"Things change." His gaze would slide away from hers, fleeing back to the comfortable gray zone he had dwelled in since he'd stopped going to work. Lurking in his den for hours, he read or hunted up Web sites for Boston terriers. He'd had one as a boy and still liked to look at their cheerful, pugnacious faces. Sometimes Janice heard his little TV go on, then off again. Sometimes over dinner he related local stories about robberies or domestic assault, stories she didn't know because he kept the paper until five o'clock, when he took his daily walk. "I honestly don't know where the time goes," he said, and fear wrapped a tendril around Janice's heart. This kind of vagueness was for old men. Jack was only sixty-eight.

Two weeks ago she had brought in the mail and found him sitting unoccupied in the easy chair, hands empty and face slack. She stared at him for better than a minute before murmuring, "You will start to reawaken, and you will remember none of what we have done here."

Jack opened his eyes, although his face remained loose. "I was just resting."

"Most people rest after they've actually done something."

"I've been doing something all my life."

"Don't imagine you're finished yet." She took another thorny breath. "The garage could stand to be swept. Up and at 'em, Tiger."

Since then she'd heard the brisk, convalescent-care tone come into her voice as she'd urged him to take a walk, get some air, for God's sake move his carcass out of the house. Maybe this was what

Alicia and the Becker sisters had been whispering about so emphatically — *Such a steep decline. Used to be such a handsome man.* Stung, Janice wanted to call them up and say, *He is still handsome.*

That night, watching him wrap his spaghetti in neat packets around his fork, she said, "Did you find the Web site you were looking for?"

"It wasn't much. Fuzzy pictures of pups. Not worth the search."

"A lot of work, just for pictures."

"I like to look at them," he said mildly.

"So why settle?" She propped her chin on her hands. "We could get a dog." The idea would shock him, she knew. They had never thought of themselves as people who might have a dog, just as they had never been people with children. They had floated free of encumbrance, and only lately had Janice started to worry that, lacking ballast, they might simply float away.

"*Get* one?" he said.

"People do it, you know. All over America."

"Well, this is a new idea." He didn't look befuddled, as she had feared, didn't break into that expression she associated with dingy pajamas and the stinging smell of urine. His narrow eyes brightened. "You're sure you want to take this on? Dogs need attention. They have to be walked every day."

"I think you could work that into your busy schedule."

He stretched back in his chair and spread his hands. "I'll name it Lucky. After me."

Janice snorted. Jack's fraternity brothers had called him Lucky Devil, when they weren't calling him Handsome Jack. The day he graduated, they gave him the mirror from the house bathroom. Janice said, "Give it a rest. You haven't been Lucky for forty years."

"Are you kidding? I've been lucky every day of my life."

She groaned happily and stood up to clear the table. He was alive after all, and she'd only needed a dog to find that out.

By ten o'clock the next morning Jack presented her with a printout of Boston terrier breeders in a three-state area. "I guess I put the nickel in you," Janice said.

"Why wait? Here's a litter that's already four weeks old. Two females, two males. We want a male — they have the spunk."

"Spunk. Oh, boy." She watched Jack efficiently circle phone numbers and underline key phrases. He put two lines under *peppery*. This would be a fine topic for the party tonight — dog stories, puppy stories, advice about training and housebreaking. She and Jack could invite suggestions for dog names. After the first round of margaritas, the suggestions were bound to get fun.

She wore her happy mood all day, through the scrubbing of the coffeemaker and the rooting through cupboards for Styrofoam cups. When she was slipping into a gauzy cotton shift for the party, Jack wiggled his eyebrows and said, "Ooh, la la" — pleasant, normal, marital lechery, for which she lifted her skirt to give him a glimpse of thigh.

The party was in half swing when they arrived, a few kids already playing street hockey while Chloe and Saralynn fussed with the arrangement of dishes on the picnic table. Beside a pear tree's cloud of white blossoms Alicia was talking with Flinn Merchant, the newest neighbor. A recent transfer from St. Louis, Flinn worked downtown as a legal consultant and lived without husband or children — a rarity in Long Acre, where she said she'd come for the community, although neighbors scarcely saw her. The woman was always hurrying — probably to the gym. She had a full wardrobe of exercise clothes and a long, taut, expensive-looking body. Women with hollows on the inside of their thighs usually had a man somewhere, and Janice guessed Flinn's résumé included at least one divorce.

Now Flinn was talking fiercely to Alicia, gesturing in Janice's direction, and Janice felt embarrassed without knowing why. She had scarcely ever spoken to Flinn beyond "Welcome to the neighborhood; let us know if we can help." But now the woman's furious stare scorched Janice's back as she slipped into the Beckers' kitchen door to fill up the coffeemaker. When she staggered out again — twenty cups of water — Flinn was waiting.

"Shouldn't your husband be helping you with that?"

"I can carry a coffeepot." Jack had gone off to stand with the men. She would have been surprised if he'd done otherwise.

"It's been my impression that he volunteers to help."

"Jack?"

"He carries my trash can back to the garage every week after pickup. I finally asked him to stop."

Janice felt her mouth flatten. "I'd say that's nice of him."

"I would too. But he won't stop. I've asked him now three times. He appears just after five o'clock, when I'm home from work."

"He's retired. He doesn't have a lot to do."

"I know that. I assume he was looking for something to do when he found out my birthday."

"Sorry. You've lost me."

Flinn's face was so tense that the flesh of her cheeks looked as if it had been pinned back. "He got on the Internet, looked up the records from my house sale, and found out my personal history. Probably my health history, too, and anything else he was interested in. Two days ago, he walked up to me and said, 'It's almost your birthday. You shouldn't be here all alone. Next week I'll come over and give you a nice birthday spanking.'"

Janice couldn't keep her gaze from flying to Jack, who stood comfortably telling a baseball story — first the wind-up, then the pitch. Even from across the lawn, she could feel his easy charm.

Flinn said, "Where I work, that comment would be actionable."

"You want to sue Jack because he made an off-color joke?"

"I don't want him walking past my house when I come home. I know he's your husband, but he gives me the creeps."

"He likes to walk. Five o'clock is convenient for him. You don't have to go outside then."

"I have a dog who has to go out as soon as I get home. That's the first thing your husband learned about me."

The frustration that rose in Janice's throat felt like soft, clammy dough. Flinn was saying, "I wouldn't be surprised to find him outside my windows, trying to peek in."

"He's sixty-eight years old," Janice snapped. "Believe me, he's too old to do the things you're thinking."

"He's not too old to bother me," Flinn snapped back. "I'm sorry if I'm making you uncomfortable, but he's been making me uncomfortable. The next word he says to me is going to get him a harassment complaint."

"Who are you going to complain to? He's just a friendly older guy who thought you could use a hand."

Flinn folded her arms. "He should — I'm sorry — be on a leash. My dog backs off from him."

"He loves dogs," Janice said stupidly. Chloe was standing near enough to listen. Alicia, too. From across the yard came Ben's laugh, a yelp as if he'd been goosed, and then Jack's dependable chuckle. The sound made Janice's mouth fill with an emotion that was not anger and was not fear, but borrowed from both of them.

"Your husband is a menace," Flinn said.

"No, he isn't." Janice knew she sounded like a grade-schooler. And then: "At least I have a husband."

Flinn took a moment before she produced a flat laugh. "I told you because I thought you'd want to know," she said.

"Like hell. You could have come to my house and talked to me privately. You wanted everybody to know."

"I wanted to know if he's done this with anybody else," Flinn said.

"And?"

"I'm not special."

Janice very much wished that her voice had not grown so thick. Still, she managed to say, "I could have told you that."

In the five minutes it took her to leave Jack at the party and reach her own back door, Janice had thought about pornography sites on the Web, about the new shoes Jack had bought for his walks, about how much walking a dog as small as a Boston terrier would require. When her brain flashed an image of Jack peeking around the door as she stepped into the shower, she stared down at the suburban throwaway newspaper that lay on the steps. She blinked until she could read the headline about scholarship winners at the local high school, eager to give back to society.

Half an hour later, when Jack came looking for her, she had turned the kitchen radio off three times. "Are you sick?" Jack asked. "I looked up and you were gone. You should have told me."

His light brown eyes glittered like river water. She said, "I hear you've been toting Flinn Merchant's trash cans for her."

"Thought she could use a hand."

"I guess you thought you were Galahad when you offered to deliver that birthday spanking."

She had to hand it to him: he looked as baffled as a child confronting a new word. "How would I know her birthday?"

"From the Internet." This part sounded right, even though Janice herself didn't use the computer. There had been so many news reports about violations of privacy.

"No wonder she's divorced. You take a gal's trash cans in and the next thing you know she's accusing you of indecency."

"How do you know she's divorced?"

"You told me. You said nobody goes to the gym as much as she does unless she's between spouses. Believe me, nobody's going to want to marry that one."

Janice studied his tense hands and shoulders. Even his elbows looked stiff. "They'll just want to spank her?"

Although he took a moment to reply, his voice was steady. "At first when I couldn't find you, I thought you were inside with Chloe, helping out. I kept watching for you to come back outside. After fifteen minutes I asked Ben. After twenty minutes I asked Saralynn. I was afraid something had happened."

"Something did."

"Are you all right?"

"What do you think?"

Jack watched her for a minute before he went into the living room, to the TV. The news was finished now, replaced by a quiz show. After a few minutes, Janice joined him, sitting in a chair across the room.

Sleep that night was flimsy, interrupted by dreams of boats and shadowy cats. As soon as the first light came, Janice studied Jack's face: broad forehead, straight nose, beautifully deep-set eyes. A throat and mouth that drooped despite the fifteen minutes he spent every morning on facial isometrics. He looked, she thought without rancor, like a hound. "Woof," she said.

In the kitchen she clattered through coffee making and studied Alicia's house across the back yard. Janice had no doubt that her neighbor was remembering what she had overheard at the party, weighing this interesting news, rehearsing how she might retell it to others. Janice would have done the same.

"Think you could be any noisier in here, Janice?" Jack stood in the doorway, showing off his lean frame to advantage.

"I haven't detonated anything yet."

He glanced at the counter, where she had not set out his oatmeal. "You're not being fair, you know."

"Am I not? Shucks."

"You won't even listen to me."

Janice was looking out the window again. "I listened. You didn't say anything that explained why a complete stranger would want to come up to me and lie."

"She's a man hater. I know her kind."

"You know a lot, for a guy who just brings in her trash cans."

"Don't you get it? She's gunning for me. She'll say anything to make me look bad."

"You?" Janice stared at her husband's righteous mouth. If she could have, she would have laughed. "You think this is about *you?* Oh, Jack, you're priceless." She could hardly breathe, watching his face stiffen under the kitchen light. She said, "I'm the one Flinn talked to in front of everybody. I'm the one they were watching. You get to be the heel, but I get to be married to the heel. To stand by my heel."

"So no matter what I do, from now on I'm the bad guy?"

Underneath the vexed whine Janice heard something that startled her — a note of desperation, and surprise. He truly couldn't believe that anyone might think ill of him. Irritation and amused affection surged through her, and she allowed the affection to win out, a bit of marital kindness he would never know to thank her for. "Sorry, sweetheart," she said. "I thought you knew."

Usually Janice and Jack made up readily after quarrels, moving ahead with the good cheer that was their trademark. This time, though, the good cheer froze into a merciless solicitude. A stranger watching them might have thought he was seeing courtesy. Jack, who rarely so much as poured anyone a glass of milk, searched out Janice in the odd corners of the afternoon and handed her steaming, watery cups of coffee. She hemmed a pair of his pants that had lain on top of the sewing machine for close to a year. A pucker crept in the left leg where she had forgotten to adjust the bobbin's tension, but he thanked her twice, and she could see him trying to take shelter from whatever storms might be on the approach.

He might have tried a little harder. Ancient slights were revisiting her, feelings he'd hurt thirty years before. When he handed her another cup of light-brown coffee, she remarked, "Do you remember the Christmas you gave me Chanel, but you gave a bigger bottle to your secretary?"

"I must have gotten the packages mixed up."

"I would never have known, but I dropped by your office one day, and she had the bottle next to her typewriter. It was so big, it made her feel rich."

"I don't even remember that."

"Two weeks ago I didn't, either," Janice said.

"Do you want me to bring you a big bottle of perfume?"

"Sure. I'll bring it with me to the Talk All Nite and see if Flinn has one, too."

She hadn't thought of herself before as a vindictive person and was surprised at the new avenues suddenly open to her. When Jack drove across town to pick up their new puppy, she made a dog bed out of a cardboard box and old velour towels. But the second the dog came in the house, his sweet, broad face making him look like a Dead End Kid, Janice cried, "Spanky! Here, Spanky!" Perking up his tiny ears, he tumbled toward her.

"Is this enough?" Jack said, watching the puppy squirm joyfully while she murmured his new name. "Are you satisfied?"

"I never said I wanted to be satisfied," she said. "Where'd you get that idea?"

"You can't just keep punishing me."

"Because you say so?" The puppy backed up a step, let out a shrill bark, and dived into her lap again.

His voice softened. "Because I'm tired. Aren't you?"

In fact, she was achingly tired. And she could hear his version of the conversation: how she rewarded his conciliation with shrewishness and met his advances with a blank wall. It was not easy to break the long habit of telling him what he wanted to hear. "No," she said, giving in.

At the Talk All Nite, the third store she visited, Janice finally found Alicia, picking through the shaggy bunches of dill. "Are you okay?" Alicia asked. "I heard you got sick at the party."

"Not exactly sick," Janice said. "I had some thinking to do."

Alicia's face was full of tenderness and sympathy and expectation. "About Jack? You needed to know."

"I put sheets on the guest room bed for him. Old habits die hard. I should have told him to put on his own sheets."

"You've been married a long time," Alicia said.

"Since God had grandparents." Janice paused. "Jack has said things to you, hasn't he?"

"Jack has said things to everybody."

"Why didn't you tell me?"

"In his day, stuff like that was more acceptable. Besides, not everyone minded hearing racy talk from a good-looking guy." She stopped, and Janice hefted grapefruit while the comment trembled between them. "I'm sorry," Alicia said.

"You could have told me." Janice watched Alicia register the years between them, the community they had built.

"I thought it was best," she said.

Janice sighed stagily. "At least I know what to do next: take Flinn out for lunch and ask about divorce lawyers."

"That seems a little quick." Alarm sparkled through Alicia's voice. Leaning toward Janice, she spoke in an urgent whisper, as if someone might overhear. "You and Jack have had a whole life together. He deserves a second chance." Alicia swallowed. "You'll hate yourself for even thinking these things."

"Everybody thinks about divorce," Janice said, the line she had practiced. It was fun to say, like playing dress-up.

"Not for more than half an hour. That's the rule." Alicia's

words came even faster, a marble racing downhill. "Pat can think about the kids' French teacher for half an hour, and I can think about divorce. Then I splash cold water on my face and go back to folding laundry." Alicia looked at Janice's stony mouth and dropped her eyes. "You would hate yourself. Just don't do anything you'll regret."

Lou used almost exactly the same words when Janice encountered her at the dry cleaner's, adding, "At our age, we don't have many options." *Our* age? Janice had seventeen years on Lou. But the other woman's face looked serious and tense, and Janice remembered the murmurs she'd heard, whispers of whispers, that Ben and his girlfriend had started up again.

Lou said, "Think twice before you do anything, all right? And then come talk to me."

"I will," Janice assured her, although Lou, with her rollicking husband and anxious mouth, was precisely the last person Janice would confide in.

Before going home, she stopped at the bakery for cream horns. Jack usually protested that he was watching his weight, but she supposed he'd eat them this time. Then she drove back to Laurel Avenue the long way. Soon Alicia would share her worries with someone, and Lou with someone else, until everyone on and around Laurel Avenue would be knitted together in a blanket of concern that Janice might leave Jack — a terrible thing, after all those years. What was marriage, except sticking together through the bad times? They'd have the conversations with their spouses every night. They'd do their best to convince Flinn. It would be interesting to watch.

Jack met her at the door when she came in and watched her arrange the cream horns on a plate, powdered sugar rising like dust. "I have been reading an article about the stock market," he said. "I have not looked up secret files."

She held out the plate. "Snack."

"I'm not hungry."

"You will be later. I thought we could go upstairs and get a little exercise."

His shudder was just a quick jerk, barely a tremor. She had expected as much. What she did not expect was the tiny, hot tears that instantly dotted her eyes.

"That might be a little beyond my reach," he was saying.

"Try."

His face was a soft mask of misery, as if he were the only miserable one in the room. He was coming to knowledge so late, and that was her fault. She had accommodated him, anticipated him, delayed his comprehension of marriage's ruthless economy. Even now, she understood the balance sheet better than he and could tell him his every debit — and hers, too, though they were fewer. She loved him so much, she could hardly bear to look at him.

"You have the right to ask," he said.

"Good Lord, Jack. This isn't a legal proceeding." She added, "Will it help to pretend?"

"No." His slow gaze traveled up the wall and rested on the door beside her head. One night, before they were married, his gaze had traveled up her like that, and she had thought she might dissolve in the sweet heat. He said, "Yes. Is this more punishment?"

"No," she said. "Yes. Do I have to say who's being punished?"

"I can't tell you what I'm pretending about," he said after a pause.

"That's okay," she said. "I can't tell you, either."

She had intended to start accompanying Jack on his walks, but in the end she didn't have the heart. Jack's face had taken on a hunted, twitchy quality. Janice didn't miss his earlier dimness, but she worried about stress. Hearts gave out at this age.

She also put away the idea of a welcome-the-puppy party, even though the notion had charmed her. Spanky was a gregarious thing, given to parading around the living room with a washcloth in his mouth. Janice had already taught him to bark when he wanted a treat. Now, as Jack pointed out, he barked all the time.

But he didn't bark the afternoon the back doorbell rang — he must have been sleeping, probably with Jack. Janice automatically blocked the kitchen door with her ankle. How quickly the new habits came. Preoccupied with her thoughts, she was startled to see Flinn Merchant on the mat, the shadows of her cheekbones sharp in the late afternoon sun. "Am I disturbing you?"

"Well, sure." Janice made a half-smile. "No offense."

"No offense. I'm coming as a friend."

"That should be interesting." The hospitable smell of fresh coffee filled the doorway, a fact Janice regretted. Flinn said, "You always have coffee on."

"Bad habit."

Flinn shrugged. "What's wrong with coffee?"

Janice shrugged back, let her in, put out milk and sugar. She couldn't think of one word to say to this angular woman, her wrists like slim tubes at the ends of her sleeves.

Seated at the kitchen table, Flinn said, "I'm here because I owe you an apology. I said things that I shouldn't have."

"Didn't you tell me the truth?"

"Not every truth needs to be told," Flinn said.

"And you a lawyer. That's a hell of an attitude."

The woman permitted herself a dry smile. "I'm off the clock." Then she said, "Look, I've caused you trouble, and I didn't mean to do that."

Janice glanced around the kitchen. "No trouble here."

"Trouble between you and Jack. I'm not a home wrecker. At least, I don't want to be."

"You're safe," Janice murmured, making a quick list: Lou would have brought Flinn cookies, Alicia taken her out to lunch. Chloe would have patted her dog. Flinn should be thanking Janice, not apologizing. "Nothing's been wrecked. You might have done me a favor."

"You don't ask for much, if that was a favor," Flinn said.

Janice couldn't get herself to stop shrugging. "If you want to stay married, you take what you can get."

"Do you mind if I tell you something? I used to be in family law. I saw a lot of couples." Flinn leaned forward, and Janice wondered how often she had produced this frank, confiding smile at contract negotiations. "Nothing is ever final. The rules get reestablished all the time. In the good marriages, people knew that."

Janice stared at Flinn's mouth. "Are you telling me I have a good marriage?"

"I didn't come over here to insult you," Flinn said.

"But you did come to judge."

The woman stayed for a glass of water and two more apologies before Janice could get her out of the house with assurances of lunch soon, yes, of course — the ritual Laurel Avenue goodbye. Soon Flinn would be a Talk All Nite regular.

Jack, reading in his den with the puppy on his lap, looked up at the sound of her step, his expression giving away nothing. "Flinn was here," Janice said. "She's awfully sorry. She never should have said those things at the party and would like us all to begin again."

"So I guess everything is dandy now."

"I'll bet Lou Lund wrote the speech for her," Janice said.

"From what I hear, Lou's listening for some other speeches." He smirked, and she smirked back. When the puppy stirred, Jack stroked the tiny shell-like ear. "You and I are finished fighting now, aren't we? What's done is done."

"I wouldn't use those words." Her spirits were singing. "We're a story. Ongoing, like Ben Lund and his girlfriend. What's done is only started."

He was quiet, either holding back a comment or trying to form one; it was always hard to tell with him. He was not glib, she had told her sister, her mother, friends across the years. What he said, he had thought about. She would miss being able to say that.

"I can't live like this," he said. "You — everybody — sitting there like a spider, waiting for me to make the wrong step. I can't live waiting for you to kill me." He glanced at the computer on his desk. "I've looked into apartments."

Janice could feel her mouth go soft, that ugly shape between laughter and fear. A lifetime spent studying the man, and still he could shock her.

"Not now," she said. "Not when you're about to get a whole new life. Do you know how lucky you are?"

"Huh. When do I start feeling lucky?" His voice was merely neutral. It could have been worse.

Her hands were shaking, and she thought briefly about how despair and thrill felt so very much alike. When she rested her hands on his shoulders, she felt them stiffen, then loosen. The first night he had ever held her, in the back seat of a Plymouth that smelled like cut grass and cigarettes, he said, "I'll do anything you ask."

"Better watch out. I'll ask for a lot," she'd said.

He'd smoothed her hair. "You don't know how."

Nearly fifty years later, his shoulders could still be the shoulders of that handsome boy. If she closed her eyes, he was in front of her. "Now," she said. "Right now."

DAILY AFFIRMATIONS

A WEEK BEFORE MY FLIGHT back to my parents' house for Christmas, my suitcases were already packed. I knew packing early was an unproductive habit that discouraged me from living in the moment, but by three o'clock one sleepless morning my self-control had ebbed, and I hauled out the suitcases for the plain relief of doing something.

It was December 12, and since September I had been focusing the meetings of Standing Tall, my support group for survivors of difficult childhoods, on the holidays. We talked about battle strategies, and I developed metaphors. "You're going to be on the frontlines. How will you defend yourselves when the choppers start coming in?" I suggested that they take home one another's telephone numbers as well as talismans to carry or wear. Myself, I packed two books of affirmations, the cassettes from the seminars I had led the summer before, and my favorite button, the one I liked to wear to workshops. It showed a stick figure tugging at a huge barbell, and it said LIGHTEN UP.

Thinking about what lay ahead, I pinned the button to my coat. My mother, who insisted on going to daily mass, had just broken her ankle on a slick spot outside the church, so she would be bedridden — *helpless* was her word — for three months. When I talked to my father on the phone, he told me she was making the whole ordeal worse than it had to be. "She won't use the crutches. She talks like nobody's ever been in pain before." I fought down my impulse to tell him to honor her pain, which he wouldn't have paid any attention to. I was thirty-three years old, living in my own apartment and attending to my own life. Her pain was their issue, not mine.

After I finished packing, I wandered into the kitchen and flicked open the freezer. I could catalogue every item in it, including the mousse cake left over from dinner with Jon in November. Binge eating in the middle of the night was another behavior I tried to avoid; it channeled into every old complex that had wrecked my twenties. I thought about this, then fished out the cake and went to the cupboard for peanut butter and bread.

In *Returning to the Body* I wrote a chapter called "Eating for Two" about this exact phenomenon. That chapter seized almost as much attention as the ones on sex, and for months after the book came out I fielded phone calls from readers who wanted to confess their late-night eating. One woman wept and admitted that she'd eaten a stick of butter like a candy bar. We talked for half an hour, and before she hung up she gave me permission to use her story. I was already at work on my next book, a follow-up that my publisher wanted to call *Into the Light*. My suitcases were stuffed with notes, a computer, and the transcripts of fifty workshops. I theorized that by writing while I was home, I could distance myself from my past and — a bonus — allow my parents to see the woman I had become.

Thinking this, I tucked another book of affirmations in my purse. Trips home always courted danger. One step into my mother's kitchen made my whole new life start to waver and float. I'd found it useful to talk at Standing Tall about my recurrent dream about home — how a dark, underwater current pulled me farther and farther from shore. When I described it, every head in the room nodded.

After finishing the cake, I crossed my legs, relaxed my shoulders, and closed my eyes. First: inhale to the count of five. Second: begin that day's affirmation. *Today I will acknowledge that healing is a lengthy process, and I will give myself all the time I need.*

I took thirty deep breaths and shifted on the couch, easing

my pants at the waist where they bit. This was the fifth night in a row I had dipped into the Skippy. Peanut butter was itself a danger sign — hadn't I counseled clients to purge their cupboards before Thanksgiving? — but my resolve was shrinking, and a dull recklessness had set in. I was sleeping through the alarm in the mornings, skipping exercise classes, and not telling Jon about any of it. He was fond of reminding me that as an adult I had choices. *He* wasn't the one going to visit his parents. "We've learned to avoid the holidays," he said when I asked him. "Damage containment."

After the flight landed in Los Angeles and I shuffled to the terminal behind a grim man carrying an enormous plush kangaroo, the first thing I saw was my father, waving hugely, grinning and hooting like a Texan. Usually it was my mother who stood leaning against the low restraining gate. She was nearsighted but never could find glasses that pleased her, so she would crane over the gate and peer at every passenger until she found me. Dad would be waiting in the car outside, avoiding the parking lot where, my mother had once read, over a hundred muggings occurred every year. But now here was my father, whooping at me, calling my nickname, which only my family used.

"Tracy. Tracybug. Hey, sight for sore eyes," he said, trying to grab me with one arm, my bag with the other.

"Hi, Dad," I said into his shoulder. "Hey, yourself."

"You don't know how glad I am to see you," he said, letting me step back so he could look at me. He was beaming.

"It's funny to see you here without Mom."

"Everything's going to feel different," he said. "We've had Mc-Donald's for dinner the last four nights."

"What, you forgot how to scramble eggs?"

"Your mother won't let me in the kitchen. She thinks I'll ruin her frying pans. But now that you're home, we've got her over a barrel. What say salmon steaks tonight?"

"Mom doesn't like fish," I said.

"I know," Dad said, wiggling his eyebrows. "But I do." He threw his arm around me again and squeezed. "It's good to have you home, Trace. You look good. Corn fed."

"I've been very busy," I said. I started down the corridor toward baggage claim — it was time to get moving, and Dad looked as if he was ready to stand there all day. "You can't imagine all the conferences and then small group work. And my publisher wants the new book by June."

"Don't count on having much of your own life. This is your mother we're talking about."

He was holding his mouth in a sour smirk, watching me. Usually it took a little longer before he started coaxing me to join in the chorus of his gripes. "You need to be generous with her now," I said. "This sort of challenge can be a good thing — a time of real growth. She's just discovering her own new needs."

"Me too," Dad said. "My need is to get her to quit complaining. When Monsignor called last night, she talked to him as if her leg had fallen off. After she hung up, she cried and reminded me that faith can move mountains."

I'd heard about her faith all my life and hadn't seen it move so much as a note card. I said, "We can fry some potatoes with the salmon — that's always nice. If you have any apples on hand, I'll make a pie."

"Now you're talking," Dad said.

We stopped at the big Thriftimart on the way home and bought seven bags of groceries; whenever I stopped to look at an item, he put it in the basket. "I don't know what we have," he shrugged, collecting both light and dark miso. By the time we got home it was nearly four, the sun low, and I pulled my snug jacket tighter against the sharp ocean wind. Dad unlocked the door, then gestured me in with a courtly sweep of his arm, and so I was the first one to see my mother crumpled at the bottom of the stairs.

"I was sure you'd been in an accident," she said. When she turned I could see how she had tucked the leg without the cast underneath her to keep warm. I could also see the urine puddled on the back of her robe.

"Mom, I'm sorry," I said, dropping the bag of groceries and squatting, letting her shoulder rest against me.

"I know you are," she said.

Dad trudged up from the garage with the suitcases, muttering as he always did about how I must have packed bricks. When he saw my mother on the floor, he said, "For Pete's sake," then set down the suitcases and bent to lift her up.

"I was trying to get to the bathroom," she said. "You were gone so long."

"Why do you think the doctor gave you crutches?" Dad said.

"They hurt. You think it's easy, but it's not."

"You're working hard to keep it complicated, I'll give you that," he said, letting her lean on him as she steadied herself on her good foot. "This is quite a homecoming for our daughter."

"Don't worry about me," I said, with idiotic brightness. "I'm tough."

My mother glanced at me and twisted her mouth. "I'm not weak. But I could never have believed the pain."

"Now that we've shared that, Mother, let's get you cleaned up," Dad said, steadying her hips while she awkwardly hopped ahead of him. "Then you can come down and talk to Tracy. She's going to make dinner for us."

"A blessing," my mother said, breathing hard. Dad turned and winked at me, and I rolled my eyes despite my best intentions.

When I finally got Jon on the phone, I told him, "It's like trying to skirt quicksand." I'd been home four days. "One foot is always being sucked in."

"This is your opportunity to work on detachment," Jon said.

"I'm detached, dammit. She talks about God's will, Dad tells her he's sick of her whining, and I yell over the fray for time-outs."

"You can only take responsibility for yourself." His voice was hushed and choppy, and I could picture him nodding, waving his hands to hurry me along. His wife was probably in the next room.

"It's such a relief to talk to you," I told him, my voice sticky and wheedling. "When I hear you, I feel like I'm standing on something solid."

"The holidays are a difficult period for everyone," he said. "We're set up to relive the traumas of our youth."

"We've got the mother lode here," I muttered, but he was still talking, reminding me not to let others define my reality for me. I didn't have a chance to tell him about watching Bob Hope on TV the night before. When I had stood up to get some cookies, my mother's face was covered in tears. "It's like something gnawing with sharp teeth," she said when I touched her shoulder.

"For God's sake, Mother, why didn't you say something?"

"I didn't want to bother you," she said.

Now Jon was talking about openness to life's richness. "I'm open, all right," I told him. "I'm taking in every morsel that my rich new life provides me."

Dad came down to the kitchen every night after the news, when I liked to have a snack. "At least you can get some sleep," he would say, breaking off a piece of whatever I was fixing. "She lies there and moans. In case I forget for one second the torment she's in."

It was so hard to resist. Already I had found myself telling him about washing her hair, when she started crying because I'd let shampoo seep into the corner of her eye. She pushed me out of the way and hobbled back to bed, soapy water streaming down her neck. "Fastest I've seen her move since I got home," I told Dad.

"Good to know something can make her jump," he said. "She lies in that bed like she wants to make a career of it."

Now that I was home, my mother was making more of an effort to get up, but her lurching progress exhausted her. She collapsed into chairs and sat, pinched and silent, for fifteen minutes before she could gather herself to speak, and her suffering face was a mask of accusation. I came downstairs later every morning and lost whole afternoons to elaborate recipes that called for stacks of phyllo and jasmine rice.

"I really would prefer plain chicken," she kept saying from the armchair we rolled into the kitchen for her. "Rich food doesn't agree with me."

"We're trying some new things," I said. I was enjoying myself; every time I suggested a menu, Dad headed to the grocery store. I had never cooked better and with his encouragement tried a chicken stuffed with chestnuts, chocolate-mint torte. "Good for the holidays," I said when I served the cashew-rolled tenderloin that, left over, made such good sandwiches. "I never eat this way at home." Mom picked at whatever I put on her plate. Sometimes her eyes were damp, though my own — frustrated, impatient — remained dry.

In the mornings I stared helplessly at my computer screen. The chapter about coping strategies was only sketched out, so every morning I reviewed my thick stack of notes and case histories. I couldn't manage to boil them down to the punchy, practical style my publisher liked. After a half-hour of twisting on the chair, I would go to call Jon.

I knew the relationship with him was not ideal, but it was a far cry from the terrible entanglements of my twenties. "More affairs than I could count. As long as men were unavailable — emotionally, maritally, fiscally, or physically — I was game," I wrote in the first book. That confession had been central to my recovery; it took all the courage I had to publish it. After the book was included in an article about recovery literature in *Newsweek,* my brother Patrick, who used to drive me wild by calling me Saint Tracy when I was a pious ten-year-old, sent a furious letter addressed to Slut Tracy. I brought it to the next session of Standing Tall as an example of how families can get in the way of our growth.

My parents didn't mention the book. I waited until two weeks after the *Newsweek* article, then finally asked whether they had seen it. Jon held my hand while I made the call.

"I'm not going to read it. It doesn't seem like something I'd like," said my mother. "But we're both very proud of you."

Now I typed: *Health isn't a goal like a high-jump record. Life throws us curves.* I sighed and wiped it out.

There was a tap at the door, and then Dad opened it a crack to look in at me. "Just making sure you were off the phone," he said.

"Never was on it. Couldn't get through."

"You've been trying."

"You monitoring my calls?"

"Now, now. Your mother frets. She thinks your publisher should be the one paying for long distance."

"I'm not calling my publisher," I said. "I'm calling my collaborator."

"Collaborator. Sounds like World War II." He raised his eyebrows at me playfully, but I swiveled back to the keyboard.

"I'll shave my head and you can parade me through the streets," I said.

"I'll leave that to your mother. Who wants you to wash her hair this afternoon. Apparently she's recovered from your last assault."

I quickly typed: *We who seek and strive are heroes, and only when the battle is finished do we see the faces of our foes.* I saved it, turned off the computer, and said, "Tell her majesty I'm on my way," pushing back from the computer so hard, my chair screeched and stuttered on the wood floor.

After I'd been home a week, I had floated well out to sea. I sat at my computer from nine to twelve and buried myself in cooking all afternoon. My mother joined me when I came downstairs, so my sautéing and mincing stopped whenever she needed more pillows or a sip of cranberry juice or — the most frequent request — help in hobbling to the bathroom. Sometimes she sat at the table and phoned one of my brothers, then handed off the phone to me. "Well," said James, my closest brother in age, "finding stories to tell for another book?"

"I'm working on it," I said evenly.

"Most of us are still recovering from the first one."

"That was about opening the door. This one is about starting the journey."

"Mary's fine, and the twins are great," he said. "They've got almost all their teeth."

"You should bring them out to visit. Mom tells me all the time how she wishes you'd let her dote on them." It was the kind of meanness I wouldn't have stooped to a month before, but I was tired. Jon hadn't answered the phone since the first call. When I took time out to read my affirmations, they felt absurdly childish, chipper as Norman Vincent Peale, and it took an act of faith to bother opening the book at all.

"It's good to see you and your brothers talking," Mom would say after I hung up. "A close family is one of the graces I pray for."

This was an opening volley, but there was no way I could have known that. She launched the full campaign on Christmas Day, after we came home from mass, which had left us undone. She had winced and gasped the whole short ride, then inside the church redirected Dad three times until he situated her wheelchair out of the way but still in full view of the priest.

After the service she held court outside in the thin December sunshine, and it took a half-hour to wheel her away from the people who pressed their cheeks to hers and told her how she never left their prayers for a minute. "And see," my mother kept saying, clutching my hand, "my daughter is home." I smiled while they nodded coolly at me. Clearly they had heard about the book. *I have nothing to apologize for,* I wanted to say. But no one quite gave me the opportunity, and by the time we came back home I felt as if I'd been flayed.

"I can't tell you the good it does me to go to mass," my mother uttered faintly, her head resting against the chair back. "I miss it so."

"Until that ankle heals, God's just going to have to understand," Dad said.

"The mass is a comfort," she said.

"You certainly are popular," I said. "It looked like you knew everybody there."

"We have a community."

"Now that people know what's happened to you, I'm sure they'll call," I said. "You won't feel so cut off."

"It's not the same," she said, twisting fretfully and waving her hand as if she would reach over the length of her cast and rub it herself. Dad and I watched her for a second, then I went over and rested her foot on my lap and got to work. "The new priest, Father Jim, he gives such good sermons — even on weekdays. You wouldn't believe."

"What are you angling for, Mother?" Dad asked.

"Nothing. I'm not *angling for* anything."

"That's good," he said. "Because Trace and I have got our hands full here."

"I just think," she said, "it would be nice if you two went to mass together during the week. It would be a fine sharing time for you. And you could tell me what Father Jim said."

I kept rubbing and shot a look at my mother's face, which was serene. "Mary Grace," Dad said, "you're out of your mind."

"I don't know why you say that. I think it's a good idea."

"Tracy and I are not going to start getting up at five-thirty to go off to mass for you. I can't believe the wild hairs you get."

"I don't see any reason that you should speak for our daughter," my mother said, trying to hike herself up in the chair. "She's perfectly capable of speaking her own mind."

I was bent over her foot, still rubbing away. "I write in the mornings," I said.

"You could manage a half-hour for mass. It would probably help your writing."

"I don't think so," I said.

She yanked her foot away from me, swinging out her leg so hard, it jerked off my lap and crashed under the weight of the cast to the floor. "So you won't even consider it. Both of you just too busy to do this simple thing for me." She sniffed hard and tried to clamp her mouth. "It's a small enough favor, God knows."

"Not everyone shares your sense of priorities, Mother," Dad said.

"You've made that perfectly clear," she said. I reached down to hoist her leg back up, but she snapped, "Just leave it alone. I wouldn't dream of putting you out."

"Oh, for Christ's sake, Mary Grace, lighten up."

"I wish you wouldn't swear in front of Tracy."

"She's heard worse," he said.

"I'll go," I said. I was clenching and unclenching my hands, trying to control my breathing. I didn't look at either one of them.

"No," my mother said, jerking her chin. "I don't want you to go now."

"I'll go. Maybe I'll find something I can use in my book."

"Tracy, sweetheart, you can't just give in," Dad said.

I stood up. "I can't stand listening to you two. When did you start going for blood? You never used to fight like this."

Dad shook his head and sighed. "Always. But you didn't notice what you didn't want to see."

"You had your head in the clouds." My mother nodded.

"Things are different now," I said, and went into the kitchen. I had made brownies and icebox bars the day before, from recipes in my mother's oldest cookbook. I put a handful on a plate and then headed for the stairs and my room, but Mother called me back.

"You know," she said, "Doris Dilworth started going to daily mass when she began her diet last year, and she was finally able to lose the weight and keep it off. Isn't that interesting? You could use a story like that in your book."

"That is interesting. Now I've got a suggestion for you. Next time you're checking in with God and asking for graces, try asking for the grace to know when to shut the fuck up," I said, and took the stairs two at a time — good exercise for the thighs.

Jon wasn't home when I called, and he wasn't home half an hour later. Grimly, I settled in for a siege, picking up the phone every twenty minutes. He would have to answer eventually. He and his wife were staying home for the holidays, taking the chance to spend time with their sons. I used his private number, which rang only in his home office. All afternoon and into the evening it rang.

At intervals I went downstairs to snack. Neighbors had been dropping by with cookies and fruitcake; the kitchen counter was crowded with fancy plates, and Mom held court in the living room. Once I ran into my father, who said, "You've been slaving away ever since you got here. What say I go out and pick up some Mexican tonight?" I shrugged, nodded. If he opened the refrigerator, he would find enough leftovers piled up to see us into the new year.

I didn't get Jon until after eleven — after one, Chicago time. "I've been trying to reach you all day," I said when he picked up the phone.

"I keep restricted hours during the holidays," he said loudly enough that anyone in a nearby room could have heard him.

"How nice. Around here it's cruise missiles."

"What good is all your hard work if you don't hold tight under fire? Remember everything you've worked for."

"Families aren't supposed to be battlegrounds," I spat.

"We grow up with myths. The first thing to do is put them aside," he said, and then, more softly, "At least you ought to be getting some good material."

"As a matter of fact, I'm not," I said. "My parents have staged a battle to the death and my mother has bullied me into daily mass."

"She can't make you do anything," he said, and I thought that finally he'd said something my mother would agree with. Even in my irritation, I was swayed by the heavy, creamy fall of his voice. "You're the only one responsible for your decisions."

"Listen, I got them to stop carping at each other for two minutes."

"Holidays. They should give out operator's licenses," he said. A moment's silence shimmered between us, a rare thing. "Is there anyone there you can talk to?"

"Jon, I'm talking to you."

"When you're in a bottom, you need lots of support."

"Good. Support me. Did you tell your wife about the apartment?"

"All important decisions should be put off until after New Year's."

The glittering silence descended again, and I pictured the lines of telephone wire shivering between us. "Look," I said. "I'm having a hard time. Things here are terrible. I need to know that you miss me."

"Of course I do."

"Try sounding like you mean it."

"I do. Of course. But remember," he said, "some needs can't be filled by another person." I could hear the wheels of his desk chair rolling over the floor, and I pictured a woman standing in the doorway of his office.

"Thanks, Jon. Good support. I'll be sure to call again," I said.

"It'll be easier when you come home. You'll remember who you really are. You'll reclaim your new life."

"If my old life lets me," I said.

I groped down the stairs the next morning at quarter to six, stuffing my shirt into my pants. Mom always put on a skirt to go to church, but if God was expecting me this early, He could accustom His all-seeing eyes to pants. Which, too tight, hurt.

Dad was already in the kitchen, dressed and glaring at the front page. "I didn't think you were going," I said.

"Once you gave in, I didn't have any choice." He sighed. "What the hell. Let's go out to the Belgian waffle place afterwards. Salvage something out of this."

"What about Mom?" I said.

"I walked her to the bathroom at two, three, four-thirty, and five-thirty-seven. If she's not dry as the Sahara, she can hold it." He fished in his pocket and tossed me the car keys. His night vision had gotten dicey, and the sky was still licorice black. "Let's go."

We didn't talk at all on the drive over and had to grope our way into the tiny chapel where daily mass was held. A dozen women were already yawning and waiting in sweatsuits and stretch pants, none of them under sixty. They swung their heads up together like deer when we slipped in; Dad and I took the folding chairs by the door. Everyone was close enough to touch.

When the priest walked in without any fanfare, the women rustled to their feet, and he smiled at them with sweet generosity. "Let's begin," he murmured. The women pitched into prayer with wonderful precision, none of them even bothering to glance at the missalettes. I tried to imagine coming here every morning in the dark, reciting prayers by heart, and then going home to make breakfast. It felt utterly peculiar.

"What do you make of that?" I asked Dad when we were back out in the chilly black air.

"I managed to nod off twice, which is about as much rest as I get sleeping with your mother these days."

"Don't tell her that. She'll count it as a victory."

When we got to the car, I turned up both the heat and the radio, and we sang along to "The Lion Sleeps Tonight" all the way to the restaurant. A waitress with eyes that looked as if they'd been set in with a wood-burning kit seated us. Dad glanced at the menu, put it aside, and cleared his throat while I was looking at the strawberry waffles. He fiddled with his napkin, folding it into a little pup tent next to his fork until I looked up again.

"You know, you're going to have to talk to your mother," he said.

"I'll pay attention to the sermon tomorrow. I'll take notes."

"Not that," he said. "You were pretty hard on her yesterday. She takes these things to heart."

"She's got to learn to back off."

Dad smiled unhappily and picked up his spoon, trying to catch his reflection in its bowl. "She doesn't realize sometimes. She loses track. But honey, she cried all night."

"Shit." I closed my eyes. "I lost my temper. I'm not perfect." I looked up to see him nodding, and my anger started to swell again. "We do everything she wants. You say so yourself. Why else are we going to church in the middle of the night?"

"You don't get it, Trace. You'll be gone in a week. When James told her not to come out after his babies were born, she cried like her heart was breaking. There's nothing in your life that matters as much as you do to her."

"So who are you trying to help here? You want me to go do a case study on her dieting friend to get her off your back?"

"She thinks you'd be happier if you were thinner. You *are* pretty big, honey."

I folded the menu closed and shook out my napkin so it had no wrinkles. My stomach growled. I knew I had the words to respond to him. I had a whole speech. But the speech had drifted away, and there was only a table separating me from my father. It wasn't enough.

"Displacement?" I said. That didn't sound right.

"Not funny, Tracy."

"I'm not trying to be funny."

"I don't need your psychoanalysis," he said sharply.

"We're a long way from the couch. I'm just wondering what it means when a father avoids his wife by trying to win over his daughter."

He flattened his hand on the table. "We play on the same team, Tracy. Don't condescend to me."

"Don't intrude on my life."

"I'm so far from intruding on you, I can barely even see you," he said. "If I was going to start intruding, I might take your telephone away. I might ask why you're the one doing the calling, and why you don't mention his name to your mother, who would like to know. I could lock up the sugar and butter and feed you lettuce."

"I'll be happy to make salads for you in the future. Better yet, I'll hand over the lettuce. You can make dinner to your own exacting standards."

The blank-eyed waitress materialized next to us and stood, tapping her order pad. "Just coffee," Dad said, glancing at her. "I can't eat this early."

I opened the menu and pointed to a photo of three waffles mortared by thick layers of whipped cream with blueberries. "That," I said. "And coffee." The air in the restaurant was warm, full of low laughter and the scrape of cutlery on heavy plates. I was so hungry, the images wobbled before me.

"That ought to help things," Dad said after the waitress turned away. "Good choice."

"We came to a waffle restaurant. I ordered waffles."

"Nothing I say makes any difference to you, does it?"

"I'm an adult. I have to make my own decisions."

"You make some piss-poor ones."

"Impressive talk from a man who's spent fifty years arguing with his wife."

Dad leaned across the table. "Your mother and I live in the same house with each other. We aren't pretending, or hiding anything."

"No," I said. "Nothing except all the things you can't wait to say to me."

Dad stood up. "You know what your mother says? She says evil takes good and makes it look bad. I *know* you, no matter what you think." He spun around and walked out. When the waitress came back, I nodded at his place, as if he were going to return in a minute, and I went ahead and ate my breakfast. Even though the berries were lost in the gummy syrup and the coffee was faintly burned, I ate every scrap and wiped the plate to get the juice, and when I finished my cup of coffee, I drank Dad's.

• • •

Tiptoeing into the chapel by myself the next morning, I still felt clumsy and shy, but the chair by the door was open and the quiet warmth of the room was comforting. I had joined my parents for TV the night before, apologizing to Mom at the first station break. They nodded, and I went up early to bed. When I left, I heard my mother sigh.

I folded my hands now and watched the faces around me, which were uniformly peaceful, as if bread were on the rise in every one of their kitchens. I couldn't imagine my mother wearing such a look. Patrick used to do imitations called "Mom at mass": preoccupied, muttering, ticking off mysterious lists on his fingers, while James and I roared.

The side door opened and I looked up to see an ancient woman supported by a walker, wearing the shapeless polyester skirt and crepe-soled shoes of a nun. Two women near the door bounced up and guided her to a chair, one on each side, smiling and murmuring. They looked as if they had done this many, many times, waiting until the sister was secure in her chair before they moved her walker to the wall.

I kept staring at her faint hair, coiled into a permanent that exposed rambling pathways of scalp. The way she tottered, she must have gotten up at three to make it to the chapel. But when she had entered, her face held the same calm, pleasant look as the other women's. If you came every morning, over enough years, did the calm come?

Abruptly tears began to well, and I couldn't stop them, although I knuckled my eyes hard. In fact, I started to cry harder and had to bury my face in my hands to muffle the sniffling. After a minute I felt a hand rest on my shoulder. "There, now," a voice said. "There. Is it someone you're crying for?"

"My mother," I whispered, and though I didn't look up, I imagined that the woman beside me was nodding.

"No prayers are ever wasted," she said. "God hears you. He'll bring your mother to his side. He sends tears as a sign."

I glanced up then, blinking to see her mild face. "It's not that simple."

"I'll pray for her too," she said, smiling and patting my hand. I was saved from having to respond by the priest, who hurried through the door, straightening his stole. Swiping my hand across my nose, I stood and felt the sense of warm, liquid collapse drain away. Beached on the shore of my recognizable life, I was back on dry land, where I stood uncomfortably waiting for mass to end.

The old nun stayed seated through the opening prayers, but she swayed to her feet during the intercessions. After the other women offered their personal requests — "for my daughter Jenny," "for my cousin's surgery" — finding comfort in the displacement of their powerlessness, as Jon would say, she spoke up. Her voice was dry as a rusk: "God's peace comes to his believers." I had no idea what she meant, and I craned my neck, trying to see the nun's face. All I could see was her wavering stance and then the unceremonious way she tipped over, dropping to her left like a carelessly balanced board.

The women were at her side instantly, straightening her legs and rubbing her hands and feet, and the priest was already moving toward her. I stood watching from the back, caged between folding chairs, as out of place as an ungainly animal. The nun coughed once, tremendously. At least she was alive. For the second time my tears surged, and I groped my way to the door and left.

Ten minutes later I was still sitting in the cold car, listening to my breath shudder and catch. I felt as if I had been slapped by some vast hand, and I could stop crying only by focusing on what was directly in front of me: a spindly tree supported on three sides by wires. No leaves. Its branches made shadows like veins in the light from the church.

Going home was out of the question. Mom would ask about mass, and I'd be helpless to control my ragged crying. Or Dad would shoot me an ironic look, and I wasn't ready for that, either. When my feet got cold enough to hurt, I started the car, but from the parking lot I turned right, away from East Gables, where my parents were.

Seventeen years had passed since I'd lived in California, but I drove with perfect memory. Jon had some expression about how adolescent knowledge is the hardest to lose. I felt more adolescent now than I had ever felt as a teenager — teary, shaken, driving because movement was soothing.

I turned onto Pacific, the first four-lane street I'd ever driven on. Windows were starting to light up; coffee shop parking lots were half full, and a wobbly mechanical Santa on top of a computer store soundlessly waved and laughed. Four stoplights down was the rec center where I'd learned to swim. Lights were on throughout the building. It was already almost seven o'clock, when morning sessions started for people who needed quick uplift before they went to work. The center had a flashy new sign out in front, listing classes and meetings for the holidays — WEIGHT WATCHING IN FRUITCAKE SEASON, QUIKSTITCH QUILTING, HOLIDAYS WITHOUT HO-HO-HO: SUPPORT GROUP.

If I had been my mother, I would have called that sign the hand of God. I turned into the parking lot from the far lane. Even if the group wasn't a good one, there would be a coffeepot going in the back.

The meeting was practically finished when I crept in — the leader, a shockingly thin woman with hair cut above her ears, was already reading from the closing statements. "We come together without fears or requirements," she read dully. "We allow each other our own needs. If you feel that you belong here, you belong."

Twenty-two women listened in the circle around her. One, near the leader, was so frantic around the eyes and mouth, she looked as if she'd vibrate if you brushed her arm. "It is our faith that all pain is to be honored," the leader read.

I knew this. I'd heard it hundreds of times, meeting after meeting, night after night. Sometimes two meetings a day, before I met Jon, when the loneliness was so sheer and bright, I burned my fingertips with matches as a distraction. Next came call and response.

"Our experience —" the leader read.

"— is the center of our being," the group chanted back.

"Our responsibility —"

"— is our own healing."

I thought of my mother, her pursed lips and fussy fingers. With some shock, I realized that she would look right at home here.

"Happiness —"

"— is up to us."

"That's wrong," I said to the woman beside me. She looked up with bloodshot eyes and shifted as if she might move, so I put my hand companionably on her arm. "I'm not criticizing. But if it was up to us, we'd all be singing."

She stood up then, shaking off my hand like water, and scuttled to another chair in time for the next refrain.

"Honest," I said, standing now and speaking clearly, to be heard over the others. "I've written a book. I know what I'm talking about. Don't you all deserve joy? I do. My mother does."

"Growth comes in knowledge —" the leader began, but the response was splintered as women turned to look at me and frown.

"Sure," I said, "but what does knowledge lead to? I know every bad habit I have. Now my bad habits are my best friends. Every day I tell myself I hold my own happiness, but I'm still coming to meetings like this." The group had fallen silent, the tense woman looking at me with a slack mouth. I took off my jacket and moved into the center of the circle, where I liked to stand when I directed groups. "We all want a map because we can't see the road. But there aren't any maps. There isn't a road."

"We find our own path," said the leader, her voice quivering. "Only by working together can we find our individual paths. We've learned that this is the only answer."

Heads were nodding, but women looked back at me, waiting for my response. I stood on a chair. "Aren't you listening? Individual paths are the same as no path. Every day is shapeless." As I spoke, the tears broke free again. I couldn't wipe them away fast enough, so that looking at the group, I sensed we were all held in the same warm, salty water. "Listen! There's a new answer every day," I said. "I'm trying to tell you."

CITIZEN OF VIENNA

THE PHONE RANG AT 11:10, almost certainly Lucy. I was watching the local news report on a four-alarm tenement fire downtown, a harrowing, gorgeous sight. The tulip of flame, three stories high, lit the night for blocks. A cigarette had been left burning near a pile of bedding. Residents had been lucky to escape with their lives. The camera closed in on a shivering group of youngsters, three of them wailing but the fourth, maybe ten years old, standing stiffly apart, holding back his tears until the cameras went away. I felt a quick stir of sympathy for him. The phone rang one more time before I turned off the TV. "Took you a while," Lucy said when I finally picked up. "My bad if you've got a guy over there."

"Don't I wish. There's nobody here but us chickens."

"Here either." Lucy's voice was a husky whisper. "I could use a man. I could use a drink. I've been turning myself inside out trying to get ready for this stupid play. Want to hear one of my lines?"

She went silent for a four-count.

"You won't have to sit up nights memorizing," I said.

"I'm onstage for sixteen and a half minutes and don't get one word. I deserve a drink. Don't even say it: I should go out and help somebody else instead of sitting in my self-pity."

"Okay. I won't even say it."

"If I went down to Central Parkway right now and found a junkie to talk to, why would watching him stick a needle in his thigh make me feel any better? Strike up the band! I found an addict!"

"You're not living down there with him. That's something to be glad about."

"If that's all I've got to celebrate, then I really want a drink."

For the next five minutes I focused on coaxing Lucy out of the kitchen and into her bedroom, where she was less apt to have stashed a bottle. On other nights, when her dry rage wasn't so far off the charts, I could get her to start thinking about her good fortune. Her rent for the month was paid. She had heat, hot water, a cupboard full of ramen noodles. But tonight Lucy was too drunk on her own misery to be grateful for salty noodles. "Everything takes so much effort, and then everything still goes straight down the shitter," she said.

"Take a deep breath. Go easy on yourself. Put your slippers on," I told her.

"I guess it would kill you to admit that sometimes life sucks."

"Give it a rest. Life always sucks. That's life's job. But you should still put your slippers on."

"Little Mary Sunshine," she said. "You want to know what really makes me want to take a drink right now? That you are the only person in the world I can think of to call. Sorry if that hurts your feelings."

"I'll live."

I could hear Lucy shifting around, putting something in her mouth. "My life stinks," she said, and I flicked the TV back on, sound off. We were out of the woods.

Although only ten years older than Lucy — thirty-five to her twenty-five — my role in her life made me feel ancient, part mother, part sage. A regular Sacajawea of sobriety, in the last five years I'd blazed the trail for a teacher, a lawyer, two women who had started a glassware business together, made a fat little fortune together, and decided to go off the bottle together. All of them called me when they felt lost or fearful, and I talked them back into the light: things were never as bad as they thought, remember the big picture. But Lucy, a temp worker who wanted to be an actor — how could anyone make a living in Cincinnati as an actor? — was more inventive than those others, better at remembering temptation, and very, very much better at talking about it. She didn't have a scrap of the beaten-down humility that usually signaled the newly sober. "Life is boring enough," she liked to say. "Don't add to the general load."

I couldn't help liking her spirit, an affection I was pretty sure she recognized without my telling her. Neither of us could stand the damp emotions. Instead, I phoned her twice a week, sent her greeting cards that I knew would give her a wry laugh, and tracked her sobriety. Since being cast as one of the wordless Citizens of Vienna in the civic theater's upcoming *Amadeus,* Lucy was 44 days sober. Before this she had been 13 days sober, 81 days sober, and 117 days sober.

"You're on the upswing," I told her now. "Every day you can be a little more proud of what you're doing for yourself."

"Actually, I'm doing it for my director. And my agent. My fans!" She produced a bitter laugh, and I heard the sizz of a match, then an inhalation. "Last night I walked around my apartment for three hours, holding marbles in my hand, just so I couldn't pick up anything else."

"That's pretty good."

"That's ridiculous. Nobody can live this way. I felt like Captain Queeg."

"He didn't drink."

"But his men mutinied," Lucy said. "I went to bed at nine-thirty. At ten-thirty I took my bottle of Seagram's out to the trash. At eleven I went back out and broke the bottle."

"That's good. That's what you want."

"Jesus, Virginia, go easy on the uplift. I called to ask you a favor. You can say no. Maybe you'd better."

"What do you want?"

If Lucy heard the guardedness, she didn't let it stop her. "There's going to be a cast party Friday night. A party-party, not just everybody piling into cars and winding up at someone's apartment. Invitations. Punch."

"Sounds like fun."

"It sounds like booze. Every director in town will be there, and I won't get a part in anything next season if I don't go. If I drink, I'll blow myself out of the water. I want you to come with me."

Now I took the four-count. Lucy had never asked me to do anything for her before. On the few occasions we'd gone out together, she had acted as if she hardly knew me. "This is up to you, not me," I said shakily. "You know the routine: Go on a full stomach. Keep a glass of water in your hand. Even if I went, I couldn't keep you from drinking."

"Oh yes you could."

"Why not ask a friend in the cast to help you?"

"Nobody else cares if I take a snootful. If you're there — don't take this wrong, but if you're there, I won't drink. I couldn't take the lecture."

Watching an ad for an RV dealership, I let another beat go by. "How could I take that wrong?"

I didn't flatter myself that Lucy was striking out at me in particular. Like a trapped cat, she was slashing at whatever she could hit. "It's easy for you. You don't remember what it's like," she would snarl whenever she was freshly sober and her mood murderous.

In fact, I remembered my drinking with absolute clarity, which bothered me. By now the details of that boozy decade should have been softening in my memory, but the old days replayed in my brain as sharp as Hollywood movies.

Starting when I was twenty-one, ending when I was thirty, I spent most of my nights closing one or another of the bars downtown. During the daytime I wrote systems-evaluation reports. I wore sharp, trim suits, drove a snappy blue Prelude even though the insurance rates strangled my budget, and loved the orderliness of my life, which was two lives: eight to five at my desk with my files and my computer and my phone, and then five until two at The Maple Room or P.T.'s or The Mulligan, where the bartender made vodka sours — better than they sounded.

I remembered Mike, the one I lived with, and the others after him. They showed up in my dreams — handsome men, athletic, mostly kind. They laughed on the nights when I, fueled and furious, turned to some overloud customer at a nearby table in a bar and explained to him that his opinions, his vocabulary, his too-tight polo shirt, and the baseball cap over his bald spot exposed him to be the worst kind of poseur, a man who thought he was intellectual because he saw the movie version of *Hamlet*. Once I heard a bartender call me "Shali, the goddess of destruction." I tucked five dollars into the tip jar along with a napkin on which I'd written *Kali*.

I didn't stop drinking after the first bout of D.T.'s, but after the second, in a saving moment of fear, I checked into a hospital. There a doctor with a flat mouth stood waiting for me to wake up. "An alcohol-damaged liver gets hard. It starts to look like a rusty engine," he said. "Yours looks like it went down with the *Titanic*."

"First class or steerage?"

"Do you think you're cute? Capillaries in your nose are broken. Your hands tremble. You're not fooling anybody."

I closed my eyes and remembered the man I'd been drinking with. I remembered sitting with him at The Mulligan, and I remembered waking in my Prelude, shaking so hard the whole car shuddered.

"Do you want a list of AA meetings?" the doctor was saying.

"Thanks all the same." My lungs, like my eyes and ears, seemed to be full of something hot and sticky. "I can handle this on my own."

It's hard to stop drinking, but it isn't complicated. Don't go into the bar. Don't open the bottle. I didn't see any reason to have strangers tell me in public what I already knew, knew, knew. Once I was back at work, I made this point — loudly, with arm motions — to a colleague, not knowing he'd been sober for five years. Some days later, he mentioned a group he knew that met for weekly counseling. Smart, he didn't talk about support or one-day-at-a-time. Instead he said, "I go for the entertainment. You can't believe the things people say."

He went with me the first few times, until I promised him I'd keep coming on my own. The promise didn't cost much; the meetings *were* entertainment, in a sitcom kind of way. I heard about other people's blundering and stupid weekends, the night one guy stole a golf cart that kept stalling out on the freeway on-ramp, the weekend a woman meant to fly to Vegas, found herself in Dubuque, and walked through town looking for a casino. "The policeman who booked me said I kept asking for The Sands. I don't even like The Sands."

My stories were nothing like those. Whetted with liquor, I got as precise as a needle. The world appeared before me as clear as a steel-plate etching, and judgments arrived in my brain already reasoned, phrased, and savage. I lost one boyfriend when, full of vodka, I said, "You have a second-rate mind. Not a third-rate, but not a first. It will never be first."

I missed him when he was gone. He had a sweet way. It was not that boyfriend but another one — Steve, with the black curls and the middle-management job at U.S. Shoe — who glared across the tiny bar table when I told him he didn't have leadership potential. He swirled his bourbon and said, "So who died and made you God?"

Steve had told me all about the conversations at work he'd edged into and been edged out of. Two men and three women had already been promoted above him, a river of personnel rushing past his windowless cubicle. I could have saved him time and frustration if he'd have let me.

Instead he shoved back his chair and raged out of the bar, pausing only to drop a twenty on the barmaid's tray. "What'd you do to him?" she asked me.

"I gave him executive feedback," I said.

When I related this story to the group, the counselor said, "You're lucky."

"I told him the truth."

"Not every truth needs telling. You're lucky he didn't come to your apartment later with a knife. He wanted to know that you believed in him."

"I could see what was happening."

"Do you know what compassion is? It's seeing what somebody else sees."

"Why would I want to do that?" I said. Then, "A joke. Do you know what a joke is?"

I was in the group for a solid year before I stopped insulting people. It took another year for me to quit sighing and recrossing my legs every time a group member spoke tremulously about gratitude and new life. I knew I'd gotten somewhere when the counselor said to me, "You are the most stubborn person I've ever met," and I felt embarrassed instead of proud.

Not long after that conversation, I stopped going to the sessions and thanked the counselor for all his help. The man, pudgy and blotchy-faced and no fool, pushed his glasses down his nose and gazed at me with plainly exaggerated patience. I said, "I'm serious. You've taught me things. I don't assume anymore that other people want to hear my opinions." I left my phone number for new members who needed someone to talk to and a check that covered the rest of the sessions for the month.

Then I stepped into my new life. If the old days had been baroque, the new ones were Shaker — functional, simple, beautiful because they were plain. At last I was at home in myself, temperament and life perfectly matched. I'd always known the stern exultation that comes with self-mastery — even my drinking years had proved that. Now I lived in the center of exultation, day in, day out, a role model.

I got sharper and more efficient at work. After a while I began to take on new projects, complicated evaluations requiring page after page of statistical breakdowns. I pleased myself with my own skill. But at just about the time Lucy invited me to the party I realized, without feeling the need to dwell on this insight, that I was working until midnight to stay too busy to drink.

The desire for booze, at first not even a yearning so much as an unacknowledged, ongoing thought, grew a little every day. It tickled the edge of my brain. Five months had passed since a man had asked me out, and I pondered that fact. Perhaps the loss of my old, keen edge had made me too ordinary. I no longer insulted strangers in public places. I was able to make supportive comments and kept my opinions to myself. I had been cast, like Lucy, as a Citizen of Vienna, a placeholder behind the interesting characters who had things to say.

A drink, I thought without thinking the words, would cure everything. In the thick, dull night after Lucy's call, my mouth tingled with the memory of silky-hot scotch, and I half-heard the *ffff* of a cork being eased from a wine bottle. I pushed these impressions away, but not too far.

So the idea of Lucy's party bubbled through me all the next day. Lucy's presence would keep me from drinking, and meanwhile I would talk to new, artistic men, stage-lovely, extroverted, game for life's adventures. I'd been in the counseling group long enough to know that a desire to drink was in fact a desire for human connection, a yearning to crawl out of the grave of loneliness. I called Lucy as soon as I got home from work. "I'll go. I'm happy to help. To tell you the truth, I'm looking forward to it."

"Goody," Lucy said.

"It's a party. Fun, remember?"

"For you it's a party. For me it's work. I'm thinking about bagging it."

"That wouldn't be smart, would it?"

"Do I have to be smart?" Lucy said, her voice plaintive. For a second I thought she was offering a rare, unobstructed glimpse of her soul. More likely, she was practicing sorrow and yearning, important emotions for an actor. "How long have you been sober?" she asked.

"Five years. You know this."

"Do you even remember what it feels like to want a drink?"

"I don't dwell on it."

"You sure don't. When somebody says 'drink,' you think 'milk.'"

"Oh, come on," I said.

"Do me a favor, would you? Then I promise we'll go to the party and I'll have a good attitude. Tell me what it feels like to want a drink. Tell me what goes on in your mouth and your head."

"Your life looks lousy, nothing seems to be going right. Or else everything is going right. Either way, a drink seems like the answer. It's not all that dramatic."

"Would you please tell me that one time you were so nuts for a drink that you were in the bathroom, on your hands and knees, licking the tiles?"

"Lucy, do you need me to come over?"

"No point. Floor's all clean now. I should stay home and admire it."

Silence swelled between us — a rarity — and I uttered the first words I could think of. "I drove drunk," I said. "And I took walks drunk. Once I found my neighbor's cat blocks away and carried it home. But it turned out not to be my neighbor's cat. My neighbor didn't have a cat. In the morning my hands and arms were so scratched and swollen that I couldn't pull on a long-sleeved shirt."

"What did you tell people at work?" Lucy said, laughing.

"I called in sick. When I did come in, I told people I had poison ivy."

"Don't you ever miss the secret life?"

"No," I said. If she'd been there to see, I would have shrugged. Every life was secret. I shouldn't have to tell an actor that.

"Byron? Do I have that right? Not Brian?"

"You can call me Lord." The man, Lucy's director, produced a cool smile and pushed the thick yellow thatch of hair back from his eyes.

"Don't even try with this one, Byron," Lucy said. She held a cigarette in one hand and a bottle of water, her third, in the other. "She'll cut you in half before you see the sword."

"My kind of woman," he said. "Want some punch?"

I shook my head. "Club soda."

"All work."

"I play. This is how I play."

"Scary," he said, and angled toward the bar across the loud room.

"He's a snake," Lucy said. "I wouldn't drink anything he brought me."

"I had that worked out already. How did your talk with him go?"

Lucy swigged her water. "There are no bad roles. A real actor brings the same intensity to a Citizen of Vienna as to Ophelia. We are here in the service of art, not ego."

"What horseshit."

"I've talked to everybody I need to. We might as well leave."

"We can if you want," I said, careful to sound indifferent. "I hate to see you give in to this jerk, though."

"What do you suggest?"

"Stay. Laugh. Let him see something about art, not ego."

"Coach Virginia. You should be wearing a whistle around your neck."

I shrugged. "I don't like this guy." Who was threading back to us, a glass of clear liquid in each hand.

"You can talk to him if you want. I'm outta here," Lucy said, turning as Byron pushed a plastic glass into my hand. I sniffed it and caught only the sharp scent of the bobbing chunk of lime. It was an easy bet that the drink was half vodka. I rested it on the table beside me.

"So. You're juicy Lucy's friend," Byron said.

"Her devoted friend. She's a good actor. How come you gave her a part with no lines?"

Byron made a boyish smile. "I have to discharge a few debts to other people. Do you act?"

"No more than anyone else. You?"

"Too much for my own good. I act the dutiful son, the fiery director, the meticulously concerned father."

"The good husband?"

"Never had that role." He brushed a strand of hair from my cheek. "Now I'm acting debonair, to win you over. How am I doing?"

"Brilliantly." A good enough actor, I lifted my face while his fingers lingered there, and let my own finger dip into my drink. When I tasted the liquid on my fingertip, it tasted like nothing.

It continued to taste like nothing while Byron told a funny story about his directorial debut, when lighting cues were so mishandled that an entire love scene was played in the dark, the actors improvising lines such as "How dare you put your hand on my breast while we sit upon this couch!" Then he segued into a story about his own attempt, as a young man, to play a love scene with a woman he'd had a crush on; he'd so stammered and blushed and trampled his lines that the woman finally said, "All *right!*" and the audience applauded like thunder. The stories were well calibrated, showing off Byron's vulnerable and yearning heart. To occupy my hands, I picked up my drink and swirled it. For show, I brought the glass to my lips.

"So what are your roles? Aside from the cool and desirable brunette?" His straw-colored hair looked soft as fur.

"Guess," I said.

"I'd cast you as a schoolteacher. High heels and tight skirts, driving all the boys crazy."

"I hope you're a little more inventive when you're staging plays." I smiled. Again I trailed my finger across the top of my drink and raised the finger to my mouth. "I'm a paper pusher, and a member of my condominium association, and Lucy's friend."

"You must be lonely. Lucy's gone."

I jerked my head up. On the other side of the crowded room three women, two very slender and one very plump, were singing, arms linked, on the piano. Against the walls fervent couples fingered collars and earlobes. One man nibbled another's thumbnail, and at the bar a loose and laughing group shouted lines I almost recognized. No Lucy in a doorway or beside the bookcase. No Lucy calling out her own lines, or singing, or opening another bottle of water. In a moment I would go look for her, but first, a trapdoor opened at the bottom of my brain and glee fell out. I lifted my glass. "As a matter of fact, I don't feel a bit lonely."

"All of a sudden, neither do I. What's so funny?"

"Do you have even one line you haven't used before?" I said.

"You don't know many actors, do you?"

"You're the first. Make a good impression."

"I'll start by getting you another drink."

I put my hand on Byron's arm, stopping him and pulling him close. In a tremendous stage whisper, I hissed, *I shouldn't be drinking.*

He leaned closer, his hand shading the side of his mouth. *I know.*

Then I found I couldn't stop laughing, even when Lucy strolled back out of the kitchen, a fresh bottle of water in her hand, and glanced across the room in time to see me knock back half a glass of undiluted vodka.

"You're a mean drunk, but you're not sloppy," Lucy said. It was seven in the morning, and the telephone receiver seemed to buzz in my hand. "For my money, it was worth it just to watch you tell Byron that he had the psychological insight of a turtle."

"He got a rise out of me," I said, pressing my fingers against the side of my head. The blood was jackhammering. "I guess this means he's a good director."

"Are you kidding? He's the worst. Every obvious move. The only thing he knows how to do is come on to women."

"Practice makes perfect. I told him so after he kissed me the second time." I paused, then forced myself: "Thank you for taking me home."

"Happy to do it," Lucy said. I heard her strike a match. "I'm in your debt. I stayed sober."

"Congratulations."

"You're still my mentor. You came to the party and kept me from drinking. So why shouldn't I say thanks?"

I pressed my temples harder. I had the clear impression I was holding my skull together. "Common. Decency." Each word rolled out of my mouth like a pebble, and the walls of my stomach tightened, although there was nothing left there.

Lucy said, "Look, Virginia, I know what's going on with you. Better than you do. You've been sober 782 years, and you've forgotten how to start over. But you are talking to a pro." She exhaled. "What do you want right now? A drink?"

"No." The idea was nauseating, mostly.

"You will. Are you crying?"

"Yes."

Lucy's voice held the tiniest undertone of laughter. "You want to think this is a tragedy, but it's not. You're starting over with a clean slate. Up till now you've been so busy clamping down on your own miserable happy ending that you've forgotten about happy beginnings. A person falls down, she gets back up. It isn't that big a deal."

I closed my eyes over my tears. Lucy's insouciance was worse than the sarcasm I'd been ready for, or the anger. I had undone the last five years of my life for an idiot boy with blond hair, handsome and brainless. Even Lucy had never blundered so stupidly, a fact that I wanted acknowledged. No sooner had I formed the thought than I heard the response as Lucy might have delivered it: *And why should you get what you want?*

"It's not that easy," I said.

"It's not that hard. Promise you'll call me tonight," Lucy said.

"I'll be typing in data. I'm going to keep my hands busy so I can't pick up anything else."

"Good tactic."

"I learned it from you," I said, hanging up before Lucy could start talking about happiness again.

For the next two weeks, the nights were unbearable. I had car keys, a fat wallet, and knowledge I could not make myself lose: the liquor store that was open late was three miles away, the one with the better selection, nine. One evening craving wrung me until I was on my hands and knees, room to room, abrading my wrists against the carpet to make a haze of pain that would block out — no, punish — my thirst. If Lucy had asked, I would have told her about this bit of drama. Perhaps she guessed.

She was calling five times a day, and I answered the phone every time. Fighting drink was like fighting quicksand, but fighting Lucy was combat — hand-to-hand, restorative. My gratitude was beyond words, which she knew. At the end of one of these conversations, I asked her how she was getting along with Byron.

"He changed my casting: I'm one of the Venticelli now. A speaking part. He watched me watch you at the party and was impressed with my emotive skills."

"If you're about to thank me, please stop."

"I'm just telling you. Luck crops up where you don't expect it." Her voice sounded prissy and stiff. Before I could ask whom she was imitating, she went on. "By the way, Byron would like you to drop by his place. He told me to tell you. I told him to get lost."

"And he said, 'What, you can't trust your mentor to make decisions for herself?'"

"Bingo," Lucy said. Byron had been right to give her a speaking role. In the silence between us rang the echo of her voice, a chiming chord of indifference, anxiety, and pleading.

I quit rubbing the carpet. "Is this about your new part?"

"I didn't ask him."

"Can he bust you back down to Citizen?"

"He's the director. He giveth, he can taketh away. So you make up your own mind. I wouldn't have told you this if I didn't think you could figure out what you want to do."

"I want to do a lot of things," I said carefully.

"I know."

"Are you asking me not to let you down?"

"You better believe it," she said.

Byron's apartment was only a little bit shabby. The drooping palms in front of the window were dusty but still green, and canister up-lights behind the piano drew the eye away from the exhausted tan carpet. On the walls were tacked several playbills, photos, and a single poster — a reproduction of Magritte's *Ce n'est pas une pipe*. I'd forgotten how young Byron was.

"Wine or coffee?" He held a chardonnay bottle in one hand, a bag of coffee beans in the other.

"Coffee." I followed him into the kitchen. "Thank you."

"I wasn't sure where you were standing now."

"Fifteen days sober? I'm not standing anywhere. I'm flat on the ground, hanging onto a rock."

"Good line," he said. He pushed the coffee grinder's lever so that the noisy clatter briefly filled the space between us. "Good lines are your specialty. You told me so at the party."

I felt an embarrassed smile hover at the corners of my mouth. "I talk when I get tanked. Then the next day I go around apologizing."

"I liked it. You were spunky."

"You make me sound like Shirley Temple."

He snorted. "Shirley Temple played by Simone de Beauvoir. So who are you playing tonight?"

I was wondering that myself. I hadn't forgotten Byron's duplicity, but his hair rolled in a heavy blond wave over his forehead and his arms were smooth with muscle. Giddiness bubbled through me, mild at first. "I'm Lucy's friend," I said.

"What else?"

"Let's see. I'm trying to make good. I'm missing my favorite TV show. I'm too old to be here."

"I wouldn't say that." He stood just a foot away from me. I would hardly have to raise my hand to touch him.

"Trust me," I said. "You want some ingénue who won't cause trouble."

"I like trouble."

"You just think you do." I glanced at the chardonnay bottle he'd left in the sink, its sides glistening with condensation. "Don't you want to put that back in the refrigerator?"

"In a while. Tell me about trouble."

I shrugged. "Even though you know your lines, you decide to improvise. But then you need to keep talking, so you use whatever words show up in your mouth. You tell truths that don't need telling. And then it's too late."

"Is that all? I must be in trouble every day of my life."

"You didn't ask about frequency."

He laughed. Sweeping a speck from the counter, he let his wrist brush against my arm.

"Your turn," I said, not quite steadily. "Talk. Tell me something I don't know."

"You're setting me up. There's nothing you don't know."

"Smart answer," I said, holding my hands an inch away from his. I danced back a step so he could follow. He was better at this than many men, leaving a gap that one of us would have to reach across. "I'm full of wisdom," I said. "Just ask Lucy."

The mobility of his face was wonderful; he shifted from desire to regret in a single beat. "I wouldn't try asking her right now. There was a party after rehearsal last night. We had to drive her home." He glanced away from me and added, "Sorry to be the bearer of bad news."

"She would have told me," I said.

"She looks up to you. She told me so three times. Red wine."

"That's not her drink."

"She told me that, too."

Turning to the cupboard to get coffee mugs, Byron presented his profile for me to ponder. He was almost certainly lying. Lucy never started drinking when her life brightened or when she had work. On the other hand, she might pick up a drink as a way to challenge her own good fortune. I knew the impulse.

"She respects your experience," Byron said. "She talked to me about how much you've been through."

I stepped toward him. His hair between my fingers was thick and soft as a fox's tail. I said, "You have no idea what I've been through."

"You know what I like about you?" he said, motionless, his eyes closed. "You're not another drone or dumb actress. You have a real life."

"You don't know many alcoholics, do you?" Just the one hand buried in his soft hair.

"I'm in *theater*. Everybody I know shuttles in and out of AA. But no one else is like you. You're special."

He opened his heavy eyes, and I didn't draw my hand back, even though the moment grew spongy. I tingled, half humiliated and half exhilarated that this vain, untrustworthy man should understand me perfectly. Already his hands were lifted to catch me, the woman ten years his senior who had come to his house because he'd given her a drink. When the words rose into my mouth, I didn't try to check them. "Oh honey, I'm not a bit special. If I was special, I wouldn't be here with you." I pulled away from him and picked up the chardonnay bottle from the sink. "Where's your corkscrew?"

His angry smile slid across his face like silk. "I'm not going to tell you."

The corkscrew lay in the first drawer I opened, and I twisted it expertly into the cork, unpopping it with the sound that always meant celebration. I held the bottle up before him, gauging what would happen to his tense, expectant expression. Then I poured a little, wanting to drink it so bad that my hand shook, and emptied the glass onto the floor between us. Not much. The puddle would be easy to clean. I rubbed my wrist against the rough cotton of my pants.

"I guess you don't like chardonnay," Byron said.

"I love chardonnay. Catch me at the right time, I'd be on my hands and knees, licking it up." I skirted the puddle on my way back toward the front door, where I had dropped my purse and keys. Byron's damp footsteps padded behind me.

"Look, is it something I said?"

"Oh for Christ's sake, Byron, of course it's something you said." I turned to face him and squeezed his arm. "Don't worry — I'll tell Lucy that you did some of your best work here tonight."

"She must have lost the lottery on the day they were giving out friends."

"She tells me that all the time." I was pleased to be able to say something so nearly true.

He leaned beside the door, his eyes quick and tight. "So where are you going now? A bar?"

"Home."

"And what do you do when you get lonely, Grandma?"

"Haven't you been paying attention? I call Lucy." I leaned forward and kissed — hard — his lovely, parted lips. Then I went home.

THE BEST FRIEND

"SUE BETTEL: DANCER." We howled. She was our favorite topic, although we rarely said more than "Sue Bettel: Dancer." Slung across the ripped, sprung dorm couches, mostly still wearing leg warmers and leotards, we would remind one another of "Sue Bettel: Dancer," and laugh ourselves weak.

Not merely plump but actually broad, Sue had round arms and a round belly and a big, round rear; she gathered her wiry red hair into an untidy, roundish bush on the back of her head. Her red plastic-rimmed glasses flew off her face on turns, and her low forehead and steep chin gave her the look of an inquisitive finch. Lazy turnout, awkward arms: the best we could say was that she danced, somehow, with confidence. Still, she had gotten a scholarship, a fact that drove the rest of us crazy. At every party we could count on some skinny girl with sinuous arms imitating a heavy-footed, out-of-breath dancer. "I," she would pant, "have a *scholarship!*"

Only once did Sue walk in on one of these imitations. Wearing a distracted, slightly cross-eyed expression, Janine Prienocski was blundering across the dorm lounge, her mincing bourrée steps, which had started off daintily, picking up speed as Janine lunged farther and farther off balance. We were yelling encouragement, and when Sue appeared in the doorway, wearing her birdlike expression, I was so embarrassed that I laughed harder, though the other girls fell silent. Janine, a pro, kept dancing.

Head cocked, eyes blinking, Sue studied Janine's wobbly legs, her thrust-out rear, the way her arms paddled the air. Then she jumped into place right beside Janine, tipping from side to side, thumping so hard that the lamps rattled. Sue had a gift for comedy. In fact, she was funnier than Janine, although I wasn't sure she knew she was imitating herself. After that evening I felt a slim tie to her, a vague admiration and a vaguer sense of debt.

We were all dance majors together at Padarette, a tiny liberal-arts college just north of Indianapolis, the only decent dance department for miles. Five years earlier a Padarette girl had been picked for American Ballet Theatre; her signed glossy hung near the department secretary's desk, and every one of us had studied that signature, whether we would admit it or not.

We cultivated what we imagined to be professional behavior: disdainful attitudes, spotless rehearsal attendance, developing what the ballet master, Georges, called body instinct. "The single position. No other," he growled. "The body knows or it does not know."

Mine sometimes knew; Janine's often knew. But Sue's never, ever knew. By our senior year I couldn't bear to watch her practice, although she chattered about auditions when we talked in the dressing room, conversations I myself started because I felt pity for her.

Not much effort was needed to talk to Sue. Her mouth was filled with observations — the widening isthmus connecting Georges's bald spots; the hangdog, lovesick looks shot by our pianist toward Clara Leekin's butter-colored hair; the lovesick looks shot by Georges to our pianist. I had never noticed Georges's hairline before, or at least not so clearly, and I certainly hadn't noticed the pianist. Janine stood behind Sue, opening and closing her hand like a beak, the gesture for "talk-talk-talk." Sue pointed, named, talk-talk-talked.

With her voice in my head, I began to take walks around the tiny campus, seeing for the first time its halfhearted planter beds and the sandy brick of the four classroom buildings. Stains the color of new plums stretched underneath the ancient air-conditioning units. Afternoon light crashed against southwest-facing windows. Sidewalks rumpled like sheets over the thick, snaking maple roots. I wondered whether I could find a way to dance these clear, new details and then wondered who would want to see them if I did.

My dancing took on an edge, my turns snapping like whip cracks even when Georges called out to remember adagio, to feel the music. Probably my new speed was the result of the weight I was losing — graduation was nearing like a shipwreck, and all of us except Sue had lost our appetites. Nevertheless, during the long afternoon classes my mind, which should have been focused on nothing but the single position, was filled with plums and maple trees. I felt new to myself, strange, a strangeness that became darkly meaningful when, for the first time, I wasn't given a solo in the end-of-term recital. Sue had one, though.

Sue's feet were softer than ever, practically rippling on pointe, and she had put on weight around her waist and back. In arabesque her profile looked wadded. Right before lunch she would practice her long solo, set to a Gershwin medley, and she was apparently oblivious to the cluster of girls staring at her from the doorway. Always at least one of them — though I was never the one — would softly oink.

Hour by hour the level of outraged grumbling rose, and we went from wondering whether she was sleeping with a teacher to assuming she was sleeping with a teacher to fury that sleeping with a teacher should be so well rewarded. "Hell, I'd have sex with Georges if he'd give me *Rhapsody in Blue*," I said, and the others laughed. I grinned, so they would think I was joking.

The resentful grumble rose to a din the afternoon Georges posted an audition sign-up sheet for a touring company. The job was chorus line, requiring tap, ballet, and jazz, with a guaranteed run and union benefits. Teachers gave permission for the studios to stay open, and everyone except Sue spent nights practicing past eleven, past midnight, past sense.

The afternoon before the audition, Sue found me in one of the practice rooms, where I'd been hammering at my time step for two hours. "You'll do better if you get some sleep." She practically had to yell; the room was a storm of tapping, curses, three different boom boxes cuing three different songs. Everybody kept turning up the volume.

"I'll do better if my time step is right," I said, clacking through it again, missing — I always missed — the tricky kick-turn-jump.

"How well are you going to dance if you've got a bottle of Dexatrim doing time steps in your bloodstream? Get some sleep."

I kept my eyes on my sweaty reflection. My feet rattled along, kick-turn-jump, kick-turn-jump. "I don't need sleep. I need to be perfect."

"Put a little pressure on yourself, why don't you?"

"Look — if you want to stay in here, then dance. That's what the rest of us are doing."

"I'm just saying it pays to stop and take stock every once in a while. Make sure that what you're doing is paying off."

"And if it isn't?" I tossed off a fast, low triple pirouette, a turn she'd never been able to do.

She shrugged. "Then change what you're doing."

I stood still then and looked at Sue in the mirror, as she was looking at me. I had four inches on her. I could lift my leg straight from the hip until my toes pointed at the ceiling. "Your talk doesn't change anything," I said.

"I'm trying to be a friend."

"No, you're not." Taking one step back, I whipped out pirouettes until Sue left the studio. Then I went back to the time step, two against three, five against four. By morning I was haggard, caffeine burning like a coal in my stomach, but I had the step.

Sue appeared at the studio fifteen minutes before auditions began. Freshly showered, she looked like a plump doll, her cheeks rosy and her soft forehead untroubled. Her clear eyes scanned her competition. I looked too, seeing what Sue did: the limps and winces, the skull-like faces, the angular, mean want. Watching myself in the mirror, I lifted my arm and lowered it, unable to soften the sharp line. At the end of the day, three girls from our class were hired, two of them girls who had rehearsed beside me all night.

Sue called every week or two from the road, reporting on the amphetamines, the B$_{12}$ shots and blood transfusions, the sleazeball audience members — and not just men — who lingered after performances. She explained life on the road and told me stories about the headliners. At first she would interrupt her monologue and urge me to talk about myself. But I resented the smallness of grades and end-of-school recitals beside Sue's glamorous, sordid backstages, and I quickly rediverted her to the footlights. Not that she needed much diverting. "Wait until you hear about the director," she sometimes began.

More and more tightlipped, I listened. A month from graduation, I had no prospects, not even teaching in some suburban studio that specialized in tap for toddlers. During the days I tried to think only of steps, tried not to think, but my steps became distracted and confused. "You lack," Georges said in front of the whole class, "enough want."

"I want," I muttered.

"Not enough." Then he turned to the next girl in line and did not look at me again.

I blamed Sue. Some small, reasonable, silenced part of me had always known that I wouldn't dance forever, that careers were built on stages in New York, not in barely accredited colleges in Indiana. I had known that my dream of the body would have to stop eventually, but I couldn't shut away the belief that Sue had brought me to unhappiness early.

After graduation I went back home to Hammond and worked as a receptionist at the studio where I had taken classes as a girl, answering phones and keeping track of the cash box. After two years I enrolled in an accounting course at Ivy Tech and there met Dan, who told me he wanted to get out of Indiana and wouldn't mind starting his own school of dance. Sue called from Oklahoma City while we were addressing wedding invitations.

"It must be in the air," she said. "I can hardly talk over the wedding bells out here." She was marrying the show's producer, thirty years her senior, already three marriages to the bad.

"This is news," I said.

"We were friends. Then we got to be friendlier." I could hear

Sue's quick, birdlike smile. "When we get to Chicago, I'm going to be soloist."

Pure self-respect forced me to congratulate her, but something else, a masochistic curiosity, prompted me to keep asking Sue about her engagement ring, the rave reviews the show had gotten, her day with Twyla Tharp. "Some mornings I wake up and don't even recognize my own life," Sue said.

"It's yours, all right. I could have picked it out of a lineup." After we hung up, I insisted on addressing every last one of the invitations, even though it was late and Dan was ready to go to bed.

What little was left of our friendship drained away without drama. I continued to hear from Sue at odd intervals as she called to announce her succession of personal victories. The marriage to her producer lasted two years, long enough to give her a season as soloist and a daughter she named Gloria. Shortly after Dan and I moved to L.A. and opened our first studio, she called to let me know she was marrying an engine-parts heir in Indianapolis and planned to open a dancing school of her own. Later I heard about another baby, and later still twins, after Dan and I divorced, childless despite years of hoping.

Once in a while, late at night after a few drinks, I would consider calling Sue to tell her about my steadily lengthening chain of studios — three after Dan left, then four, five, six. I also invested in a little production company to help a friend, a job that let me feel as if I had my own small scrap of power in this city full of powerful people. Some vestigial store of pride always kept me away from the phone. Still, I imagined the conversations so acutely, I might as well have gone ahead and run up the phone bill. With great clarity I saw and resented the state-of-the-art floor her husband's money had allowed her to install, the students she had recruited from New York and eventually sent back there, her children, who were, every one of them, Pavlovas. "You and Dan didn't have any kids, did you?" I could hear her asking.

Maybe twice a year the old fury swept over me, and for days at a time I didn't answer the phone, afraid of what might come out

of my mouth. I was emerging from one of these interludes, working at home on billing, when the phone rang. Without thinking I
picked up the receiver. As unlikely as it sounds, in the moment of
buzzing, long-distance transmission I knew with damp certainty
exactly who was waiting for me.

"Hello, Mona!" she sang out, as she had always done.

"Listen," I said, "I'm sorry, I was on my way out the door."

"I just want to ask you one thing, a favor actually. I don't think
you'll mind."

"I'm very busy. You know, last month I opened my sixth studio."

"We're expanding too. Two regional companies want us to provide training to their dancers. I gave an interview about it to
Dance magazine."

I rubbed my eyes. "I'm supposed to be in Pasadena in fifteen
minutes, and it's a twenty-minute drive."

"You don't let time get away from you. I was just saying so to
Gloria. She's graduated from high school; can you believe it?"

"That's what kids do," I said, although I was startled. Sue had
sent me a picture years ago — a tiny, saucer-eyed child with dark
hair caught in fuzzy pigtails.

"She's six feet tall and weighs 119 pounds. She looks like a ther-
mometer and thinks she should be a fashion model. She wants to
go to L.A."

"Sue, I've really got one foot out the door."

"She's convinced that she'll take the world by storm. She
doesn't know a thing about the world, or about storms, either. But
her heart is set on this. So I thought of you. You could help her,
give her advice. Show her how to make a career with the beautiful
people. Don't you have a production company?"

I couldn't keep from snorting. "Who do you think I am, Swifty
Lazar? The company makes two commercials a year. Me, I teach
seven-year-olds to plié."

"But you live there. You know people. Anyway, it could be ex-
citing, hearing about the photo shoots and all. I'd trust her with
you. You don't have a houseful of other folks needing your attention." Her voice grew subtly louder, as if she had moved the tele-

phone closer to her mouth. "Of course I'd pay for her rent and meals."

I was scrubbing at my eyes. "I can afford to feed a 119-pound teenager. But I'm not up to taking in a stranger right now."

"A friend," Sue said, and before I could point out the distance we had traveled since friendship, she added, "I know you need to get going. Just think about it, and I'll call again this weekend."

"Nothing will change."

"She thinks she's going to set the town on fire. Who knows? Maybe she will, with you there to help her fan the flames." She chuckled comfortably.

"I was never the one to start fires." I was practically gargling with outrage but didn't suppose Sue heard that. Her ears never discerned anything so obvious as impatience or irritation. Instead, she listened for desires that pulsed and bloomed only in secret — a long, helpless wish for a child, for instance. A sudden curiosity about someone else's child. Like a quick animal, Sue sensed reflexes and defenses; she smelled alarm. What she almost certainly sniffed now was the scent I couldn't control, the first acrid whiff of capitulation.

I happened to be watering the patio plants the afternoon Gloria arrived. Hearing her pull into the driveway, I looked up from glistening begonias to see a girl emerge from a beat-up convertible, her body unfolding like the spindly legs of a compass. I held my face in an expression that I hoped was cordial, then felt it jerk into something less practiced when she bounded up the steps and looped her long arms around me. "Mona! You're here! I'm here! Finally!"

She beamed, a few strands of her springy hair tangling in a low branch of the olive tree. "Indiana to L.A. — some miles! I wasn't sure Kansas was ever going to stop. But I kept reminding myself that you'd be at the end."

"Like a pot of gold."

She laughed, and I studied her. What could Sue have told this lanky girl? Her smile shone like a spotlight.

"I've got so much to tell you." Gloria bounced back to the car and tugged at a colossal suitcase that barely cleared the lip of the trunk.

"Let me help."

She shook her head. "Mom said if I was old enough to be out on my own, I'm old enough to pull my own weight." After a final yank the suitcase thudded free. "Anyway, I'm stronger than I look."

"That's good to know." She looked strong enough to lift a small cat. Sue hadn't exaggerated about her child's shape; Gloria was a long tube of a girl, with no curves at all. When she bent to hoist her suitcase, her vertebrae made a bony ridge under her T-shirt, and her stretch pants hung from her hips without a bulge or crease. But she didn't have the sleepy, blank air of many ultra-thin girls. She chirped, she hopped, she chattered; the air surrounding her seemed spangled. She raced up the steps to the front door, so clearly delighted to have arrived that a smile pulled at my mouth, and when we went into the kitchen, I gave her knobby shoulder a squeeze.

"I feel like my life is finally starting, right here, right this minute."

"Whoa, girl. You're bringing a lifetime with you. Don't go denying your wholesome Midwestern girlhood. Around here, it'll make you exotic," I said. "Would you like some coffee?"

She shook her head at the coffeepot. "I brought celery juice. Want some?" I made a face, and Gloria laughed. "That's what Mom says, too."

"How is your mother?" I would have liked to hide the cardboard dustiness of my words a little better, but Gloria only grinned.

"How do you think? Twenty different directions, forty different projects. When I was packing to come here, she wandered into my room and told me that she was sending me to you because you're the best help a girl could ask for. I asked her what that meant and she said, 'Mona's always got the answers.'"

I reached into the refrigerator for milk. This shining girl would want to hear about pranks, escapades, close calls with boys, not a years-long string of phone calls in which Sue detailed her wildly unfair gift for the main chance and the windfall. "Your mother's got me mixed up. She's the one with the answers."

Gloria sighed and grinned and frowned at me. "You're just as bad as she is. I should have guessed. She's always said you're her best friend."

"Has she, now?" I said.

She cracked open her can of celery juice. "Are you surprised?"

"It's been a long time, that's all. We haven't actually seen each other since college."

"Well, she says best friend. She says it all the time."

In the shower or car, safely unobserved, I fretted. Things hadn't been going well for Sue in the friend department if she thought I was her best one. A best friend would have encouraged Gloria to talk about her mother and pointed out Sue's many virtues. A best friend would not slide around the mere mention of Sue's name. A best friend would certainly not spend nights envisioning scenarios — illness, bankruptcy, a long-term imprisonment — that would force Gloria to stay with me for a lifetime. I was ashamed of myself. But the girl whooped from room to room, a boxcar of delight, and she pulled me into delight with her. The house grew rich with the smell of her almond oil. She insisted on baking leaden oat muffins, which she brought to me for breakfast, and her laughter chimed in every corner. Often she returned from her runs clutching little bouquets of geraniums and nasturtiums that she left in the coffeepot. In the bud vase she plunked a stalk of celery.

Gloria carried her mother's knack for clowning, Sue's way of enlivening every detail until the world seemed fresh. While I cleaned up after dinner, Gloria mimicked the vacuous models and their hyperarticulated walk, the coked-up receptionists at the agencies, the fumbling, frustrated beginning photographers. Her specialty was the creamy agents who never quite said yes, but never ever said no. I applauded, then taught her how to curtsy three different ways.

At work I started to teach complicated steps. Bored with my class of intermediate nine-year-olds, I nudged them: "Extend those legs. Or else bend them. You've got bodies; do something with them."

Eight girls lifted their legs exactly as high as they'd done before.

Plump Ellen Martin, biting her lip, managed to raise her foot another half-inch and sweep her arms above her head, a moment of shining ambition that lasted until her balance listed and she clattered to the floor. The girl behind her mooed.

"She's outdone every one of you," I said, as Ellen hauled herself back up.

I was annoyed by their mean titters and at the same time felt glee rising like a challenge, rung by rung, up my rib cage. Pulling the blushing Ellen to the center of the room, I gave her an easy combination: one little turn, a tendu kick, a low arabesque. "Hold that. Now hitch up your shoulder. Look down your arm. Bend your knees. Hold it. Hold it!" And plump Ellen, legs bent and arms long, was suddenly as angular and mean as a cat, like the tough MTV dancers that all the girls tried to imitate.

"I thought this was supposed to be ballet," sulked one of the blond Laurens. She wore heavy, expensive ankle warmers, appropriate for a girl who never broke a sweat.

"I'm giving Ellen some options. When you work as hard as she does, I'll show some to you." After they left, I blocked out an old routine in front of the mirror, making up steps where I couldn't remember the original, throwing in trashy MTV squats for the hell of it. I watched myself making the old moves. I hadn't lost much.

My spirits were still frothing when I came home and found Gloria sitting motionless in the living room — no TV, no radio, an untouched manicure kit beside her. She hadn't minded so much when LuCille with the long, long neck had gotten the department-store ad, but now Dania, featuring her stubble of brick-colored hair, would carry the cruise wear shoot. Slumped on the couch, Gloria studied her bony toes. "Dania knows people. LuCille knows a director. She's got a flat nose, but she knows a director."

"Gloria, people know each other. That's normal." I felt my carbonated spirits drizzle away. "You don't stop knocking on doors now. You knock harder."

"Every door is locked before I even get to it." Her voice quivered. "Do you have any idea how that feels?"

"Yes," I said.

Fishing in the manicure kit, she picked up an orange stick and started working over her cuticles, ramming the soft tissue back from her fingernails. "I can keep going to auditions. If I'm lucky, I'll wind up in a crowd shot for a Toyota Sell-a-thon."

"Most of us wind up in the Sell-a-thon," I said, studying her wide-set eyes. Even downcast, they shone. "You figure out whether a Sell-a-thon is better than nothing. If you can't be the star, is it good enough to be close to the star?" If we were both lucky, she was too absorbed in her fingernails to hear the break in my voice. "For what it's worth, I know you deserve much more than a crowd shot. You deserve a spotlight."

Gloria took a moment to produce a complicated smile. "You are such a mom. Sometimes I feel like I never left home."

I reached across the coffee table and massaged her foot, closing my mouth against all the words about mothering, about protection, about the ways that girls with second-rate talent acquired a first-rate career. "Something will come through for you. You'll see," I said. "You'll find a way. Your mother wouldn't have sent you otherwise."

The words hung a long time before Gloria said, "Tell me something. I've spent a lot of time wondering. Why did she stop performing? Would you have stopped?"

"Hard to know." I drew my hand back. "I never had your mother's successes."

"She toured for a year and now she runs the Swan Lake School of Dance in Indianapolis. She's not exactly Balanchine. She kept telling me that I wouldn't be satisfied out here. Do you think she's satisfied?"

Gloria shone her appraising gaze on me, and I wondered whether it had occurred to her that I also was not exactly Balanchine. Hurt sidled to the edge of my brain, and I ushered it into the center. "What do you think? She's your mother, not mine."

"Jeez. Sorry I asked."

"Don't you think I want to know? Shoot, I'm dying to know. You tell me: Does she figure she's on the plus side of her tally sheet? When she looks at her life, does she see every show she was never in, or does she see success after success, a whole chorus line of wonderful achievements that you get to be one of?"

The shift in Gloria's expression was quick; what had in one instant looked like curiosity became judgment, calculation, a mask of cheek and lip and brow. Her smile, when she produced it, was an artifact. "Words right out of Mom's mouth. 'It's all in your perspective. If you don't like what you see, then change how you're looking.'"

"And?" I said, plowing forward, hating myself.

"I look all the time." She shook out her hair. "I'm starting to get the picture: a double exposure. You over Mom."

"Your mom over me."

She shrugged and left the table, hips forward, her hands thrust into her mass of hair, a model model if you asked me.

After that I caught Gloria watching me at odd moments. I saw her mother's evaluating eyes, the tiny motions of her finger as she made the swift calculations of my life: divorced, no kids, a so-so business that would one day close its doors without anyone noticing, part ownership in an advertising production company whose products I scarcely paid attention to. I wasn't even in the Sell-a-thon; I was in the used-car lot, kicking tires for customers who would leave before discovering how well I knew my product and how much I could tell them.

Then a photographer invited Gloria to dinner. She sputtered with brittle laughter when she told me. "'I know a little bistro that hasn't been ruined yet.' Leer, leer. The guy probably has a poster of Hugh Hefner in his bathroom. But he knows people." Her arch voice glittered.

"There's nothing wrong with going out to dinner with a friend," I said.

"He's no friend."

Gloria's shoulders rested against the wall, and her flat pelvis jutted forward like a low smile. I wiped my dry hands on my shirt. "In that case, don't go."

"Mom would tell me to make him into a friend. She believes in friends. Not exactly your way of doing things."

I snapped, "Gloria, I took you in because your mom and I were friends. So I'll say what she would say: Make this guy your friend. Or tell him off. But figure out where you stand and then stay there."

"Aren't you going to tell me what to do?"

"No," I said, and then, "I just did."

Two nights later she went out with the photographer, returning home at one-thirty. Although I was furiously awake, I didn't go in to see her or turn on my light. A week later she had a job, her first, one of five models jumping on a trampoline while wearing very tight jeans. "Greg — the director — liked my hair," she said, swigging celery juice on a quick tour of the kitchen.

"Call your mother," I said. "She'll want to hear all about it."

The next day, the first day of Gloria's trampoline shoot, I hoped to lose myself in work, but the inch-and-half along the Hollywood freeway encouraged me to ponder and reconsider my contribution to Gloria's newfound success. By the time I got to the Glendale studio my whole nervous system pulsed like a wound.

Six applicants for the tap teacher position looked up when I came in. Every one of them had a two-page résumé, Equity, and expensive, professional photos. Every one of them reeled out complicated combinations while wearing a smile that only hinted of rent past due, the craving for a cigarette, every problem in their lives that would be solved by this job. Depressed, I went ahead and let the last applicant really dance. She got louder and quicker, tapping like a jackhammer, and finished with a pirouette that dropped to a full split, old-fashioned razzmatazz that flooded my mouth with bitterness.

"Hooray for Hollywood," I said, and she produced a 1930s smile — teeth and dimples.

"Talk to me a little," I went on, while she scrambled back to her feet. "You're very good. But what are you going to do if things don't work out? You know the odds. What's your fallback plan?"

She shrugged, tapping softly, her feet patting the floor like small animals. "I'll just keep trying."

"But what if trying isn't enough? You can find yourself at forty with nothing to show for yourself but wrecked feet and a studio apartment in San Bernardino."

"I'm doing what I love right now." She dimpled again. "I really don't like to talk about it."

"I'm trying to find out who you are." Still wearing my street shoes, I began to tap with her, an easy shuffle. "I know you can dance. Everybody can dance. Tell me why I should hire you. You and nobody else. Please."

She stopped. After another beat, I stopped. Fingering her long red braid, she smoothed her finger over her mouth, then leaned forward and pressed her lips against mine. I was so stunned that my lips parted before I jerked back, dizzy, appalled, at the edge of tears.

"I didn't ask for that," I said, backing away from her until I could hang onto the barre for support. "What do you think is going on here?"

"Not giving me a job, I guess."

Clutching the smooth wooden rail, I said, "I need to hire a teacher."

"Do you want to hire me? I'm very good with kids." Holding her palms out, she added, "No touching them. I know the rules."

Still shaking, I saw her to the door, then went home half an hour early. I drove fast and badly, twice cutting people off on turns. Convinced I had crossed some important milestone of degradation, I watched my thoughts careen: I would come home to an empty house. The police would find no trace. Gloria would return weeks later with bruised lips, broken fingernails, and a brain rinsed free of memory.

But Gloria was home, waiting in the corner of the foyer. Her arms — long, long sticks — dangled at her sides. "What's wrong?" I said.

"I can have another job after this one. Greg says there's somebody else who wants to meet me."

"And?"

"And here you are, witnessing the launch of my thrilling career." She laced her hands behind her head, then let them fall back to her sides. "I can't take this. I'm going home."

"You are home."

"Home-home. 'Back home again in Indiana,'" she sang.

I took a careful breath. "Your mom wanted you to set the town on fire."

"Not this way. She told me once that nothing was more stupid than girls who slept with two-bit investors to get a spot in the chorus."

"But —" I began, then closed my mouth. From the other side of the hall, Gloria faced me, barely casting a shadow. I said, "Come into the kitchen."

She watched while I unsteadily poured a glass of celery juice, the smell like salty copper, and slid it across the table to her. "Your mother was not the best of the dancers when we were in school," I said.

"I didn't see how she could be. She's terrible now."

"But she still got roles. She had a stage career. Most of us didn't. I didn't," I added unnecessarily.

Gloria nodded. "'Never expect the world to play fair.'" I recognized Sue's hard vowels and rushed cadence.

"Watching her made me think about how things work. She taught me that talent isn't the only thing."

"'If you can't go in the front door, go in the side,' she used to tell me while she brushed my hair. She doesn't mind the side door."

"No," I said.

"She notices things. What kind of soap people like, what time they go to bed. A lot of people like all that attention. My dad did. My stepdad does. His girlfriends think she's terrific."

"Wait," I said.

Gloria's face was as bland as an apple. "I'm just telling you. When you grow up with my mom, you learn to pay attention. First she married a producer who romanced every boy in the chorus, then she married the King of the Hoosier Playboys. She didn't want to get another divorce, so he moved his girlfriends in with us. Two so far. I think she sent me to L.A. before he could bring in Número Tres."

Air vanished from my lungs. "I had no idea," I managed to say.

"She likes to have one person in the world who thinks her life is terrific. She loves that."

"I had no idea. What kind of a friend doesn't know the first thing about her friend's life?"

"Her best one, I think," Gloria said, and watched me shake my head. "'If you want to dance, then dance.' From the book of Mona. She quoted it all the time." I had never said such a thing. Those impatient, rushed words sounded like Sue's, not mine — unless at some point I'd taken them from her, as I had so much else. "You were the great shaping influence of my youth," Gloria was saying.

"Your youth isn't over."

"I guess not. She sent me to study at your feet."

"Your mother —" I listened to the words hover between us, as they had done since Gloria arrived. The room, like every room in the house, was bulging with Sue. I could hardly breathe through all the Sue. And now here was Gloria, presenting me with her mother's despair, for so long my sole desire. I felt the despair as if it were my own. "Your mother —"

"Will be happy to see me come home."

I snapped my head up. "Pay attention, Gloria. She's got her own work to do, and you're not finished here. In fact, you haven't started."

"I've started, all right. It's a little late now for the clean slate."

"Nothing is clean. Who do you think taught me that?" Reaching across the table, I took a sip from Gloria's can of celery juice, which was brackish. Luis, my partner with the production company, owed me a favor. He didn't usually do commercials with young women, but he could start. I had just the model for him. "Your mother sent you out here, to my house. While you're here, I'm your mother, do you understand? Listen to what I tell you. You're listening to your mother from now on."

THE PENANCE PRACTICUM

FATHER DOM was pleased with his reflection in the mirror. To the front of his cassock he had stapled a big dot cut out of white paper; below the cincture he had stapled two more. Tonight was the seminary's Halloween party. He was going as a domino.

He was ready to enjoy himself, although the party was one of the things that had turned iffy around St. Boniface. Some of the younger seminarians, shiny men of God who ran every five minutes to look something up in one of John Paul II's encyclicals, had raised objections: the proper end-of-October celebration for Catholics was the Feast of All Saints, not Halloween.

"We'll celebrate the All Saints mass," Father Dom told the stern contingent who came to his office. "We always do. But the Halloween party is harmless. People like dressing up."

"The magisterium has not approved Halloween as a holiday for the faithful," said Sipley. His beefy face, above the Roman collar he'd worn every day since taking his first vows, was implacable. Two of the men behind him shook their heads. Father Petrus called this group Rome's hall monitors.

"It isn't forbidden," Father Dom said.

"We won't be attending," Sipley said.

"There'll be punch," Father Dom said wearily. He wouldn't

miss them, but he hated to add mortar to the wall separating the men who fluently discussed the mystical gifts of the Holy Father from the rest of them, eating pizza and telling jokes down the hall. Father Dom had bought the pizza.

He smoothed one of his dots. He himself had been on the admissions committee the year Sipley applied. Even then the man was talking about Holy Mother Church, coming on like cutting-edge 1600s. Still, the committee had voted to admit him. The committee had voted to admit every applicant, all five who sought one of the thirty slots. St. Boniface's picking-and-choosing days were long gone. But every time Father Dom thought about a priesthood filled with Sipleys leaning over their pulpits and confidently instructing their congregations, his heart hurt. Father Dom had never felt as certain about anything as Sipley felt about everything.

Hearing voices in the hallway, he opened his door. Several men were heading toward the lounge, laughing, dressed for the party. McCarley wore a cardboard cone taped over his huge nose; he'd drawn lines of scurrying bugs around the end. "Anteater," he said cheerfully. Father Dom's spirits started to rise.

"I hope you have a good sacerdotal defense. You never know when the magisterium's going to be checking up."

"Anteaters are God's creatures. Nobody can challenge me. What about you?"

"I'm a domino. I intend to impart valuable lessons about tipping over."

Behind McCarley, Terley shook his blond hair out of his eyes and fiddled with one of his pencils. He had a dozen or so, sharpened and taped to his shirt as if they'd been shot into him. There was always at least one St. Sebastian. And beside the two men, to Father Dom's delight, walked Joe Halaczek, dressed in salmon-pink Bermuda shorts, a plaid shirt, dark socks, and sandals. A cushion under his waistband gave him a burgher's paunch. "I give up," Father Dom said.

"The Race Is Not to the Swift. It's a concept costume," Joe said. Then his voice took on its usual marshy unease. "Is that all right?"

"It's perfect," Father Dom said, hoping the white leather belt came from the secondhand store and not Joe's closet. Someone must have helped him with this — the concept of a concept costume was beyond him. With his frightened hands and unsteady eyes, ordinary conversation was often beyond him. Father Dom could hardly bear to think about his arriving at a parish, this damaged lamb attempting to lead the obstreperous sheep. But right now it was a hoot to watch Joe stroll along, hands behind his back, imitating a confident man.

"We tried to get him to come as Joan of Arc, but nothing doing," said McCarley. Already his cardboard nose was starting to work loose.

"I was afraid someone would set me on fire."

"Only if you had started hearing voices," Father Dom said, smiling when worried Joe glanced up.

Inside the lounge, festivities were puttering along. Four men shared the couch in front of the TV, talking and half watching an NFL roundup. Another group was playing darts. Everybody else was hovering over the snack table, making a clean sweep of the buffalo wings. Most of one pizza — cheese — was left.

"'The Assyrian swept down like a wolf on the fold,'" said Father Benni, the rector, nodding at the decimated food.

"At least they're not letting the pizza get cold. Where's your costume?"

"This is it. The Good Priest." He folded his long arms and assumed a benevolent expression, and Father Dom forbore reminding him that generations of students, reacting to his firm command, had called him Sheriff. "Bing Crosby will play me in the movie. I don't know who's going to play you."

"Robert Redford." Father Dom reached over to the table and snagged a wing.

"What do you think, Joe?" Father Benni said. Joe's head snapped around when he heard the rector say his name. "Do you think Robert Redford could play Father Dom?"

"It wouldn't be easy. A man of Father Dom's experience," Joe said carefully.

Father Petrus, standing nearby, snorted. "Hey," Father Dom said.

The rector was still looking at Joe. "Have you asked Father yet? I think this would be a fine time."

It wasn't a fine time, whatever they were talking about — Father Dom both did and didn't want to know. Joe was braiding his fingers, looking at the carpet, and the color had dropped from his face. When Joe spoke, Father Dom had to lean close to hear. "Father Benni would like to observe our class tomorrow. I told him I'm not the one who makes the decisions."

"You are, actually. You can say if you'd rather not be watched." At this moment Father Dom would happily have strangled the smiling rector, who was of course within his rights.

"What's the point of the class if you're not watched?" Joe said.

"The practicum is the best of all the seminary classes," Father Benni said. "Getting feedback is a real gift. You're able to see yourself as others see you. I miss that."

Joe's face was expressionless beside Father Benni's basking, nostalgic smile. Father Dom said, "We can give you a taste of the old medicine, Greg."

Father Benni said, "I was seminary champion in practicum. Everybody wanted to confess to me because I gave the easiest penances."

"What made you change?" Father Dom said.

"I haven't changed," the rector said sunnily. "I'm a lamb. Isn't that right, Joe?"

Joe was studying his shoes. "When I first got here, the fifth-year guys told me that you were easy." His mouth twitched. "They said you were easy, but to go to Father Dom if I had anything bad. He forgave everything."

"That's why we have him teach the practicum," Father Benni said equably. Glancing at Joe, he added, "It will go fine. You'll see." His voice was full of reassurance, but Joe's proto-smile had dissolved, and Father Dom guided the rector to the other side of the room.

"The practicum isn't Joe's best class," Father Dom said quietly. From the couch came a small whoop; the TV was showing a beer ad that everybody liked.

"I'm not sure Joe has a best class," Father Benni said. "His paper for Mission & Ministry was a page and a half. In homiletic practicum he fell apart completely — got up and just couldn't speak. He doesn't look like a man on his way to ordination. He looks like a man on his way to the electric chair."

"So what do you want?"

"To be reassured."

Father Dom studied Joe, standing in line for darts. He lingered at the side of the group, not the center, smiling at someone else's joke. But there was no rule that said the priest needed to be the life of the party. Plenty of parishioners would appreciate Joe's gentle manner, his ability to listen rather than talk. While Father Dom watched, Joe hitched up the cushion that held his shorts in place — his concept costume, worn in wistful good faith.

"No problem," Father Dom said.

Problem, all right. No course could be designed better than the penance practicum to showcase Joe's shortcomings. Every week, in front of the rest of the class, the students role-played priests hearing confession, with Father Dom as the penitent. He tried to keep things light, presenting goofy sins — once he'd played a woman who had visions of the Blessed Virgin saying to her, "You must wear natural fabrics." Sometimes the hardest thing for the students was keeping a straight face.

After the simulation the other students provided feedback, pointing out where the role-playing student had done well and where he showed room for improvement. The men were considerate with one another, but there were still so many ways to fall short — hints gone unheard, hobbyhorses saddled up. In their responses the students revealed themselves, which was why Joe had been ducking the role-play all semester. Now Father Dom would have no choice but to call on him. He'd have to call on Sipley, too, who volunteered all the time.

Father Dom lay sleepless until three-thirty. Then, moving softly — the walls separating the priests' rooms were like cheesecloth — he turned on the light and started reviewing notes. His desk drawer was stuffed with class outlines, files he kept because he'd been trained to keep files, though he almost never returned to them. Now he was grateful. Surely these hundreds of pages held some forgotten scenario that would demonstrate Joe's particular gifts.

Working without method, Father Dom riffled through the syllabi, glancing now and then at a note he'd written. He searched for a confession that required from the priest more sympathy than guidance, some transgression that would turn Joe's shy heart into a bridge between the penitent and God. No splashy sins like murder or embezzlement. Nothing requiring close discernment or tiptoeing among competing ethical schemes. Nothing about girls, it went without saying. Simply the extension of forgiveness, which had always seemed to Father Dom so easy.

At one time that ease had worried him. He had yearned to be valorous, rich in the grace that comes from spiritual struggle. He had worked with burn victims, telling them how a turn in life's road, even a terrible one, could be the beginning of a happiness never guessed at. "How, exactly?" asked a sixteen-year-old girl, gesturing at a face that had become a cluster of shiny ridges when she stumbled into her parents' sizzling barbecue grill. Another patient, once a mother of three, had been folding laundry in her basement when the house caught fire. Of all her family, only she was still alive, and every day she cursed God with brilliant inventiveness, then yelled at Father Dom, "Are you going to forgive *that?*"

He did. The more he looked, the more he saw only God's carelessness, work left undone when God got distracted, when God moved on to something else, when God went to get a cup of coffee and left Father Dom's mouth filled with inadequate words. Father Dom had been called, he knew, to be God's hands and voice in the world. He was just sorry that God couldn't find a better class of servant. Helplessly, he got the woman more ice chips and rested his hand tenderly on the side of her bed. Anybody could be forgiven for cursing in a world where somebody like Father Dom was left holding the bag for the Infinite.

He tried not to think about these things anymore. Seminarians of his generation had been taught that every priest was given his particular struggle of faith — the struggle, Father Dom's novice director had said often, that would last a lifetime. But Father Dom turned instead to the easier tasks of ministry, which were so plentiful — teaching, outreach. He could be a good priest without trying to solve the questions of suffering that even Augustine admitted were insoluble. He could help Joe.

He read until early gray light began to seep into the room and it was time to go to chapel. There he prayed his usual wordless prayer with more than common urgency, through breakfast, rising only when it was time to start class.

In the classroom students were seating themselves and pulling out their folders and books. Joe volunteered to fill the water pitchers. Then he volunteered to get cups. His face was the color of dust. He stopped beside Father Benni and murmured something; Father Dom watched the rector shake his head and gesture for Joe to sit down as Father Dom stood up. This week's assigned reading had centered on difficult confessions, surly or abusive penitents. It was important to have coping strategies, Father Dom said.

"You have to *listen*," said Hernandez, a thin-faced student with a smile like sunrise. "Don't just listen to what they're saying, but how they're saying it. People bring in their shame and guilt, so they're angry. If the only person nearby is the priest, they'll get mad at him."

"Have you ever had a penitent threaten you, Father?" Sipley asked Father Benni.

"I had someone pull a knife," the rector said. "He said he would cut out the screen between us to get to me."

"What did you do?"

"Gave him three Our Fathers and a Glory Be." Father Benni waited for the mild laughter to die down. "All you can do is be a priest. Of course, that's a lot."

Father Dom returned to the text, dragging out the discussion as far as he could, but after half an hour every syllable had been covered, and Sipley volunteered to do the first role-play, striding to the front of the room where two chairs stood, separated by a screen. The burly man kissed the stole lying on one chair, placed it around his neck, and said, "Hello, my son," as if he'd been doing these things all his life.

Father Dom pulled out a dependable scenario: the teenage boy who liked to kill cats. Once a student had sputtered, "You did *what?*" But Sipley was smooth, listening through Father Dom's resentful confession — his mother, he said, had forced him to come — and then talking about the sanctity of God's creations. "We are called to be good stewards," Sipley said. "Our job is to protect the defenseless."

In the discussion afterward, everyone praised Sipley's clarity. Joe said that he admired Sipley's calm demeanor. Hernandez suggested that Sipley might have spent a little more time exploring the reason the boy was tying firecrackers to cats' legs. Sipley nodded, taking notes.

An anxious silence took over the room when Father Dom asked for further comments; the air seemed to prickle. Joe was already trudging to the front of the room, where he hung the purple stole around his neck and sat down. "Okay," he whispered.

Reciting the opening prayer and adding that it had been six years since his last confession, Father Dom wondered if he looked as nervous as he felt. He hoped so. A good priest would try to put a parishioner at ease.

"What brings you here today?" Joe finally asked. His voice was faint. Sipley jotted a note.

"I didn't think I'd ever come to confession again. I don't really believe in this. But I just saw my doctor. He says I'm HIV-positive." Father Dom paused. "I'm twenty-six years old."

He had gone over Joe's transcripts. Part of the young man's fourth-year field education had been hospice work; he could draw on his experience with real patients, people he'd known and liked. But now, while Father Dom waited, Joe didn't say anything. "Are you there?" Father Dom said.

"Go on."

"Did you hear me? I'm twenty-six years old, and I'm HIV-positive. I just left the doctor. You're the first person I've told. I'm not sure I can tell anybody else." Father Dom left room for Joe to ask about his family or to murmur that the church was a good place to come to. "How could this happen to me?"

The silence stretched and thickened until Father Dom felt anger start to buckle his thoughts. What was the matter with Joe? All he had to say was *Are you afraid? Do you feel alone? God is with you, even now. Especially now.* A kid who tied firecrackers to cats could figure out that much.

"The only place I could think to come was here," Father Dom said bitterly. "Don't ask me why. It's not like the Church has ever helped before."

"Have you made plans for your death?" Joe said.

Air actually seemed to fly out of Father Dom's lungs. When he looked up, every one of the students was writing. Even Sipley looked stunned.

Joe was still talking, his voice like sand. "You need to study the teachings of the Holy Father and then accord yourself with them. The Church is very clear about the sinfulness of homosexual behavior. You should have come here sooner."

"That's not good enough," Father Dom said. He'd never mentioned homosexuality. Twenty-six years old! Maybe that sounded old to this reedy voice behind the screen. "What am I supposed to do now? I need help."

"There are several hospices in the area."

"What is the *matter* with you?" Father Dom said. He stuck his face up close to the screen. "It is your job to care."

In the long silence, Father Dom imagined Joe standing at the top of the cliff. His hands were tucked safely up his priestly sleeves while Father Dom slipped off the edge.

"Peace be with you," Joe said.

Father Dom opened and then closed his mouth, unable to think of one more thing to say. The students were silent until Sipley, of all people, laughed. At that small, embarrassed noise the others laughed too, looking at their feet. Even Father Benni, whose lips had been tight, joined in. Only Father Dom remained silent. When Joe stood up, Father Dom saw the dark spots on the stole where the boy had sweated through it.

"I want to be a priest." Joe's voice was desperate.

"Why?" Father Dom said.

Father Benni called a faculty meeting that afternoon. "What are his strengths?" he said, palming back the thick hair he was normally vain about. He didn't have to explain what had happened in the practicum. Word was out before lunch.

"He pitches in," Father Petrus said. "He's not a shirker."

"Or a know-it-all," Father Wells said.

"There's a real sweetness there," said Father Lomax, who didn't generally talk in these meetings.

"I know we all like Joe," Father Benni said, "but this sounds like we're describing the president of the Altar Society. How would he do with a headstrong parishioner? With a parish council? Can he lead?"

"He hears a call," Father Dom muttered.

"Calls can be misheard," Father Benni said.

"You think he doesn't know that?" Father Dom stared at the whorls in the table's laminated surface. "He goes around listening all the time. Priesthood is the one thing he wants, and he's terrified that we're going to take it away from him."

"That's hardly our job. Still, when I compare him to some of the other men —" Father Benni shook his head.

"That's exactly why it's important for Joe to be here," Father Dom said. He wished he could curb the desperation rocketing through his voice. "He has his own gifts. The seminary isn't supposed to turn out identical priests, each one perfectly sure of himself, rolling off an assembly line with his collar in place and his opinions set for life." He stopped under the weight of the rector's sharp gaze, then added, "A little uncertainty isn't a bad thing."

"What I saw in your classroom was not enough uncertainty," Father Benni said. "If that had been a real confession, the poor man would have left the church and walked in front of a bus. Joe did everything but push him."

"Why don't we assign him a mentor?" said Father Lomax. "Someone he can talk to, who has better judgment."

Father Dom couldn't hold back his sigh. Was the mentor going to follow Joe to his parish and slip into the confessional with him? But Father Benni was steepling his fingers, pondering the suggestion, and Father Dom's imprudent heart lifted.

"Joe might improve if he's taken in hand by someone at his own level," the rector said. "He might be less defensive. Some of the men have volunteered to help."

"Greg, you're not thinking of assigning one of the students?" Father Dom said.

The rector nodded, apparently indifferent to the horror in Father Dom's voice. "It's win-win. A fine opportunity for growth on both sides. Besides, none of us wants to stay up as late as the students do."

Fathers Wells and Berton, those toadies, laughed. Father Dom said, "Students don't have the experience. They think they know more than they do. Joe needs trustworthy guidance."

"He's had the benefit of your guidance for four years," Father Benni said. "I'd say it's time for a new approach."

"Just not this one," Father Dom said. The priests laughed and pushed back their chairs. Dependable Dom, always good for a joke. He stayed at the table until he and the rector were alone in the room. "Nobody wants Joe to succeed more than I do," Father Dom said. "But it's going to take a miracle."

"Good. That's our turf."

"Right," Father Dom said bitterly. "I keep forgetting."

Father Benni chose Sipley to be Joe's mentor. And he chose Father Dom to oversee Sipley — to mentor the mentor. Father Dom was overscheduled with classes and field experience and his outreach program at the youth center, but he was glad for the assignment. Every night Sipley came to him to describe Joe's progress, and Father Dom imagined Joe as a fragile boat that he could still see in his spyglass.

"He's shy, is all. Once you get him in a situation where he's comfortable, he opens up." Sipley was sitting in Father Dom's office, cradling between his big hands the cup of coffee Father Dom had offered.

"Where is he comfortable?"

"You should have seen him in the soup kitchen. He was jawing with everybody who came through. 'Hey, how's it going, you want gravy with that?' And nobody gave him a hard time. I think they could see what he is." Sipley shifted his bulky thighs on the hard chair. "In his way, he really brings out the best in people."

"But can you imagine Joe setting up the soup kitchen and overseeing it? A priest needs to show initiative."

Sipley shifted again. Even in his discomfort he gave the impression of being fundamentally comfortable. "He's heard a call, Father. It isn't up to me to question that."

"It is up to the rector and me to question that." Looking at Sipley's polite, averted face, Father Dom added, "In the service of the Church. Joe will be a representative of the Holy Father. And we're asking you to help us make sure he can be a good representative."

The speech had the desired effect: Sipley leaned forward and rested his elbows on his knees. When he spoke, his resonant voice was confiding. "Joe's never going to be a take-charge guy. He's all heart. But if he's working with somebody who can direct him, he'll give a hundred percent. He wants this so much."

Father Dom analyzed the young man's ruddy face and broad, chapped hands. Everything about him breathed with vibrancy. Had he ever wondered why quailing Joe could be drawn to the same priesthood Sipley was so confident about? Had he thought about the role of a man in society but not of it, safely shut away from human contact by vestments and a collar? Probably not. Sipley himself wanted to be a priest so he could tell people what to do.

"I can't believe there's no place for him," Sipley was saying.

"We're still looking," Father Dom said.

Sipley nodded. "If you don't mind my asking, Father — did you question my call, too?"

Startled, Father Dom said, "You don't present the same issues."

"But still."

Sipley's wide-set eyes were alit with new curiosity. This chance would not come again. "Of course we did," said Father Dom. "There's no such thing as an automatic priest."

"All my life people have told me I was born to be a priest. My mother, for one. Half the time it's a compliment."

"It's not something to be taken for granted."

"So I'm being tested? Is that why you asked me to help with Joe?"

"You're likely to pass," Father Dom said. "Don't lose any sleep over this." But he could see already, as Sipley stood and shook Father Dom's hand, how the young man's body was bright with new energy. Father Dom should have been grateful; his own weariness had increased a hundredfold.

In the days that followed, Father Dom expected Sipley to lay siege to Joe, intent on their mutual salvation. But Sipley was a better psychologist than Father Dom had given him credit for. He met Joe casually, in the halls or over coffee, and twice he reported to Father Dom that he hadn't spoken with Joe that day. "Figured he could use a vacation from me."

Father Dom was giving Joe a vacation, too. Aside from the weekly meetings of the practicum, he saw Joe only from a distance — in the library, the dining commons, on the walkway in front of the soccer field. When he believed himself unobserved, Joe took his place easily with the other men, and from time to time he tipped back his head in laughter. But as soon as he saw Father Dom, his gaze dropped again, and dread clung to his pale, chewed mouth. Father Dom understood that Joe had assigned him the role of the enemy, obstacle to Joe's happiness. The perception wasn't wrong, but still Father Dom felt stung.

Every day he defended Joe to one priest or another, pointing out how the young man was the first to help clear tables, the first to donate to clothing drives for countries rent by earthquakes. He heard the words' puniness as they rolled out of his mouth. Everyone in the seminary was waiting for Joe to prove himself with something more than a clothing drive. In these priest-starved days, when Father Lomax predicted that St. Boniface would have to start ordaining dogs, it was a special humiliation to be reevaluated, and Father Dom knew that Joe felt persecuted.

So Father Dom was relieved when, after three weeks of mentoring, Sipley told him that he had a new idea about Joe, a breakthrough plan. "It's nothing that you'll object to. I've put in a few phone calls, and I'm waiting to hear."

"Give me a hint, in case the rector asks."

Sipley paused. "The battle is not to the strong."

"That's not going to be much help if he presses me for details."

"Joe just needs the right chance to shine." Sipley beamed. As always, he was confident in the goodness of his actions. But Father

Dom wondered if the young man remembered the end of the passage he had quoted: "all are subject to time and mischance."

A week passed before Father Dom returned to his office and found a note tacked to the corkboard. *Could you join Joe and me in the dining room? We'd like to propose something.* Father Dom turned left, toward the cafeteria, worrying at a hangnail as he walked. *We.*

The dining room was empty except for the two men sitting by the window, whose heads swung up in unison at the creak of the swinging door. Sipley said, "Thank you for coming, Father."

Father Dom seated himself beside Joe. Since the young man was pretending he hadn't edged away from the table, Father Dom pretended he didn't notice.

"An opportunity has come up," Sipley said after Father Dom turned down coffee or iced tea. "I think it's too special to miss. One of the staff members at St. Thérèse House had to leave, and they need someone to step in right away. Joe and I could go together."

"Are you serious?" Father Dom said.

"It's a special opportunity." Joe's voice was dim. "Our men don't usually go there."

They sure didn't. St. Thérèse House was a two-story facility downtown for terminal children, youngsters dying from cancer or brain lesions or frenzied infections Father Dom had never heard of. Children went to St. Thérèse House when they couldn't survive another faltering transplant or more scorching chemotherapy. A hospice for six- and seven-year-olds, it drew patients from three states away. Doctors in the area were proud of the institution, which appalled Father Dom. Sweet Jesus, it was not something to be proud of.

Although he had never been in it, he realized he could describe the place as if he'd lived there. For every child who died with a face filled with light, three others left this earth looking puzzled or disappointed or so crocked on morphine they couldn't feel the oils of the last rites being thumbed onto their foreheads. His stomach turned heavily.

"Their people are trained," Father Dom said.

"They're short-handed," Sipley said.

Joe studied his clear brown tea, and Father Dom automatically thought of Gethsemane. He wondered whether Joe was also thinking of that utter despair. In a brief burst of viciousness, Father Dom hoped he was, then was ashamed of himself. "When would it start?" Father Dom said.

"That depends on you," Sipley said. "There's only so far the staff can bend the rules. We can come, but a faculty member has to supervise."

Father Dom opened his mouth and shut it again. "I don't have medical training," he said.

"The staff will be keeping an eye on the patients," Sipley said. "They want someone to keep an eye on us. Since you've been working with Joe and me, I thought you should be the one. Of course, I could ask somebody else."

And somebody would agree. Priests always went: the jails, the hospitals, the shuttered, stinking houses. "Beats reality TV," Father Wells had said one day after a visit to the prison, his eyes blazing. He might very well go to St. Thérèse House and train his gaze on those withering children. His gaze would also land on Joe, helpless at the bedside.

"I'll go," Father Dom said, lifting his chin. "I'll *go*," he added, not that Sipley or Joe had asked a second time.

St. Thérèse House smelled like apples. Most of the children ate through feeding tubes, but one or two could manage soft foods, and every morning ferocious Sister Lupe, who looked thin even in sweatpants, made a fresh batch of applesauce. "At lunch you will feed them," she told Joe and Sipley. "Until then you will visit with the children who are alone." The two young men nodded, as did Father Dom, standing a step behind them. Sister Lupe glanced at him with flat eyes, then led them down a corridor.

Bedrooms unfolded in wings from the central hall, and in either apple-smelling direction lay children, one to a room. The children were bald and gray faced, lying in what looked less like sleep than suspension. Parents, murmuring steadily, sat close beside the beds.

"How long do they stay here?" Sipley was asking.

"Two weeks, typically," Sister Lupe said. "The one you're going to see has been here almost three months, our longest ever. You're getting her because she already knows all of our jokes." Father Dom tried to imagine a joke coming out of Sister Lupe's lipless mouth.

"What does she have?" Sipley asked.

"Leukemia."

"Where are her parents?" Joe asked.

Sister Lupe's smile was vulpine. "Several agencies would like to know." She breezed into the girl's room, then looked back and gestured impatiently for Joe and Sipley to follow. "Look, Cindy. Father Sipley and Father Halaczek are here to see you. And Father Dominic." The girl smiled at them with half her mouth. Father Dom didn't know whether she had lost motor control on one side or she meant the expression to look ironic. "Hi."

Bruises ran in chains up her arms and ringed her neck, and around the bruises her skin was a dry noncolor. Her skull made a hard dent in the pillow. Father Dom guessed she was twelve years old, but he could have been three years off in either direction.

"They're going to visit with you until lunch," Sister Lupe said.

"That's a long time," Cindy said.

"It's good for you to see new faces," the sister said, already on her way out of the room. "Enjoy yourselves, Fathers."

Cindy's expression was clearly long-suffering, and Father Dom revised his age estimate upward. "Are you here to talk to me about dying?" she said.

"Not if you don't want to," Sipley said. "What's on your mind?"

"No offense, but I'm scared of priests. It's not good news when you guys come around."

Joe reached behind his neck and unsnapped his collar. "I don't have to wear this. I haven't been ordained."

"You're in training?"

"I'm on probation. I messed up, and I'm being given one last chance."

"So you're here to show your stuff."

Joe nodded, and Cindy said to Father Dom, "What does he need to do?"

"Just be with you."

"Some test." She closed her eyes. Father Dom had stood beside hospital beds for twenty-five years; rarely had he seen a face so dwindled, her forehead collapsed as if someone had stuck a thumb into it. He flattened his wet palms against his thighs. Sipley and Joe were talking to her. He could slip out of the room and no one would notice.

"Well, do it," Cindy was saying to the young men, her eyes still closed. "I'm not going anywhere."

Joe said, "What do you want to talk about?"

"You talk. I'll listen."

Father Dom's stomach seemed to tip. Shamefully, he couldn't stop thinking that he was breathing the air that had passed through Cindy's diseased membranes. He pulled a tissue from the box on the ledge and held it before his face as if he were going to blow his nose.

Joe said, "Our Father."

"No," Cindy murmured. "I don't like that one. Do your own."

Joe smiled crookedly. "Please. That's the only good prayer I know."

Cindy didn't open her eyes. "Sister Lupe says the best prayers are one word. What's your word?"

"Please," Joe said promptly.

"Keep going."

The smell of apples billowed softly from the corridor. "Please. God," Joe said, the word like a cough. "You are in heaven. And your name is — praised." His white face was damp, and he stood at a tilt, as if every muscle in his body were locked. "I could use some help," he said to Father Dom.

"What do you want me to do?" Father Dom hadn't meant to sound savage, and he was embarrassed when Cindy looked at him with interest.

"Aren't you supposed to be telling me about heaven?" she said.

"Ask Father Halaczek. He knows," Father Dom said, a bit of malice to add to his lifetime sins of evasion and cowardice, sins he yearned for now as his eyes slid away from the girl's cheeks, molded to the bone. All a priest could do was plead for her release and hope that pleading would do some good. Joe knew that lesson as well as Father Dom. Joe, who pleaded so much, knew it better.

The young man grasped the corner of Cindy's sheet, his hand tightening and releasing, his voice shaking. "Please. Your will is going to happen," he said, then broke down. Pressing his hands against his face, he stood beside the bed, his shoulders racked. "This is the worst thing that's ever happened to me," he said. "And it's going to get worse." He wheeled around to face Father Dom, who had backed up until his shoulders touched the wall. The smell of apples rose around him, and his nausea was roiling like a sea. "Isn't it?" Joe said.

"Yes," said Father Dom.

"Are you going to stop my ordination?"

"No."

"Why not?"

Sipley said, "Fathers, we're here to pray for healing." He began to move his lips unselfconsciously, a powerful man who could probably hold the seventy-pound girl in one hand. Here, Father Dom realized, was the test Sipley had set for himself: to halt death's advance, even though death was on the march. Death had already won. Father Dom wondered when Sipley was going to acknowledge that.

"Why not?" Joe repeated, louder.

"Who else would come here?" Father Dom said.

"I don't think you're supposed to say those things where I can hear them," Cindy said.

"Father Dominic is a special priest," Joe said. "You're lucky to even see him. Why don't you lead us in prayer, Father? We need guidance."

Joe probably didn't hear the rage that rang through his words. And Father Dom would forgive the boy — just as, when he looked at Cindy's shrunken, darkening body, he already forgave her parents for running away. In the end he forgave everybody, which was half the reason Joe would never forgive him.

Father Dom dampened his lips to say something unobjectionable about faith and perseverance. He breathed in the apple-drenched air. The instant he opened his mouth, he vomited where he stood. Sipley managed to get a basin under Father Dom's mouth for the last of it, but the room was full of the stink, and when he finished Father Dom could not lift his swimming eyes.

"Usually I'm the one who does that," Cindy said.

"I'm sorry," he murmured, afraid to say anything more. Sipley was probably warming up to quote St. Paul: the Spirit expresses itself in outcries that we ourselves do not understand. If Sipley said one word, Father Dom would retch again.

"Father," Joe said, "you should have told us you were ill." He pulled a chair beside Cindy's bed.

She said, "Do you mind not talking?"

"I'll get you something to drink." Joe's thin voice wavered. When Cindy shook her head, he said, "We have such a long day ahead. Let me get you something. Please."

ONE FOR MY BABY

A LESS WATCHES PATRICK slip into the back of the high
school auditorium, where he tiptoes behind the last row.
He is trying to be silent even though the door booms
shut behind him like a cannon shot. The length of the fifty-row
hall stretches between him and Aless, but still her heart shudders
as if he, her chum, her buddy, were breathing into her hair. This
collapsing of distance is just one of the things she hates about being in love with Patrick.

On stage, Aless is coaching Melanie Montrose, who has been
cast as Guinevere in *Camelot*. Every note she sings above D tilts
and wheezes and loses its balance, but Melanie's loose gold curls
tumble down her back, and Aless suspects that the girl's parents
have donated handsomely to Our Lady of Mercies for the last four
years, longer than Aless has been here.

Patrick lifts his hand in greeting, and Aless waves back, unable
to control her happy hand. She works in the same building with
the man and can't keep her heart from bucking every time she sees
his red-gold hair. Dragging her gaze back to Melanie, she says,
"Think about what you're singing. Your heart is torn between
duty and love. Your heart is *torn*. Try it again."

The accompanist gives the note and Melanie launches herself
back into the ballad, her pretty features squeezing as she imagines

herself remaining nobly silent about her ruinous desire. The song might as well be Aless's anthem, and Melanie is murdering it. Humming the right note to herself, Aless scoots off the stage to join Patrick and says, "I should make you leave. Friends don't let friends listen to Melanie Montrose."

"Why'd you cast her?"

"An audience needs something easy on the eyes. Also, I'm interested in keeping my job. Why are you here to listen?"

"Listening to Melanie beats listening to my own thoughts." In a flash, his amiable expression starts to droop, and Aless steels herself. Patrick's sorrow comes like a German train, exactly on schedule. "I was thinking about Eleanora," he says. "I never knew that sorrow would be so durable."

Aless nods, pushing the muscles of her face into a look of sympathy. Since his wife died almost a year ago, Patrick has been giving voice to his grief, talking about his emotions in the direct manner the wife encouraged. Aless doesn't care for it. His old moody detachment put a little space between them, space that she spent her time trying to violate. Now when Patrick says these things, he feels too close, intimate in every wrong way. She has to resist the impulse either to draw him to her or shove him back.

"I was going through student files, thinking about where I could recommend that Jason Sanders and his 1.3 average apply to college, when the floor opened up beneath me." Tears shine in his leaf-green eyes. "I miss her so much."

"I know," Aless says. She lets Melanie move into the second verse, for which the girl has worked out arm motions. She has spotted Patrick and beams at him, as all the girls do.

"Thank you for listening," he says to Aless. "Thank you for listening again. You should get some kind of Golden Ear award."

"What's a friend for?"

"You're a better friend than most. Nobody else would put up with me." As if he is getting a readout from Aless's brain, he adds, "It's been going on too long, this grieving."

"It's not like a class. There's no final exam."

"I need to do something. And I have an idea."

From her second-row seat Aless can see Melanie, approaching the half-step interval, tighten her abdomen. This time she comes closer to hitting the note, and she grins through the rest of the measure, confidently enunciating "dark despair."

"Sustain the energy," Aless calls to the stage, then says to Patrick, "What?"

"This isn't the place. Will you come over for dinner on Saturday?"

He has invited her to his house a hundred times, but still he sounds winsome, and she tightens her own abdomen to keep her voice from swaying.

"I have rehearsal that afternoon. It may go late." She nods toward the stage, where Melanie is hurtling through the last notes a beat ahead of the accompanist, her arms outstretched as if she's crossing a finish line. "Still a few bugs to work out."

Patrick produces his crooked smile and taps her wrist. Aless's bone rings like a tuning fork. "Don't break my heart. Seven o'clock."

Her querulous last note still wobbling through the air, Melanie curtsies to Patrick, who looks as if he might just be bullied into applauding. Aless can't bear it: signaling the accompanist, she vaults back onto the stage and repeats the last verse about the misery of silent love, actually hitting all the notes. To take over like this is showing off, but Melanie needs to know what real singing sounds like. Patrick, Aless notices with vicious satisfaction, looks rapt, as he always does when she sings.

After she finishes the chorus, Aless looks at Melanie and says, "Next time, *count.*"

Melanie flings waves of blond hair over her shoulder. "I'm a singer, not a metronome."

Aless jumps back down to Patrick, who mutters, "For Pete's sake, Less, don't encourage her to sing again." She feels herself turning toward him like a plant to the sun.

She met him five years ago, in her last year as a voice major at UCLA. Aless needed a pronunciation coach, and he answered her ad, casting an uneasy eye on the sheet music she handed him.

"*Geliebte, schön Tod.* My lover, beautiful death? This is not healthy," he said.

"I don't have to mean it. I don't even have to know what it means. I just have to sound like I believe it."

"What if I tell you it means 'I want a hamburger'?"

"Fine by me. I'll sing that with more feeling, anyway."

His smile took its time. When it was finally installed, she wanted it to start from the beginning again.

"Why do you study voice?" he said.

She shrugged. "I'm a loudmouth. Why do you study German?"

"I'm a Nazi."

"Liar. You've got *lazy* written all over you. What's the German word for *lazy*?"

"There is no German word for *lazy*," he said, slung across the only chair in the room.

Aless kept herself awake that night, imagining Patrick's fine shoulders over her in the bed, although she might as well have imagined herself, with her unreliable upper register, at La Scala. The handwriting was on the wall. The *Handschrift,* she thought, and then, digging deeper into her high school German, *die schlechte Handschrift,* the bad handwriting on the wall. She saw no reason to tell Patrick that she knew a little vocabulary of her own, even if she couldn't pronounce it. The German word for *lazy* was *faul.*

Instead of dating, which she did with the few straight boys in the theater department, she and Patrick went to bars together, low-rent dives that smelled like sour bar rags and had names like Bluey's. He called them "authentic," and she laughed at him. She also laughed the night that a regular patron in checked pants that showed his bony ankles slammed into their table, glared, and told them to go back to their disco. "I have a right to be here," Patrick said after the drunk caromed away. Patrick had had a few drinks himself.

"Just don't expect him to be thrilled to see you, Joe College."

"That is so unfair." His face turned dark and self-important, which happened sometimes when he was deep into the gin. "He should respect me. I am a seeker."

"What are you seeking?"

"Same as you. Enlightenment."

"Leave me out of it. I like the dark spaces."

Even his scowl was handsome. He went to the jukebox and punched in "One for My Baby," then came back to the table and pulled her out of the booth.

"Go," he said.

Maybe he thought sopranos who sang art songs didn't know Harold Arlen. She propped her hip against the table, pretending it was a piano. "It's quarter to three — there's no one in the place except you and me." Concentrating on a loose jaw, as her teachers were always reminding her, she stroked the notes as if they were breakable. The bar quieted around them, and Patrick looked at her with startled attention. By the time she was done, people whistled, except for the guy two tables over, who was sobbing.

"I didn't know you could do that," Patrick said. He gazed at her until she shrugged and looked away. The cocktail waitress was never nearby when you needed her.

"You're — transformed," Patrick said. "Will you sing something else?"

"What, for free?"

"I thought you were an artist."

"Who in the world told you that?" A blue neon light cast a thin shadow down his jaw, and the urge to touch it was nearly irresistible.

A bulky Lakers fan — cap, shirt, shorts — called to them from the bar. "Hey! Hey! Can you sing 'New York, New York'?"

"No," said Aless and Patrick on the same breath, and she felt her heart expand.

Still, she never should have sung for him. Twice in the next month she found him lurking outside her practice room, and when she hummed in the car, he stopped talking. In the face of his ravenous gaze she wanted to scratch herself or break things. One night at Willie's, where it was Dollar Tuesday, she caught herself singing along with the music video, saw his moist eyes, and said, "Don't you have a test coming up?"

He lifted his glass. "Day after tomorrow. Whatever doesn't kill me makes me stronger." Then, a beat later, "Don't you have a call-back tomorrow?"

"No," she lied. A month before she had been foolish enough to let him know about an audition, and he called her three times a day after it was over, asking if she'd heard anything. If she had gotten the part, he would certainly have sat in the front row on opening night with his girlfriend du jour. Brooding over this, she almost missed his news: he had been chosen as August for the Fresh Men of UCLA calendar.

"You're not a freshman. You should have graduated two years ago."

"I am still fresh enough to be exploited for my beauty."

Aless shrugged. "Say no."

"The money from the calendar goes to battered women."

"A picture of you in your briefs will work for the good of women?"

"I'll do it for the irony," Patrick said.

"Like hell," Aless said. She was on autopilot, thinking about Patrick without paying attention to him. He was carrying on about the calendar, subtly bragging, nudging her to tease him. Not until he said "I have met someone" did her head jerk up. She had missed some crucial transition — now Patrick's face looked unguarded, and he shyly stirred his drink. Ignoring Aless's profound silence, he told her about finding this new woman — Eleanora — in a bead shop. She sold him some dope. "She hardly uses it herself, but she believes in the free market. When she makes more than her target profit for a month, she gives to the food bank. I bought her a cup of tea."

"You helped her hit her target. She should have got her own tea."

"She's a masseuse. And she teaches yoga."

"She doesn't sound like your type," Aless said.

Patrick shrugged. "She's very real. She knows things I've never thought of asking. When I'm with her, I feel like I've landed on the planet of happy people."

"Send back a signal to the home station," Aless said.

He did better than that: he invited her to join them for lunch the next day. Aless invented a rehearsal, and he invited her for the day after. "Eleanora will like you," he said. "Eleanora likes performers." He created sentences that would let him say her name.

At home, Aless reminded herself that Patrick had never dated the same woman for more than a month. Even so, her breath fluttered when she entered the sandwich shop in Santa Monica. Patrick leaned across a table toward a woman who had long, straight hair and an earnest expression. She looked as if she carried finger cymbals in her woven purse.

"Namaste," Eleanora said, bowing as Aless neared. "The holiness in me greets the holiness in you."

"I know," Aless said. "I took a yoga class."

"Your name is really Alessandra. You should embrace that."

"My parents were hoping I'd have a career in opera." Aless made a smile. "Patrick says you sell dope."

"It is restorative." Eleanora's face took on a proud cast, as if she had invented marijuana and found it good.

"After I smoke, I wake up feeling like a litter of cats has walked through my mouth. It's fun while you're doing it, though."

"We meet where we stand today," said Eleanora. "Who knows where we will stand tomorrow?"

"I'm not going anywhere," Aless said grimly. On the way home, she promised herself, she would stop at a liquor store.

She had been prepared to be overshadowed by a woman with a face like a rose, or whose laughter chimed. But with her long, straight hair and long, straight nose and chin that jutted like an accusing finger, Eleanora intoned apothegms about universal oneness while Patrick looked at her with an expression dazzled and lost.

That night Aless filled a juice glass with gin and toasted *l'amour*, which made every moment new and precious. Without love, a person might scarcely know she was alive. Her mouth numb, she sang every aria she knew — two — while the radio played "Mood Indigo."

Two nights later, Patrick invited her to dinner. A week later, to lunch. He showed her Eleanora's pastels. He brought over Eleanora's dope. He called her first when he and Eleanora decided to get married.

Aless might have been able to sustain the disappointment of

her young career, whose highlight so far was singing a radio-station jingle at a dingy studio in downtown L.A. She could have put off her ambition and waited for her big break, distracting herself with the occasional date with the occasional man. But she was living in actual fear of Patrick's visits and phone calls, the way he subpoenaed her to witness his happiness. Without a whiff of the old irony, he proudly announced that Eleanora planned to follow her yogi to India for six months. Patrick would go too, of course, and he wished he could convince Aless to join them. But since he could not, would she care to housesit while they were gone? The next day Aless found Our Lady of Mercies High School in Lompoc, not far from the high-security federal prison. The school was in immediate need of a teacher of voice and theater and required no teaching certification.

Aless took a long lease on an apartment in a building with a pool. Six hundred students were nearly adequate to block Patrick's memory, although the post cards that came from India assured her that he had not forgotten her. She would love it there. So many kind people!

After he and Eleanora returned, Aless expressed sympathy for Eleanora, who had contracted an intestinal virus in Delhi. Patrick assured Aless that the illness was not communicable, and she did not ask him how it had communicated itself to Eleanora. She was thinking of this with pleasing dislike late one night when the phone rang, too late to mean anything but sorrow.

"It's Eleanora," Patrick said, and then his voice washed away in tears. At that moment, pressing the telephone receiver against her ear, Aless could not have identified the emotions she felt. "She's dead."

Dizzied by her illness, she had been struck by a bus while crossing the street. The scene rose before Aless: Eleanora, her head unsteady, wandering idly in front of a charging commuter van. Her last thought might well have focused on the soul's movement from one plane to the next.

Patrick was in pieces. "Where can I go? She was my whole life."

"It's terrible," Aless murmured.

"Can I come to you? I need someone who understands."

"Of course," she said. But she hadn't understood just how much understanding he was asking for. While Patrick was in Lompoc, he arranged for an interview with Aless's principal. Pleased with his breadth of experience, the old nun granted him a tidy office where he counseled students, offered college and career guidance, and sometimes pinch-hit for the German teacher. He managed to see Aless most days, on lunch duty if nothing else. "I always knew we'd end up together," he said one day over fish sticks.

"This isn't the end of the line," Aless said. "You don't know what's around the next corner."

"Eleanora would have liked to hear you say that."

"I know," Aless said.

"You keep her alive for me."

"It isn't just me. She's in everything you see." Aless stood up to get a second cup of coffee, improbably good — all the faculty drank it like fiends. These platitudes were the best she could do. If Patrick didn't push any further, they could stand for kindness.

Over his second glass of wine at dinner, Patrick says, "I'm holding myself back. Eleanora wouldn't want to see me like this."

"That's true," says Aless, dabbing at her forehead. Hot light flickers from the candles clustered on top of the refrigerator. A group of them stands also on the TV. Six are burning on the tiny kitchen table where Aless and Patrick are eating elbow to elbow. Eleanora made and sold candles, but Aless is pretty sure Patrick has run through the inventory she left behind. Tonight's assortment, along with the ghostly shadows they cast, are commemorative.

"But I can't just wake up and be different. I tried."

"How?" Aless says. She's on her third glass.

"I took some classes after she died. I went to a dating service." He has the grace to drop his eyes. "In the end the only thing I could do was come here."

"Aless's repair shop for the bereaved and brokenhearted." She hears the nastiness of her tone, and half-accurately adds, "I think of Eleanora every day."

"She's the sort of person you remember. I want to find a ritual that seems right for her," Patrick says. "Something that will finish the pattern of her life."

"Her life was full of giving. She gave to others," Aless says, the words losing their shape in her mouth. She is *tanked*.

"Old Lester-Less. I wonder where I would be if I lost you, not her."

Aless glares at her wineglass. "Where would you be?"

"Back in India, probably. Eleanora was my soul mate, but you're my — head mate, if there is such a thing. You see the same world I do. I wanted to see the world Eleanora lived in, but the best I could do was glimpse it. It was like she lived in a soap bubble."

"Yes," Aless says.

"I want to memorialize that," he says, and Aless has not drunk quite enough yet to tell him that a soap bubble cannot be memorialized. "For one thing, it's time to scatter her ashes."

"Do you have a place in mind?" she says. If he wants to go back to some ashram, she'll offer to counsel students while he's gone.

"There's an outcropping up in the foothills that she loved. You can see in every direction; she said it was a place where the world gathered its energies. If we drive to Tahoe, it shouldn't take more than a day or two."

She squeezes her eyes shut, then tries to get him in focus. "Let me get this straight. You and I drive to Tahoe, hike into the mountains for a day or two, and another day or two back, and drive home?" She doesn't know which is more absurd, the idea of taking off a week when half of *Camelot* hasn't been blocked yet, or the idea that she can hike four days up and down a mountain. Has Patrick looked at her? She weighs 105 pounds and has trouble carrying a half-gallon of milk into her apartment.

"The weather is clearing now, so we shouldn't have to worry about snow."

"Patrick, honey, remember who you're talking to. Voted Least Likely to Walk Across the Street If She Can Drive. I couldn't survive a four-day hike."

"If I promise to carry you over the hard parts, will you do this for me?"

"That is not a promise you want to make."

"Don't you tell me what promises I want to make. Who else could I spend four days with?"

Once again, the space between them feels as if it's collapsing, and Aless might as well be falling into his arms, right through the table and bowl of spaghetti that separate them. She would agree to hike to the Taj Mahal with him.

"This is the portal to my next life. Do you want me to enter it by myself?"

"No," she says, as if he doesn't know. Patrick is not the only one confronting a portal, and Aless is already clambering through.

The pigeons seem excessive. Patrick calls them doves and intends to release them as part of his ritual. Their cage is lashed to his backpack, and he claims not to notice the cumbersome weight swinging behind him any more than he notices the weight of Eleanora's ashes, the box holding them a discernible square inside his pack. Aless drops farther and farther behind, trying to avoid the tiny feathers and bits of filth that fly from the cage toward her mouth.

The tawny dirt path isn't steep, and Aless is able to keep up with Patrick so long as she isn't expected to talk. Caught in his own thoughts, he is making the hike easy for her, and in the absence of his usual monologue Aless acutely hears other sounds — their crunching footsteps on the sandy dirt, her huffing breath, remote stirrings that she hears without recognizing. At a clearing he points down the slope. "We saw a bear there once. A mother."

"How did you know?"

"Eleanora knew."

"Were you afraid?"

"It was a long way away. Eleanora blessed her." Patrick keeps staring downhill, and Aless steps back, shifting her own gaze to the sky. Across the valley floats a hawk, one of the few birds she can identify. The quick wind that curls around her is tangy with pine. On the drive from Lompoc she vowed to maintain what Eleanora would have called a right attitude and to respect the ritual Patrick has chosen. But he is trying to conjure a bear, and Aless is left with her unruly thoughts, which now include stories of hikers mauled by wild animals.

"I try to think that she's still here," Patrick murmurs.

"Yes."

"If I could just see things the way she did." The pigeons' prattle ascends a tone, then settles back to *cdllcdllcdll*, indifferent to Patrick's sorrow.

"I keep seeing chipmunks diving into their holes," Aless says carefully. "I think they're chipmunks — they're very quick. Look at the sky. It doesn't look that blue at home. She must have loved it here."

"Love was her great gift. She could love a garage."

"But you didn't want to leave her ashes in a garage," Aless says.

"You know what they say — funerals are for the living." Sluggishly he starts up the trail again, and after a few beats, Aless follows.

She wishes she could ignore the stinging burn down the front of her shins, her thirst, her overall unhappiness, which is not improved by the soundtrack from *Camelot* circling through her head. The pigeons maintain a steady, liquid gurgle, and Aless is ready to sacrifice them right now. Still, she sees the dejection in Patrick's shoulders, his trudging gait. And she can't help remembering what they are here to do.

"Feel the wind," she says. "And look." She points at a tree ahead of them, although Patrick doesn't look back to see her. "It must be two hundred years old."

"Not much, for a tree."

"Eleanora would have blessed it." When he doesn't lift his head or answer, she plows on, "She would have loved that tree. She is a part of it now."

"Aless, stop," Patrick says, turning so fast that the chittering birds are tossed to the side of the cage, which they do not care for. "It's a tree, okay? It probably has ants and wood rot."

"I thought I was saying what you wanted to hear," Aless says stiffly. She hasn't heard Patrick sound like this in years, and her heart trips.

"I didn't ask you to come so you could do third-rate imitations of Eleanora."

"It wasn't third rate," she says.

He shrugs the pack to straighten it on his sagging shoulders, loosing another chorus of protests from the pigeons. "Why did you agree to this?"

"Your friend comes to you in grief and asks you to help with that grief. It's a pretty lousy friend who says no."

"Even if you think it's crazy?"

"I never said that," Aless says.

The pause hangs between them. Eleanora used to talk past these halts in the conversation, while Patrick looked at her adoringly and Aless looked at a chair or a wall and thought about love's obduracy, not to mention its blindness.

He says, "Eleanora always told me that I could learn from you. She said that even though you were undeveloped and your energy was negative, you had learned how to inhabit other lives. In order to escape your own limitations you poured yourself into other people."

"I had no idea she had so many opinions about my limitations," Aless says.

"She thought it was a good thing when you came up to Lompoc to teach. You were just hurting yourself in L.A., trying to have a singing career."

"And why would that be?" Aless says tightly.

"Eleanora said it was too much tension around the mouth. She offered to give you specialized massage. I don't know if you remember."

She remembers clearly. The idea of Eleanora probing with her skinny, sandalwood-scented fingers around Aless's mouth and neck seemed creepy. Still does.

"She felt sorry for you. You wanted so much."

Aless's voice has retreated into her throat. "To want something is to be alive."

"It was hard, stretching between you two," Patrick says.

"I never asked you to stretch."

"You are my friend," he says.

They stare at each other, the sky around them so brilliant that it seems to transcend blue and leap to some other color, beyond words.

Patrick says, "Have you ever watched yourself sing? Your face changes. You become somebody else. I always thought it was deliberate."

"A singer has to open up the muscles of her face to shape the sound. It's not mystical." She hopes he will not remember her many classes in mime and musical theater. She owns two copies of *An Actor Prepares*.

"Another dream gone." He swings back onto the trail, the pigeons on his back chuckling, and she lets them get five steps ahead. Then, arranging her face in the shape of grief, she forms her lips around the melody. *"Geliebte, schön Tod."*

"Is that supposed to be funny?" Patrick asks.

"No," she assures him. It's supposed to be mean.

"We'll get to the ridge tomorrow," Patrick says after they have finished their dinner — two cheese sandwiches. Because this is his pilgrimage, he insisted on carrying their provisions, although he had little room in his pack, what with the box holding Eleanora's ashes. Aless is famished, a state not likely to improve after Patrick pulls out a baggie with a skimpy joint and lights it. "Here's the end of what she left. After this — what?"

"We'll drive home and get a drink. In the morning we'll go back to work."

"I'm supposed to be changed."

"That will come when you scatter the ashes." Since he likely can't see her in the fading light, she shrugs. The words might be true.

"What if nothing changes? What if everything is exactly the same, except that I don't have her ashes anymore?" After giving her the first hit, he draws hoggishly on the joint, inhaling half of it. Aless watches the spark end travel up the paper.

"Get the candles out of your apartment. Take up jogging. Make a date with somebody."

Patrick is nodding. "Sensible. It's what anybody sensible would say. It's just" — he gestures with the joint but does not pass it to her — "not what Eleanora would say."

Aless's stomach roars, reminding her of the bear, blessed by the ineradicable Eleanora, the Undead. "Here's what Eleanora would say: 'Every moment, every world is coming into being. When we observe that, we honor and join in all creation.'"

"Stop it."

"'Our senses are the small door through which we enter the infinite universe.' 'In darkness we seek light; in light, shade. Harmony is constant evolution.'" It isn't hard to capture Eleanora's breathy tones or to arrange her face into Eleanora's expression of rapture. It isn't even hard to feel rapturous, given her lightheaded hunger.

"She believed those things."

"I am escaping my limitations."

"You're just making sounds."

"What the hell do you think she did? Who knows if she ever had an actual thought?"

His expression cracks apart, and he staggers up from the fire before Aless can say anything else. Blundering toward the stand of scrubby pines behind them, he knocks over first his backpack, then the birdcage that he covered with his vest when the sun went down. The pigeons yelp, startling Aless, who didn't know they could make such a shrill sound. They remind her of Melanie Montrose. Aless takes one good breath, then scrambles up to help Patrick. The cage is rolling away from him.

The site where they have camped is flat, but it slopes on one side — gently at first, then dropping straight to canyon. Patrick is crashing behind the cage, bellowing and ripping his way through waist-high brush. For a moment Aless, her brain spongy from marijuana, follows him, but then she sees the footpath. It zigzags next to the bouncing, screaming cage, and she races down it. She thinks she's racing. Pointy branches rake up her arms, and Aless has no trouble imagining Eleanora's spirit in them, as she can imagine Eleanora in the vine that snarls around her ankle. She trips twice before she finally snags the wire handle and pulls it to her, the hysterical birds beating their wings and screeching. When Patrick catches up, she is cradling the cage, rocking it and murmuring to the terrified birds. Beside her lies an empty potato chip bag that she has smoothed out and will carry back to camp.

Eleanora is around them like a fog. From a distance, though Patrick will later deny this, something roars.

The morning sun vaults into the sky with an alacrity that strikes Aless as malicious. She feels as if someone went over her with a Brillo pad during the night, and the sound of Patrick patiently striking match after match to start a fire scratches on her nerves.

"Did you sleep?" he says. She's surprised he knows she's awake. His eyes are fixed on the thread of flame under his cupped hand.

"I dreamed I was running down a mountain."

"There's a lot of that going around."

Patrick pours water into the dented saucepan and opens a foil pack of coffee. The pigeons are preening as best they can inside the cage, apparently untouched by their trauma. Aless hauls herself from the sleeping bag, her shins like chipped glass. "How far is the ridge?"

"This is it."

"You said it would take two days."

"This is a ridge, too. And it's close enough." He blows on the little fire, his face unreadable.

"I don't think this is a time you want to cut corners."

"Nothing is being cut. Don't worry, Less." Coaxing the water to a desultory boil, Patrick is not behaving like a man on the verge of a ritual. He is still wearing the bright green pajama pants he slept in. He takes fifteen minutes to brew up bad coffee and set two more cheese sandwiches on the plastic plates they used the night before. When she joins him, he bows his head long enough to murmur "Namaste" — the holiness in him greeting the holiness in his cheese sandwich. Then he looks at her with the same mild, unreadable face. "How is the show coming?"

His eyes are level, his voice steady. He rarely asks her for simple civility. "It's a train wreck," she says. "The boys only want to rehearse the fight scene, Lancelot can't dance, and you've heard Melanie."

"So you're hoping for a miracle."

Aless thinks for a moment. "At the fall recital a girl skipped an entire verse and just stood there while the orchestra kept playing. I mean *stood,* her hands in her pockets, staring at the stage. Her proud father had a video camera. He never saw a thing wrong."

"What do you call that?" Patrick says.

"High school." She sees where he's going with this, pursuing the miraculous in a fifteen-year-old girl's meltdown. She also sees the sweet, merciless light picking out the new wrinkles beside his eyes. He is too old to be groping to make up a ritual, which means that Aless is too old to be abetting him. She can hear Eleanora's fluty voice: *We always have the tools. We have only to recognize them.*

"Let's get going. It seems cruel to keep the doves in their cage any longer."

"Right now? Like this?" The two sleeping bags are still lumpily unfurled, the embers from the little fire glow, the torn coffee pouch is stuffed into Patrick's unwashed cup.

"She won't mind." Patrick picks up his pack and the noisy cage and walks to the top of the slope. He stretches his arms above his head, then bends until his nose grazes his knees. From her long-ago yoga class, Aless recognizes the Sun Salutation. Standing fussily straight, he rolls his shoulders and flattens his palms against the small breeze. "Tadasana: The Mountain," he says.

While he adjusts his posture, she has time to take in the view and wonder how different things would be if they hiked all the way to the original spot. She can't help thinking that Patrick is keeping that place from her, now that she has smirched the memory of his beloved, even though the thought is unworthy — of him, if not her. She wonders if she would be a kinder person if she were not in love with Patrick. More patient. More giving. More like Eleanora, who loved everything, and whom Patrick had the good sense to love while he could.

"You can move," Patrick says without shifting his mountain stance. "This isn't church."

"I'm meditating," she says.

"Don't you need a learner's permit?"

"I am letting the spirit move me." Cautiously, she rubs her jaw, its clean line such a good feature for the stage. At one of her last auditions, before she left Los Angeles, the director said, "There's nothing loose in you." She winces, remembering how proud she was of that.

Patrick finally slumps out of Tadasana, rolling his neck and shoulders. "Are you ready?"

"This is your show," she says gently.

Taking the box from his pack, he flings the first handful of ashes in an arc before him, as if he were sowing seed. The ashes fall gracefully from his hand, and a few pieces glitter when they catch the light. The moment looks like something from a movie. Reaching back into the box, he sows the ashes again and again, handful after handful, impressing Aless with the sheer amount of Eleanora. She takes close to ten minutes to be scattered, and then Patrick steps back from the ridge, rubbing his arm. "Now the doves."

Like a magician's assistant, Aless hands him the cage. He has to nudge the first bird out, so tightly are they packed, but the others spill behind, and two of the six start to fly, landing a few feet away and pecking at the dirt. The others cluster near the door, making their *cdllcdll* sound. None of them shows the least desire to take flight.

"This is funny, isn't it?" Patrick says.

"In a way." It hurts her to look at his befuddled face, so she charges down the slope, pounding her aching legs on the dirt, waving her arms and shouting. The pigeons rise, fanning out over the canyon, panic making their fat bodies spurt through the air. Moving even faster is the hawk who appears like a dot in the sky, dropping onto one of the pigeons and carrying it away. Patrick has been looking from side to side, one hand shielding his eyes. He might have missed the hawk. He says, "Eleanora would have loved this," which could go either way.

"I do, too," says Aless, moving back up the slope to join him.

"Now I have nothing."

"Health. Education. Your life stretching before you."

"That's not what I mean. I really have nothing. My hands are full of nothing." His hands are actually covered with fine ash, though it seems tasteless to point that out.

"You were right," he is saying. "Now that her ashes are gone,

I'm changed. Things are not the same. It's time to embrace life."

Aless lifts her face. Patrick has promised to carry her. When she opens her eyes, she sees he has not moved, but he is smiling at her.

"Would you teach me to sing?" he says.

For an interesting moment, the world turns white. Aless can't even see Patrick, although she hears his smooth voice, which has asked so many things. The asking never stops, nor the giving.

"Open your mouth," she says. "Then make the biggest sound you can."

He lets out a little croak. "More," she says.

His second sound is almost the same; she can see self-consciousness freezing his mouth. She taps his jaw, which she has never touched before. "Bigger! Yell! Raise the roof!" To show him what he should be doing, she opens her own mouth and lets sound pour out. For a moment her roar obliterates everything — wind and bird calls and distant, prowling creatures. Patrick stops and looks at her admiringly, and she gestures at him to join her. He opens his mouth again and does a little better.